dead
and ...

Calba

"I still can't believe she's dead. She was so funny on her show. She seemed so sweet," Gabby said.

Jen sighed. "She wasn't that sweet. I hate to say it. Everyone who worked at the Yummy Channel had a beef with her, but I can't believe she's dead. I wonder what's going to happen with the network."

"Bess's Bakery was always my fail-proof, go-to cupcake spot," said Gabby. "I hope they keep it open and just change the name or something."

Jen described the policeman who had questioned her in detail, describing his broad shoulders, shiny badge, and perfect hair. His eyes—especially his eyes. They were hazel with flecks of green, a color that Jen couldn't get out of her head. "You should have seen the way he calmed down the room when everyone was running around in hysterics."

"Didn't he give you his card or anything? His badge number?" Gabby asked helpfully.

"No. I think he was about to but his partner called up one of the publicity guys from the Yummy Channel. Plus I want to lose twenty pounds before I see him again. At least ten . . ."

death, desire, and dieting

a diet to die for

A SKINNY MYSTERY

SARAH STEDING

Pocket Books

New York   London   Toronto   Sydney   New Delhi

Pocket Books
A Division of Simon & Schuster, Inc.
1230 Avenue of the Americas
New York, NY 10020

This book is a work of fiction. Any references to historical events, real people, or real places are used fictitiously. Other names, characters, places, and events are products of the author's imagination, and any resemblance to actual events or places or persons, living or dead, is entirely coincidental.

First Pocket Books paperback edition July 2013

POCKET and colophon are registered trademarks of Simon & Schuster, Inc.

For information about special discounts for bulk purchases, please contact Simon & Schuster Special Sales at 1-866-506-1949 or business@simonandschuster.com.

The Simon & Schuster Speakers Bureau can bring authors to your live event. For more information or to book an event contact the Simon & Schuster Speakers Bureau at 1-866-248-3049 or visit our website at www.simonspeakers.com.

Manufactured in the United States of America

10 9 8 7 6 5 4 3 2 1

ISBN 978-1-4516-8468-1
ISBN 978-1-4516-8469-8 (ebook)

a diet to die for

prologue

Billy smiled and waited for a woman and her swarming mass of children to come to a consensus on a cupcake order at Bess's Bakery. Watching this lady's caravan of chaos was like watching an episode of *Sesame Street* dubbed over by an episode of *Jerry Springer*. One of the kids had a trail of sticky drool running down his chin and a smear of what Billy hoped was chocolate on his shirt. Another had extracted all the napkins from one of the dining area's chrome napkin dispensers and tossed them around like candy from a parade float. And this mom, hair all frizzed out like she'd stuck her finger in a socket— Billy thought she looked like a rat in a cage, red-rimmed eyes and all. He didn't get why anyone would raise their kids in New York City, even if they were millionaires. Trying to survive this city was crazy enough when you were flying solo.

Billy tried to mediate from the other side of the counter to get them moving. Bess's was closing early this afternoon, in like twenty minutes actually, and he was the only one working right now. He cleared his throat. "So you want one chocolate cupcake and two vanilla, and one peach cobbler cupcake with ginger buttercream frosting? And then the strawberries and cream to go?"

The woman nodded, then heaved a great sigh. "Wait, cancel the peach cobbler cupcake. I forgot I'm starting a diet."

Good luck, lady, thought Billy, shrugging. *No one can resist the siren song of Bess's Bakery. You're in the wrong place if you're on a diet.* He smiled and reached into the case for a vanilla and placed it squarely in the center of one of the bakery's distinctive checkerboard plates. He froze as the largest of the little people let out a high, long shriek.

"I said I wanted *s'mores!*" the little girl screamed. "You never listen to me!" Billy turned up the wattage of his smile and tried to channel his inner mellow.

"S'mores then," the mother said, shrugging at Billy. "Instead of one of the vanillas." The baby on her hip was pulling her hair, the napkin kid was now lying facedown on the bakery's black-and-white checkered floor, and the third child was still moaning about being ignored. The mother lowered her voice. "Just add the peach cobbler one back on too."

Billy nodded at her and smiled. Why fight it? Bess's Bakery wins every time. He was lucky because he could eat as many cupcakes as he wanted to without gaining weight.

He rang the lady up and helped the next customer in line. It sucked to be running the show alone, but on the plus side, there was nobody to share the tip jar with, either. And no one to make some stupid stoner joke when he dipped into the back to drop Visine in his eyes. All in all not a bad deal.

He wasn't trying to be a Zen master or anything, but he kind of prided himself on being able to just stand here with a smile and help this lady and her crazy kids if it meant they'd have a better day. He could do that. That's just how he liked to live his life. *Pay it forward, man.*

He'd told his boss Charlie that it was *no problem* when he'd explained that Billy would be running the show alone for a few hours while the rest of the staff made preparations for Bess's big party. All week Charlie had been down his throat about it as if Billy couldn't handle the extreme pressure of serving cupcakes without an army to back him. *Sorry, Charlie. Not rocket science.*

The party was a big schmoozy, boozy affair with all the Yummy Channel celebrities and executives to toast her hundreth episode of *Bess's Bakery*, the Yummy Channel show by the same name as the very bakery that employed Billy. Reruns must not count, Billy figured, because if they did, it would be like the ten-millionth episode. The Yummy Channel party planner who had put the whole shindig together was none other than Billy's ex-girlfriend, Jen *get-this-party-started* Stevens. The party sounded fun, and Billy was looking forward to seeing the lovely Jen. Jen got him this job a year ago, when he was out of work. He reminded himself to say thanks again when he saw her tonight. He liked this job. It was a keeper. He got paid. He ate cupcakes. His coworkers liked to bitch about Bess's attitude and being *underpaid* and *overworked*, but Billy never had any problems with Bess. Some of the other Yummy Channel staff drove him crazy when they stopped by, but for someone whose name was on the door, Bess Brantwood was pretty hands-off when it came to the kitchen and the counter. Just how Billy liked it. To him, the job was sugar and butter; it was a piece of cake.

The girl he usually worked shifts with, Daisy, bitched more than anyone else about how unfairly the bakery was managed. At the party tonight, Daisy had to wear this special little outfit and walk around offering mini cupcakes and champagne to reporters or whomever. Daisy told Billy that it was total crap because *cocktail waitress* wasn't exactly in her job description. She was a cupcake connoisseur. Billy laughed at her when she showed him the little outfit they'd asked her to wear at tonight's party. To be honest, he had felt a tiny bit shafted that he had to work in the back doing food prep until he saw that stupid white bow tie. Now it was like, *whatever*. He didn't want Jen to see him looking like a high school prom date. He liked working with his hands at the bakery instead of staring at a computer all day like other people, but he really didn't want to lose his dignity by putting on a penguin suit to wait on his ex and her party guests.

The woman and her pack of kids had taken over a corner of the restaurant. They were the only people in the dining area and while he was waiting for them to finish up and ship out, he read the new Stephen King novel discreetly under the counter. He flicked his eyes up to the family every minute or two. The mom fluttered around, getting everyone napkins, breaking up fights while the kids demolished the cupcakes. When she finally sat down, for just one moment, she totally relaxed. Billy witnessed it. There was just this one split second when she was sipping her cappuccino, and then she took a bite of the cupcake, and the sun hit her face, and she closed her eyes a little bit in some mixture between relief and ecstasy.

Even a year into this job, Billy still loved to see the customers enjoy Bess's famous cupcakes. It was totally rewarding. And then the kids spilled their milk, started begging for more cupcakes, and emptied sugar packets out on the table, crying, freaking out. The mom tipped the stroller over as she was backing out of the bakery, dropping all sorts of kid stuff and then bending down to shove it all back in. When they finally took their mobile disaster out the front door, he went to the table with a spray bottle and a rag and mopped up the evidence of their visit. Billy wondered if that one fleeting moment was worth it.

Billy liked to think of cupcakes as the great unifier. All different types of people frequented Bess's Bakery. Tourist families in matching windbreakers ordered one of each flavor in heavily accented English. Hipsters, with their beards and plaid, enjoyed the ironic pleasure of a good cupcake: the good, clean fun of the baked goods. They made fun of the Motown sound track and checkered tablecloths, but Billy could tell they loved the kitsch. But today the customers had slowed, and the party set-up would be under way as soon as Charlie and Jen got here, so as soon as the family left, he slid into the alley for a quick toke.

The alley wasn't an alley per se. It was actually just a small parking lot area with a Dumpster where Bess got dropped off when she came into the bakery, which only happened about once a month. A couple of times paparazzi had spotted Bess going in and camped out for over an hour in the dining room, much to everyone's annoyance. Bess had griped about it in the kitchen, but then walked out and charmed the pushy reporters. She even gave them all free cupcakes. As

Billy leaned against the wall in the alley the afternoon sun dropped lower and shadows began to shoot across the pavement. A needle of sunlight glinted off the Mini Cooper that pulled off of Ninth Street and into the alley—Charlie's Mini Cooper, with Jen in the passenger seat. Billy quickly pinched out his joint and stuck it back in an Altoids box. He grabbed a mint before shoving the box back into his pocket. *Shit.* He should have put the CLOSED sign up already. He looked at his phone. Quarter after six. It was staying light so late now, and the weather was so nice. The evening had snuck up on him. He hurried back inside and hoped they hadn't seen him.

They had seen him, of course, and Charlie railed into him right away. Jen smiled and shrugged, and Billy smiled back. She looked great. Maybe a little wider than the last time he saw her, but her dress was tight in the right places. Her curly hair tangled all up on top of her head. She didn't stay and talk though. She was off and moving. That girl was always moving. Billy smiled to himself. Even when they were younger, she could never keep still. After he'd unloaded the car and listened to Charlie index everything he'd done wrong, Billy began whistling and unpacking the glassware. He liked knowing that Jen was up front somewhere and he'd see her again soon.

Charlie and Jen's arrival triggered a whirlwind of activity. Daisy showed up a few minutes later and Billy laughed at her bow tie. She scowled at him and angrily began to frost cupcakes. He hoped her annoyance didn't rub off on the desserts. You gotta respect the sweets. He took a place alongside her and got to work. When the cupcakes were ready, he began setting up trays of cupcakes and sparkling wine. A couple of other waiters gradually flowed into the kitchen to pick up the trays, and Billy started to get into a rhythm—wash a tray, arrange a tray, then the tray would come back empty and he'd do it over again.

He was just beginning to really feel the rhythm when his groove was interrupted by a squawking car alarm, coming from the back lot. Charlie's fucking Mini Cooper. *Nobody wants to steal your car, Charlie,* thought Billy to himself. He grabbed the keys from Charlie's desk, and when he cracked the back door, he was accosted by the shrieking rhythm of his least favorite city noise. A chill rushed in around him despite the day's warm weather. Sunset always looked eerie in this alley, with the surrounding buildings' shadows creating a hidden valley of darkness.

Billy stepped outside. As the sirens and horns beat on his eardrums, he pointed the little black wand thing at the car and clicked off the alarm. The momentary relief in his ears was quickly filled in by the sounds of the city and nearby bars and restaurants. He heard a woman's high-pitched laugh, and a man's deep baritone joined her. The warm weather was bringing everyone out to live *la vida* New York. The New York life, baby. No matter how expensive rents got, he'd never leave it. A car door slammed, and a honk sent a burst of warning into the evening. Another breeze brought in the aroma of tasty fried things and alerted Billy to the distinct probability that some patrons of nearby bars might be using this lot behind Bess's as a pisser.

He saw an open book lying on the pavement next to a crate. Was it his Stephen King? No, definitely not. It was nice, hardcover and leatherbound. He picked it up and flipped through. It was a journal with swirly handwriting on each page. It seemed out of place here, and it definitely hadn't been here earlier when he'd come out to smoke.

A sense of unease tugged at him and he figured he should probably take a look at Charlie's car. Maybe someone had thrown a bunch of stuff from an upper-level apartment in a lover's spat or something. He looked up, but didn't see anything unusual. He turned toward the Mini Cooper but stopped dead in his tracks. A long, cream-colored arm stretched motion-less out on the pavement from behind Charlie's car. Billy did not want it to be what he thought it might be. He saw crooked fingers, with nails painted dark red, like red velvet. He waited a second, hoping to see them move. When they didn't, he took a wide, cautious path around to peek at the other side of the car, and when he saw the body it was eerily familiar: a slim woman with auburn curls fanned around her face. She lay on her back, her knees bent, and leaning against the back tire, her purse spilled out next to her.

He rushed over to her. Her heart-shaped face was unmistakable, with her turned-up nose and sprinkling of freckles. Billy had last seen her that morning, on TV. It was Bess. His boss's boss, the original cupcake lady, the Yummy Channel star. Billy wasn't the kind of guy who sat around and watched morning talk shows, but he'd been killing time, surfing through the channels, and he'd stopped on the show for a second. She was grinding some cloves and cinnamon together with a mortar and pestle. She looked up and winked at the audience with those big blue eyes. He remembered the way her fingers had looked, sprinkling glittering sugar into the spice mixture, and he could still hear her Southern twang when she said, "There it is, sugar and spice and everything nice. And y'all, don't worry about a little mistake. When in doubt, just add a little more butter."

Now, here on the dark gravely pavement, she was so pale that she almost seemed to glow in the twilight. He hesitated to touch her, but when he pressed his fingers into her neck, searching for a pulse, she seemed warm. Hot even, like she had a fever. He pried her eyelids open, hoping she'd respond, but her big blue eyes looked blank and empty. Billy had no idea what to do, but his hands seemed to work on their own, digging into his pants pocket, pulling out his phone. He shoved the journal in the back of his pants, not wanting to throw it back on the ground. First he dialed his sister inexplicably, then he quickly hung up. He scrolled through to find the number to his roommate's cell phone but stopped. Who did you call when you found your boss in the alley behind her own bakery? Oh. His brain snapped back into place. He dialed 911 and set the phone down next to him on speaker while he bent down and tried to remember the right thing to do, tried to breathe life into her lungs. He pushed down on her chest with his hands, willing her to breathe, and trying not to hurt her. Should he move her? No. Never move a hurt person, right? *Shit*, man, he didn't know. He kept trying, thinking about every movie he'd ever seen where somebody almost died, and then at the last minute, the person sat up, sputtering, coughing, and the laugh track echoed everyone's relief. *Come on*, he thought. *Sputter, dammit.*

chapter one

When Bess was five minutes late, Jen texted her. "Still coming? Just checking in. :)" She immediately regretted adding the smiley face after she sent it. This was not a smiley-face situation. The phone read 7:05 p.m., and Bess should definitely be here by now. If she didn't arrive soon it would be a train wreck instead of a celebration. Jen felt anxiety gather in the pit of her stomach. The guests weren't supposed to arrive until 8:00 p.m., but the press would be there any minute. The press loved Bess Brantwood—they ate her sugar-coated celebrity up with a spoon. For some reason reporters didn't flock to her, Jen Stevens, Yummy Channel event planner, in the same way. Jen stared out of the plate-glass window into the late afternoon and willed a Town Car to turn the corner and Bess's red head to come bouncing up to the door. *Deep breaths.*

Jen turned and looked at the room. She hadn't had to decorate too much because the dining area at Bess's Bakery was already pretty festive. Chandeliers of different sizes hung from the ceiling, catching the light and twinkling, and the walls were painted pale blue with a bold yellow trim. Her cute checkerboard-patterned dishes with bright, bold colored rims brought the whole look together. Jen twisted a sparkly garland around the staircase that led to the upper seating area and made sure that the NO ADMITTANCE sign to deter customers and guests was blocking the entrance to the basement steps. She used removable wall adhesive to affix twenty-by-twenty-four-inch framed prints of still shots from all one hundred episodes of *Bess's Bakery* throughout the dining room area. Bess's cooking show had the highest ratings of any cooking show in the Yummy Channel history. The cupcake master's sweet Southern charm melted the hearts of viewers, and Jen thought the pictures she'd hung really captured her essence. They conveniently left out what a nightmare Bess was behind the scenes.

The bakery looked beautiful, indeed, and the cupcake tower that she'd set up with Billy's help next to the podium looked like a fairy-tale spire. Jen had scooted a table by the door, faltering only slightly in heels that she rarely wore, and arranged gift bags for the guests to take as they left. Six sterling silver vases filled with bright zinnias lined the counter that sep-

arated the kitchen from the dining area, and four
larger-than-life cardboard cutouts of Bess were dis-
played around the room as tastefully as possible. Jen
had tried to talk Bess out of the cutouts, but she'd
insisted. With an ego like that, Jen thought that Bess
would at least be on time to the party. Bess was fashionably late to other Yummy Channel events, but Jen
had just assumed she'd stay on schedule with this one.
Jen fingered the ribbon on one of the guest bags and
turned from the door. This would teach Jen to assume
anything when Bess was involved.

To soothe herself, Jen popped a chocolate buttercream mini cupcake into her mouth from one of the
trays placed around the room. That would be the last
one for tonight, she promised herself. Her dress was
already so tight she couldn't afford to eat any more,
even with two pairs of Spanx sucking in the inches of
pudge she'd put on in the last six months. Plus, it was
Fiesta Friday, and she was looking forward to meeting
her friends at Mexican Max's after the party tonight
for a late-night drink and snack. She closed her eyes
as she chewed the cupcake, savoring it. *Delicious.* The
caramel sauce drizzled over it made it even more
amazing. Bess's Bakery—the show and the bakery—
were famous for a reason.

Jen licked her lips and watched the manager, Charlie, setting up platters, stacking the little cupcakes into
fancy pyramids, fanning little powdered sugar bei-

gnets into a perfect arch. Billy was in the back, and she hoped he was working hard. He was just so laid-back, and it drove Jen crazy. That was the reason why they hadn't made it as a couple, though she had to admit that he seemed like a good fit at the bakery. She was relieved he was working in the back tonight. She was self-conscious enough in her tight dress without her ex staring at her fat ass.

Anyway, everything was coming together for the party. Everything except the guest of honor. Channeling anxiety into action, Jen walked along the wall to straighten the picture frames. Bess Brantwood expected perfection on her show, in her bakery, and at all events which bore her name. She was a tough boss, but Jen thought it was mostly worth it. Working with Bess felt glamorous, like riding a shooting star. But Jen didn't feel particularly glamorous at this moment as she tugged at the hem of her dress to make sure it wasn't riding up too far on her hips. She grabbed another mini cupcake. They were so good, so rich and sweet that if no one was looking, she could eat the whole tray. However, since she was in public, wearing a dress that barely fit, *this* was the last one. Definitely the last one. *Where was Bess?*

Working closely with a diva wasn't exactly good for her own ego. Jen preferred to work with some of the other stars of the Yummy Channel, like her sweet friend Maya Khan, star of the cake decorating show,

Khanfetti. Maya's show was filmed in the Yummy Channel studios for the first two seasons, but last season Maya took her show on the road and traveled from town to town surprising deserving viewers with perfectly amazing custom-decorated cakes in the shape of their favorite things. Sometimes even working on events for self-proclaimed *man's man* Will Riley—king of the deep fryer—was better than Bess. Bess's barbs, attacks both personal and professional, could break even the thickest skin. Between the constant criticism and the unlimited access to amazing cupcakes, Jen had put on fifteen pounds over the last six months or so. And that was on top of the "freshman fifteen" she'd gained over a decade ago and never lost. It all began when she started dating Billy, as a matter of fact. She could still blame him for it, right? All the cans of beer and ramen noodle dinners that made up their courtship had taken their toll on her tummy and rear, though now at thirty, Billy was still as slim as the day they met. It annoyed her to no end. Jen wiggled again in her dress, silently begging the material to give a little bit. She bargained with the Spanx god that if she could just get through the night she'd either lose weight—or more likely buy a bigger dress.

When it was 7:12 p.m., and still no sign of Bess, Jen stepped outside onto the sidewalk to call her again. The humidity swirled up off the pavement, warmer than when she'd arrived at the bakery a few hours ago to set up. Unseasonably warm for early May, she thought as she squirmed, feeling her corsetlike undergarment constrict around her. She paced back and forth in front of the door, her heels clicking on the pavement, her thighs brushing together, and sweat forming everywhere. When Bess's voice mail finally picked up, she resisted the urge to scream "WHERE ARE YOU, %&*!?" into the phone. Instead, she cheerfully chirped, "Bess, it's Jen. What's up? I *hate* to nag, but when are you coming? The guests will be arriving in forty-five minutes, and the camera crews before that. Call me back—or just *show up!* I'm sure you're on your way. Please *and* thank you."

Jen pressed "end" and stared at the phone, willing it to ring with some information that would ease her nerves. She realized she'd left one major stone unturned and scrolled through her phone to find Bess's assistant's number. Giselle. She pushed "dial" and pressed the phone to her ear. Where the hell was Giselle, for that matter? With Bess, Jen presumed, and as usual, responding to the star's every beck and call. *Assistant* was an unsatisfactory title for Giselle's job duties. An *assistant* would have called ahead, come early to help set up, maybe even collaborated with Jen on some of the event details. A more accurate description of Giselle's job was *Bess Wrangler* or *Diva Management Expert.* Perhaps *Wild Animal Handler.* It was

Giselle's job to make sure Bess didn't fly off the deep end, so when Giselle's voice mail picked up after the first ring Jen angry-whispered into the phone, "PLEASE get here now! You're late! *Where is Bess?*" Since Jen doubted anyone of Giselle's age-group actually listened to their voice mail, Jen followed up with a text: "Call me!" She leaned against the brick doorframe outside, poking at a crack in the pavement with her peep toe, forcing deep breaths into her shapewear.

A car door slammed, drawing her attention up at the street. The traffic had let up from the earlier gridlock that gums up Manhattan streets during rush hour leaving the streets relatively clear. A reporter and cameraman climbed out of a van parked in front of the bakery and walked toward the doors, chatting amicably about their luck getting a good parking space in this neighborhood at this time of the evening. Jen stepped aside and opened the door for them. They were thirty minutes early. Just Jen's luck. "Welcome," she said, greeting them warmly.

"Hey, how's it going? We too early?" the cameraman asked, shifting his heavy, tattered canvas bag on his shoulder. The reporter, Callie Rogers, cocked her head to the side and smiled at Jen. Her teeth gleamed and her makeup was perfect, and her earrings looked expensive. But what left the biggest impact on Jen was Callie's weight. She was stick thin except for two enormous breasts, and looked disproportioned like she might tip over. Jen put on a wide smile and tried to embody cool confidence. Callie was a special reporter on the evening news. Just famous enough to feel entitled, and unknown enough to be viciously ambitious. It wasn't Jen's first time at the press rodeo, though. She'd dealt with reporters nonstop since joining the Yummy Channel.

Yes, you're too early, dummies. The Yummy Channel camera crews aren't even arriving for another twenty minutes. "No, of course you're not too early!" Jen lied. "You're the first, though, so I think there's a special glass of champagne for you inside." Callie's blond shoulder-length bob looked shellacked in perfect waves and subtle curls. Callie's hair did not so much as sway as a breeze came through, cooling the tiny layer of sweat that had beaded up on Jen's forehead. The reporter gave a dainty shiver, her bony hands coming up to cradle her elbows. Jen rolled her eyes. No one could possibly be cold on an evening like this. She turned to the cameraman and laid her hand on his back, ushering him inside. "And there's some great microbrew beers in there too if you're into that! Just ask one of the waiters." He lit up, gave her a nod, and headed inside.

"Any chance of getting an exclusive with Bess before we start here?" the reporter asked, holding her ground. The press loved covering Bess Brantwood because the viewers loved Bess Brantwood. Jen had heard a reporter from Channel Six say that they've never gotten more glowing fan e-mails than when Bess was on. Bess had an undeniable on-camera appeal. The problem was that she was fully aware of her appeal, and used it to her advantage to act like a diva. "Last time we had an interview scheduled, Bess came down with a sudden case of the flu. Or at least that's what her assistant told us." Callie smiled at Jen conspiratorially.

Jen snapped into diplomacy mode. Jen knew that Callie knew that Bess had probably completely fabricated the excuse because something better had come up, but Jen wasn't about to gossip about it with a reporter "Oh! Well! I think she's made a full recovery, and if she has a second before we start, I'll send her over to you for five minutes," Jen promised. She made an awkward move to head inside, hoping that her choice in undergarments was slimming enough to be worth the discomfort. This must be what women in New York in the 1800s felt like, corseted and squeezed within an inch of their lives.

"Is everything okay?" Callie asked, narrowing her eyes as Jen squirmed. "You seem uncomfortable."

Out of the corner of her eye Jen saw Billy amble into the dining area from the kitchen, carrying a rack of glassware. Charlie directed him to the counter and he hefted it up, almost pushing off one of the flower vases. He straightened it with a goofy grin and literally stopped to smell the flowers. Classic Billy. How can anyone be that laid-back at a time like this?

"Yes, I'm great!" said Jen, gulping in a breath when she saw the time was now 7:20 p.m. "Everything's great!" She wasn't lying, exactly. There was no reason to panic yet. Things could still be great. They *would* be great. Where was that waitress with the champagne flutes and cupcakes? She could really use one of each about now. At least with a mouth full of cupcake she wouldn't be able to talk to Callie anymore.

She excused herself and walked into the kitchen doors, letting them swing back and forth on their hinges. A couple of people dressed in service uniforms milled around, leaning against the walk-in refrigerator and chatting, waiting for the action to begin. "Bill. Hello," she said, spotting him standing by the long stainless-steel counter used as a decorating station. "How's it going?" Without waiting for an answer, she continued. "Listen, have you seen Bess?"

"No Bess," Billy replied. He smiled his usual slow and easy grin. "Hey, you look really pretty tonight. You have a minute to talk?"

A flutter of nostalgia skipped through Jen's chest when she stared into Billy's goofy smile, but she could not be sucked into a circular, pseudo-philosophical *what-does-it-all-mean* conversation with him. Not now. Probably not ever again. "I obviously do *not* have a minute, Billy," Jen snapped, but then she felt like a shrew and softened her voice a degree. "I'm running a party for one of the biggest networks on television and the guest of honor has decided to go AWOL. I have to find her."

"Oh man." Billy looked as lost as a kid who'd missed the school bus. "Did you check her office? She's, like, never in there, but maybe she is hanging out there tonight? I mean, if I had an office, I'd be there all the time, hanging out, filing papers and stuff."

Jen gave him a quizzical look and grabbed one of the puff pastries he was arranging on a tray. She ducked into the hallway toward Bess's office. It was a short hallway off the kitchen, with only three doors. One was marked MAINTENANCE. Jen turned the knob, but it was locked.

She kept going, her heels clacking against the linoleum, and passed an employee bathroom and shook her head. She could smell the stale smell that she recognized from college. Weed. *Subtle, Billy.* Only the light scent of mint masked the skunky odor, the still-familiar breath mints he'd always carried with him.

The light was off in Bess's office. This door was locked too, and Jen didn't think anyone had been down here tonight. Jen peered in through the glass window in the center of the door and saw nothing special. It was a small, neat office, decorated with a few photos up on the bulletin board, a computer with a perfectly lined-up keyboard and mouse. Jen spied a case of Bess's signature healthy tea, which cost $6 a bottle, by the file cabinet. She'd spotted another case in the walk-in fridge when they'd been unloading. She rolled her eyes at Bess's extravagance and stomped back down the hall and instructed Billy to come find her immediately if he saw Bess in the back.

Nearly a half hour later, fifteen minutes before the guests would begin arriving, the bakery's front seating area was already fairly full, cameras perched like big black birds around the room with their operators chatting among themselves. Jen circulated through the room as it grew more populated, checking on everything and constantly keeping an eye out for Bess. The life-size Bess-shaped cutouts kept getting her hopes up, then dashing them.

Jen greeted familiar faces as she made her way through the room. Her main secret to a great event was to make each person she spoke to, staff or guest, feel like the guest of honor. One of her first bosses out of college had told her that, and she still thought of it every time she worked an event, especially when she was stressed about the last-minute details coming together. She buzzed over and made sure the camera crews had what they needed and that the staff was prepared. Jen found the waitress with the champagne flutes and grabbed one. She made eye contact with

Thomas Wegman, president of the Yummy Channel, and grabbed a second flute from the tray. His ruddy, round face disappeared seamlessly into his shirt collar, and a bump of a chin protruded below his mouth as he stared down into his BlackBerry. It was time to fess up that things were not looking good for the evening's soiree.

"Hi, Tommy," Jen said, handing him the flute. "You looked empty-handed."

Tommy looked up, thrusting the BlackBerry he'd been stabbing at with his finger into his pocket. He laughed a deep, appreciative rumble. The Brooklyn-born-and-raised exec looked like a grizzly bear, but to Jen he seemed warm and kind. He reminded her a little bit of her father, who had also loved to eat and laugh. Tommy seemed to genuinely enjoy other people, which made him a good CEO. It also made other people instinctively feel at ease around him, which Jen imagined worked to his advantage in negotiations. "As a matter of fact, I am empty-handed." Tommy took the glass and dinged it against Jen's. "Thanks for noticin'." A moment of silence passed as they sipped from their glasses.

"Have you tried the chocolate cupcakes with the caramel sauce?" Jen spun her head around, her curls fluffing out from her face as she tried to locate one of the circulating waitresses in the white bow ties.

Tommy smiled at Jen but waved off the offer. Jen

eyed his strained shirt buttons and approved of his decision. The last thing the president of the Yummy Channel needed was another cupcake. She wasn't judging him, of course. It's that Jen was glad that even though she was overweight, she wasn't necessarily obese. Yet. She had to be careful, though. It was a fine line. Jen got up her nerve. "Tommy, I have to tell you. Bess isn't here yet. I can't find her. She won't answer the phone. I'm sure she's on her way. You know how celebrities are!"

"Did someone say big-time celebrity?" Yummy Channel chef Will Riley asked. Tommy gestured to his phone and stepped away, hopefully to try to find Bess. Jen was sure that Tommy would track her down. He had a way of keeping his stars reined in even when they were up to their most obnoxious behavior. However, Jen absolutely did not want to be stuck talking to Will. He always stared at her cleavage and told dirty jokes that were just clean enough not to get him fired in a sexual-harassment scandal.

"Will," Jen greeted him coolly, straightening her posture as he sidled up alongside her.

"In the flesh," he greeted her. What a lot of flesh there was, noticed Jen. But more than his size, Will's clothes just never fit well. Loose shorts and baggy button-up shirts with crazy prints just seemed to draw attention to the bulging and swelling of his body. His belly curved out over his waistband, though his rear was flat as a pancake. A double chin swung under his face like a pendulum. He was snacking on a cupcake, opening his mouth wide with each chomp. Jen prayed she didn't look like that when she ate cupcakes. She looked down at her dress and self-consciously sucked in her belly and plucked the fabric away to try to conceal her own chub.

The moment she broke eye contact and looked down, Will reached over and slid a hand up Jen's arm and onto her shoulder. He was quicker than he looked. Jen stepped backward awkwardly, nearly losing her balance. She did not do well in heels. "Whoa!" she squealed, trying to regain her footing, a trail of goose bumps rising where Will's hand had made contact with her. He'd had a few drinks already, Jen could tell.

Will attempted his most winsome smile. "So, where's our star?" he asked. "It's a little late, even for Miss Thang to make a fashionably late entrance."

"She'll be here," Jen said, raising her voice slightly above the chattering guests.

"It would be a shame if she missed her own party," Will said, sarcasm dripping from his tongue, along with cupcake crumbs.

Jen prickled at Will's thinly veiled competitiveness. "It's her party, Will. Maybe if you play nice you'll get a big party on your hundredth episode of *Deep Fried and Spicy*." Will's show had been getting a lot of attention lately. They were the trifecta of Yummy Channel stars. Will Riley, Maya Khan, and Bess Brantwood. The three jockeyed with one another for attention, each trying to commandeer the channel's resources. Lately the pressure had been making staff meetings intolerable.

Bess was the diva, Maya was an artist, and as obnoxious as he was, Jen fully acknowledged that Will's show was really fun to watch and viewers thought he was great: edgy in all the right ways. Jen tried to stay out of the stars' antagonistic relationship, but since she was the event manager for them all, she got pulled in from time to time.

Jen looked at her phone to check the time again, pulling it from the small sequined clutch she carried. She was annoyed. No, *pissed off*. Bess had acted childishly before, but not even showing up to her own meticulously planned celebration was over the top. Who did she think she was? Tommy stepped back over and Haley Parnell joined them, having suddenly materialized.

At a staff meeting once, Tommy had said his favorite spice was cinnamon. Haley Parnell said hers was cayenne. Jen thought that somehow encompassed the whole of their personalities. Haley was the vice president of programming for the Yummy Channel and Jen had never met someone so efficient. Tall and lanky, she seemed to have a bottomless reserve of energy. And lipstick. Her lipstick was always perfect, as was her long blond ponytail. Not a hair out of place, not a smudge outside of her lip liner. Jen couldn't help begrudge her the lipstick, considering Jen had never found a shade that actually worked with her own light, freckly skin tone and blond curls. That, and the fact that Haley must eat every meal on the treadmill, if she ate at all, made Jen wonder if she modeled herself after CEO Barbie. Clothes fit Haley the way they fit a Junior's Department mannequin at Macy's.

"So Bess didn't show up?" Haley asked, narrowing her eyes at Jen. "Where's Giselle?"

Jen shrugged. "She's not here either. I tried Haley, I promise, I tried everything. I called her, I called Giselle, I left messages, I sent texts." A tray of champagne passed by and Jen grabbed another flute to try to quell her growing discomfort. Liquid courage. Delivering bad news to someone who could fire her, even if it wasn't her fault, would always make her heart beat faster.

Haley looked at her watch and considered the situation. Jen looked at her phone and saw that it was nine minutes to 8:00 p.m. She looked to the front door and saw the first few *real* non-press, non-Yummy-Channel guests start to come in. David Brantwood, Bess's husband, walked in right after Maya Khan came through the door. Jen squinted, hoping to see Bess enter after her husband. Once her eyes rested on Maya, though, she couldn't tear them away to look back at Haley. Jen felt frozen, staring at Maya with her jaw open. *Holy cow!* Maya must have lost thirty pounds while filming out on the road over the last twelve weeks or so. Jen vaguely remembered Maya mentioning something about a low-carb diet, but it didn't seem like she was taking it very seriously—until now. "Jen? Hello? I said, *is the mic set up?*" Haley asked for the second time.

Jen snapped her focus back and nodded to Haley. Haley squinted her clear blue eyes at Jen. "Good." Then she spun toward Tommy. "Tommy, excuse me for speaking so candidly, but this cannot continue. Bess has taken advantage of her status with us for too long. She needs to start being a team player, or we're going to have to make some changes."

"Bess has special circumstances, Haley, you know that. She gets very anxious before big events."

"Who doesn't get anxious? That's why Xanax was invented," Haley said, throwing up her muscular arms, seemingly disgusted. "With all due respect, I don't care about Bess's nerves *at all*. If she can't stand the heat, she should get out of the Yummy Channel kitchen. Why do you make excuses for her? This is a profession. Everyone else employed by the Yummy Channel has to show up and be held responsible and part of the team, and she should too." Jen blushed, uncomfortable at being part of such an impassioned conversation between her bosses. Will, still standing next to her, didn't seem to mind in the least. Jen coached herself to be invisible and not to wobble on her heels as she felt the champagne blush her cheeks.

Haley held eye contact with Tommy for a moment, their eyes shooting encoded messages back and forth. The ponytail whipped around again and Haley spoke to Jen. "If she's still not here at about five minutes after eight p.m., I want you to go up and thank everyone for coming, just to stall," she demanded. Bess had prepared a twenty-minute speech reflecting on her past hundred episodes. It would be hard to fill that giant void and keep the guests entertained.

"Um," Jen hesitated.

"Want *me* to go up there and say something to everyone?" Will Riley offered.

"No," Tommy, Haley, and Jen said in unison. Apparently Jen wasn't the only one who noticed the competition among the big personalities of the Yummy Channel.

"I'll do it," Jen said. Her dress felt like a torture device though she was thankful for the two layers of Spanx if she was going to get up in front of a room of rolling video cameras. "No problem. When Bess gets here she can do her thing too."

"Exactly," Haley agreed. She thought for a moment, pursing up her strawberry-rimmed mouth. "No need to get fancy. Just thank everyone for coming, and raise your glass for a toast to Bess Brantwood and a hundred fabulous episodes of *Bess's Bakery*." Haley pantomimed a toast. "You can point out the gift bags and the cupcake tower too." She pointed to the dessert display with her manicured fingers. The exec took a step back and looked at Jen. "Don't forget to stand up straight. The camera adds five pounds." Jen's cheeks felt hot. Several more guests had come in now, and the room was alive with chatter and movement.

"You can do this. You'll be fine. It's your time to shine, Jen, why not get a little credit for the wonderful event you put together? Go on up whenever you're ready. Once the camera crews see you up there, they'll start rolling. Wait until you see the red lights go on." Haley pointed to the podium sitting atop the small platform she and Charlie had set up earlier.

Jen nodded and pointed to the ladies' room off of the dining area. "I'm just going to go freshen up." She reapplied her lipstick and checked her phone once more to see if Bess had come back to planet Earth. Someone was in one of the stalls, and Jen peeked under, hoping to see Bess's feet. No such luck. The person in the stall was wearing brown loafers that Bess wouldn't be caught dead wearing.

It wasn't the public speaking that spooked Jen as much as it was the fact that she'd have to see herself on camera. She loved being in the television industry but hated the idea of being on the other side of the camera. She didn't want all the attention. Especially when the camera added weight to her already robust frame. Jen washed her hands and sniffed the lavender-scented soap. It was refreshing. She noticed a basket of small brightly colored packages on the counter and picked one up. It was a sample-size package of XyloSlim diet pills. She shook her head. It seemed really wrong to have these in the bathroom at a Yummy Channel party, but the company was a major sponsor. The annoying XyloSlim commercials injected minute-long guilt trips into almost every show in the Yummy Channel's delicious lineup. This meant that Haley and the Yummy Channel advertising team were always trying to wedge XyloSlim products into Jen's events no matter how much the stars protested.

Jen took a deep breath and pushed out of the bathroom, nodding to Haley and ascending the steps to the podium. The room had filled up even more, but everyone quieted down as she stood there smiling out into the audience. Then red lights on the cameras began to blink on. Jen took a deep breath and, instead of picturing everyone in their underwear, as her high school speech teacher had advised, she focused on the cupcake tower next to the podium. Her eyes lingered on the frosting whipped up in beautiful scallops, the glittery sparkle of sugar on top of the glaze. It looked magical, and Jen wanted to dip her finger in it and taste the sweet frosting melt over her tongue.

"Ahem." Jen cleared her throat, and the reverb of

the microphone echoed through the room, ripping everyone from their conversations. "Thank you for coming!" She wished she had a glass of water or something cool to press against her forehead. "I'm Jen Stevens and I helped coordinate this exciting event to honor Bess Brantwood." A crash sounded in the back, and what sounded like a yelp. It sounded like Billy, Jen thought. She hoped he hadn't hurt himself on the dishwasher or something. Jen looked out over the crowd as heads turned to the kitchen door.

She looked around the room for something that could help her focus, but all she could see was the red lights on top of the cameras rolling. She tried to breathe as she noticed the kitchen door swinging open and Billy's head pop out. He was sucking in deep breaths and his skin seemed drained of blood completely. "It's Bess," he said, his voice raspy. "She's . . . I mean, I think she's dead. In the back."

For a moment, everyone froze. Then a wave rippled through the room as the cameramen turned their cameras toward the kitchen in unison, and people started running back behind the counter and into the kitchen to help. Jen saw David Brantwood sprinting toward the back, with Maya Khan on his heels. Will Riley pushed through the room too. Callie and Ron's camera was the only one still facing Jen.

I should help too, Jen thought. Her thoughts seemed fuzzy, though. Suddenly, without intending to, she felt like she was floating, reaching out for the cupcakes, reaching out in front of herself, reaching for the spar-kles and dollops. The cupcakes rushed closer to her mouth, as though they wanted her to have them, all at once, all of the tempting flavors at the same time. *The cupcake display really does look beautiful,* Jen thought. *Bess is dead,* Jen thought and then she couldn't seem to breathe at all. A lovely pink swirl and the shock of sweet icing glazing her tongue was the last thing she remembered as she teetered forward into the tower of cupcakes.

chapter two

Jen described the evening to her friends later that night but found herself unable to remember two crucial details. The first was exactly how many glasses of champagne and how many cupcakes she'd consumed before going up on the podium. The second was the name of the very handsome policeman who had rushed to her aid, untangling her hair from the cupcake tower. She'd woken from her dead faint, bewildered and clutching his hand. After a moment she assured him she was fine, and he took a handkerchief from his pocket and gently wiped the frosting from her face. He left her with the handkerchief and rushed to the back when a hiss of static and a bark of a voice sounded through the radio he wore on his belt. He'd been one of the first of many officials wearing NYC badges that had walked through the door of Bess's Bakery after Bess's body was found behind the building. Gabby and Elizabeth sat on the edge of their barstools after midnight on Friday night, heading toward the wee hours of Saturday morning—as Jen tried to describe the horrifying course of the night for them over late-night nachos and margaritas.

Time seemed off to Jen. It had only been ten minutes since she'd flagged down a cab outside Bess's Bakery. Jen couldn't believe that she was there, at the bar with her friends, after everything that had occurred that night. It seemed surreal that Bess Brantwood's dead body had been found only four hours ago. She looked at the time display on her cell phone, trying to understand. She arrived at Mexican Max's exactly five minutes after the detective who'd taken her information cleared her and the other employees to leave.

The night had gone so violently wrong. She was still a mess from her fall. Her hair looked like an eggbeater had whipped her frosting-coated curls into stiff peaks, and her makeup was running down her face. She tried to clean herself up after she fainted into the cupcakes but didn't have the energy to reapply makeup or comb out her tussled hair. She focused back on her friends, trying to fill in the blanks in the story. "Well, I guess it started with the caramel, which was fantastic, and then there were these little berry-flavored—"

"Jen!" Elizabeth yelled, disturbing the couple dining on chimichangas next to them. "We don't care about how many cupcakes you ate. What did they say happened to *Bess*?"

"*And equally important*"—Gabby shot a soothing look at Elizabeth, who tended to be too blunt when she got flustered—"are you sure *you're* okay? That's a nasty bump on your forehead." Gabby reached out and touched Jen's forehead gingerly, like a mother tending to a small child. She took her hand away and rubbed her fingers together, wiping off remnants of colored sugar.

"I'm sorry. When I'm stressed I just think of food. Yes, I'm okay. But you should have seen me. I was covered in frosting and cake. I know it's so insignificant compared to Bess's death. But I just can't believe I fainted because my Spanx were too tight. I feel sick." Jen reached for a nacho and scooped up extra hot salsa. "I mean, not *sick* sick, just sick thinking about how much weight I have gained." She looked again at her nacho, knowing it probably wasn't the key to a fit figure.

"I'm just worried about your health," Gabby said carefully, twisting her long black hair around one finger, a nervous gesture she'd had for all the years Jen had known her. "What I mean is, you just *passed out*. Should you be drinking margaritas? And maybe some chicken soup or something would be more nourishing than nachos?"

Elizabeth nodded her head in agreement, her big

blue eyes wide and glossed lips pressed together emphatically. "Jen, if you're complaining about your weight, and you're passing out, because of too-tight shapeware, you need to take a look at what you're doing *right now*." Elizabeth had started her own business as a life coach three years ago, after getting an advanced degree as a licensed counselor. Her quick success wasn't that hard to understand. She was just not hung up on people's feelings, so she could tell it the way it really was. Also, she was easy on the eyes. Elizabeth's river of highlighted hair trailed down her compact, fit body. She worked out constantly, at least five days a week, and Elizabeth always dressed to impress.

Jen looked up at her friends and shook her head. "Stop it. I just need *this* right now, guys." She gestured to the bar in front of them, with the plates of nachos and half-full glasses of margaritas. "The night was horrible. I want a drink. I want my friends. I want food. I am going to be fine. I'm not the one who died." Jen shrugged. "Not tonight, anyway."

"Okay, okay," Gabby relented. "I'm just concerned about you."

Jen noticed super-fit Elizabeth, queen of the treadmill and the eat-only-when-you're-hungry mind-set, turn her head away. Jen wanted to smack her. This wasn't the time for judgment, but Jen could feel it coming from Elizabeth in spades.

Jen knew this wasn't the time to obsess about her weight. She reached for her drink. "Anyway, they haven't said for sure what happened to Bess yet, but I heard an officer tell Tommy, our boss, that the medical examiner said it looked like cardiac arrest." Jen remembered how Tommy's face had been white, even the natural ruddiness of his cheeks faded and pasty. He'd sat by himself all evening, still clutching his BlackBerry like somehow it contained an answer to how this could have happened. Bess's husband, David, had sat alone too, though Jen noticed that he'd still been standing by the detectives when they released the other guests and employees. He didn't seem like he had anywhere else he wanted to go, and just kept pacing around frantically.

"A heart attack? She's only thirtysomething, right? She's practically our age," Gabby murmured.

"She's forty," Jen said. "It seems really wrong. She had such a healthy lifestyle, except of course for the butter in her cupcakes and, you know, the negative and poisonous attitude. But she seemed to make up for that by working out, and she was always drinking healthy teas and watching what she ate." Jen scooped up the last nacho. "Sorry I'm hogging all the nachos. It's just that now I need something savory to even out the sweet from the cupcakes earlier," Jen rationalized then crunched, enjoying the texture and flavors of the chip and toppings. The salsa and jalapeños burned her tongue and the sour cream soothed it. She tried not to think about the calories she was packing in. She needed comfort right now, in the form of nachos.

The three of them sat in a row at the long bar at Mexican Max's. They perched atop barstools, Jen in the middle. Their tradition of meeting once a month for Mexican food and margaritas, no matter how crazy their lives and jobs and relationships got, kept them connected and sane. The tasteless, chintzy, bedazzled scene, and the comically large sombreros on the wall seemed garish to Jen after a morbid evening, but the normalcy of the food and her friends' company made her feel as if life would continue to go on even after the unthinkable happened.

"After Billy came in with the news, and I made my *graceful* exit from the podium—aka plunged face-first into dessert—the cop who showed up first helped me up while his partner went out back."

Gabby interrupted. "That's *our* Billy, right? Your ex? You got him a job at the bakery a while ago, right?"

Jen nodded. "He started there about a year ago. I didn't really get him the job. I just told him about the opening and put in a good word for him. It was strangely comforting to have him there. You know how he's always just really mellow? Well, he and I sat next to each other, and Maya Khan sat with us, and we just sat there. Maya and I talked a little bit, but when one of us would get upset, Billy just kind of calmed us down with his stoner philosophy even though he'd just found a dead body. *The circle of life, man.*"

"Hmm." Elizabeth didn't approve of Billy from the first time that Jen brought him over for electric skillet macaroni and cheese in their dorm room during their freshman year of NYU. "Well, I guess it's a plus that he's so chill under pressure," Elizabeth agreed.

"You know who else was chill under pressure? The cops. Especially the one who helped me. When I came to," said Jen, "a few people were standing around me, and the cop was talking to me so softly. Everything was out of focus and then kind of snapped together and these hazel eyes were staring down at me."

"You should post a missed connection online: *you were investigating a death; I was covered in cake,*" Elizabeth offered.

Gabby choked on a giggle despite herself, and then shot a look at Elizabeth, as if to say *inappropriate.* Jen took a gulp of her margarita. After the champagne and sugar rush earlier that night, Bess's death, passing out and coming to, she was having a hard time keeping her thoughts organized. "Let's see, what happened next? When I texted you guys, I guess it was about a quarter after eight p.m. Around then?" Gabby looked at her phone and confirmed the time of the text.

Jen continued, "Then the ambulance drivers arrived and they spent a few seconds on me making sure I wasn't concussed. Officer Hazel-Eyes's partner went around and put up that yellow tape in front of the front door and then took everyone's name. The detectives came around and asked a few questions, mostly about everyone's relationship to Bess: coworker or friends. Everyone was a coworker, though, except for the press people. They weren't letting anyone leave or walk around or anything. They cordoned off the upper seating area and made some of the guests who were sitting up there come down.

"Then when the police finally let us go, it was all at once, after the crime scene investigators had gotten what they needed, I guess. They said they might follow up with a phone call." Jen hoped that she'd get a call from the officer that had helped her. She'd like to thank him personally. She'd also like to get more details about what happened to Bess tonight. It seemed so bizzare. "It was all much less *Grey's Anatomy* or *ER* than I expected," Jen concluded. "I kept expecting them to come back and say that it had all been a mistake and that Bess was being taken to the hospital to recover."

"Those shows are so fake!" Gabby said. "We love them. Marco and I watch the reruns all the time."

"Me too," Jen said, a wry half smile twisted on Jen's lips.

"This would make a good episode of *CSI*, actually," Elizabeth suggested. Jen and Gabby looked up. Elizabeth went on, her voice dropping. "Really. How did a healthy forty-year-old have cardiac arrest?"

"I can't even wrap my mind around it," Jen said. "I still can't believe she's dead."

Jen paused for a moment and then added, "It is so weird. To be honest, I feel kind of guilty. I was so angry with her for not showing up, and there she was, dying behind the building. I never went out there when I was looking for her, but Billy said that he goes out there pretty often to get some air. He said she definitely wasn't out there until after seven-forty-five p.m. He said he was positive."

"She was so funny on her show. She seemed so sweet." Gabby sighed.

"Well . . . she actually wasn't that sweet," Jen jumped in, being totally honest with her friends. "Everyone who worked at the Yummy Channel had a beef with her, but no one said that tonight. No one said anything about it to the detectives or so much as hinted at it," Jen said. "Still I can't believe she's dead. I wonder what's going to happen with the bakery, the show, and her whole empire?"

"I hope the bakery stays open for selfish reasons. Bess's Bakery has been my fail-proof, go-to cupcake spot for the last five years," said Gabby. "It is the best in the business, and I would know. Last year I did a write-up on my blog of the top cupcakes. I must have tried twenty-five." Gabby patted her soft belly. "She has a legacy to be proud of, at least."

A television was mounted on a swivel brace above

the bar, in between a pair of sparkly maracas and an ominous Día de los Muertos mask. After the program that had been playing silently on the screen ended, Jen looked up to see herself, pink cheeked and visibly nervous, standing on the podium in the center of Bess's Bakery, next to the glistening cupcake spire.

"Jorge, can you turn the TV up? Quick, please!" Elizabeth called out to the bartender. He looked questioningly at her. "Jen's on TV." She pointed up. Jorge put down the bottle of tequila he held and grabbed the remote, aiming at the television. The shot changed and the volume rose as Callie began speaking and the headline "Tragedy at Bess's Bakery" appeared underneath her handheld microphone.

"A tragedy tonight in the East Village as Bess Brantwood, owner of Bess's Bakery and star of a show on the Yummy Channel by the same name, was found deceased outside her establishment." The screen cut to a shot of the emergency vehicles that had pulled into the small parking space behind the bakery. It was dark, and you couldn't make out much, except for a momentary flash of a white sheet as the paramedics loaded the stretcher into the ambulance.

The shot switched back to Jen on the podium, this time moments later in the footage. Jen could see her reaction at the exact moment when Billy had come forward. A look of aggravation had crossed her face first, and then it crumpled a little bit. The shot switched back to Callie outside the front of Bess's Bakery. Callie went on, "The celebration was in honor of the hundredth episode of the *Bess's Bakery* program, which will air as planned according to VP of Yummy Channel Programming Haley Parnell."

Haley's pert face filled the screen, her lipstick perfect and freshly applied as always. "We are so incredibly saddened by Bess's death. I don't have anything more to say at this time, but we will issue a press release when we have more information. Until then her family and friends are in our thoughts." Haley always knew the right thing to say, Jen thought.

Callie interviewed a few people walking by outside, who all praised Bess's cupcakes and the show. "This is a real tragedy," a woman clutching a small dog said. "What a loss to the community," a man in a too-tight Yankees cap said. The shot switched back to the police at work, and Jen caught a quick glimpse of the policeman who had rescued her. In the shot that played on the news, he was walking across the room quickly. She didn't remember him walking across the room like that, powerful and equine. Watching the officer on the screen was like watching cut scenes from an extended version of a movie she'd seen a hundred times, and she had to recast her view of the night. The realization hit her that she didn't remember that because she'd been unconscious. He was probably rushing to help her when he first arrived.

The reporter at the desk thanked Callie and closed with, "We'll keep you updated with developments on this case. For more on this story, visit us online." Jen, Gabby, and Elizabeth continued to stare at the television several seconds into the next story, which covered a workers' strike in China. Elizabeth nodded when Jorge asked if he could turn the volume down again. Jen looked down. She could feel Jorge, her friends, and everyone else sitting at the bar looking at her. She'd taken her Spanx off earlier in the bakery's bathroom, so her belly pushed even harder against the material of her dress. She looked like she was smuggling a loaf of bread under her dress.

"Oh my god," Jen said, reality hitting her hard. "Oh no."

"What is it?" Elizabeth asked, reaching over to comfort Jen. Gabby leaned in and looked at Jen.

"Oh no. No, no, no. If the news channel has footage of me on the podium, and footage of that cop rushing toward me *after* I fainted . . ." Jen trailed off and buried her head in her hands.

"There must be footage of everything in between as well," Elizabeth read her friend's mind.

"Including my fall into the cupcake display," Jen finished the thought. "I'm sure that nobody would post *that*. Right? They wouldn't do that."

"Well, they didn't show it on the news tonight, so

that's a good thing," Gabby offered hopefully. Jen tried to remember, but everything was so fuzzy.

Elizabeth picked up her iPhone and let her fingers fly over the surface. "I don't think it's online. Not yet, at least. But listen to this—all these people on Twitter are saying Bess's death is probably an overdose of drugs."

"Who is saying that?" Jen demanded, peering over Elizabeth's shoulder at the glowing screen.

"Just people. No one official, just gossip," Elizabeth said, scrolling through. She looked up. "But, they've got a point. It doesn't seem like Bess died of natural causes. I just don't believe it. Whenever there's a sudden death like this, especially a celebrity, it's always something like anorexia or drugs, right?"

Jen shook her head. "I just don't think that makes sense. She's not anorexic. I don't think she was morally against drugs or anything but she was too driven and cared too much about her image. Once she fired a guy on the spot for saying that she looked tired and offering her a 5-hour Energy. And she was always drinking healthy teas and doing juice fasts and stuff. She didn't seem like the druggie type."

Elizabeth smothered a laugh. "No offense, Jen. You're so good at so many things, but sometimes you can be so naive. I don't even think you'd notice if someone was doing drugs right in front of your face."

"Hey, I'm the expert on druggies after dating Billy for five years," Jen said, defending her street smarts. She'd seen a bong or two in college, thank you very much.

"Oh please," Elizabeth said. "There's a difference between a *stoner* and a hard-core potential-overdose *druggie*, don't you think?"

"For sure," Gabby said. "Anyway, you only got mad at Billy when he kept sniffing out your secret stash of chocolate when he had the munchies!" The three women began laughing at the memory but quickly regained control.

"I feel like a creep laughing when Bess is dead," Jen said as their laughter tapered off, a rush of guilt moving in and clouding her eyes with tears.

Gabby reached over and patted her back. "It's okay to laugh. Your life goes on, honey. From what you've said, I bet if the tables were turned, Bess would not waste too much energy crying over you."

Jen considered this. "You're probably right," she agreed. "Bess was really not a particularly compassionate person. The last time I saw her she said that she'd make sure that I got fired if a single thing went wrong at this event."

"Ironic," Gabby stated. "Something went wrong, but there's not much she can do about it now." Jorge brought over an order of hot wings, along with another order of margaritas.

"On the house," the bartender said, placing the dishes in front of them. "Your favorite. Looks like you have had a hard night."

"Thanks, Jorge," Jen said gratefully, digging in. After finishing a wing in record time, and wiping her mouth of the sauce and oil, she looked up. "I forgot to tell you about Maya Khan. While she was out on the road filming the last season of *Khanfetti*, she lost like thirty pounds or something. She looks like a Kardashian now, all curvy with a tiny waist."

"What's her show about again?" Elizabeth asked.

"Oh, it's so good," Gabby gushed. "I love Maya Khan. She goes around to people's houses and helps them surprise-ambush their friends with these incredible custom-decorated cakes. She's so talented. It's so cool that you guys are friends."

"Yeah," Jen agreed. "And now she's talented *and* thin *and* newly single. We sat together and caught up a tiny bit while the detectives went around checking everyone's identification and getting phone numbers. We just watched them. We were both in shock, I think."

Jen had still been light-headed when Maya sat down next to her near the podium. Everything had seemed so odd with Billy on one side of her and Maya on the other. She felt so foolish for fainting, so disgusting covered in the sugar and cake remnants. The lights had been unnerving, flashing red, blue, red, blue, out of the front window.

The four uniformed servers sat together with three of the kitchen employees and Charlie, huddled on the steps that led to the second level. One young server burst out crying, a loud wail. Jen heard her mumble that it was all so sad. The other party guests and employees milled around. Thirty people without direction in the dining area made the space seem crowded and dirty somehow.

Though their crews weren't manning them, the cameras were still rolling, their lenses and telltale red bulbs trained on different areas around the room. Quiet conversations erupted and then were extinguished. After blocking off the kitchen, the two policemen stood upright, unsmiling, by the door.

Jen found herself watching her officer intently as he filled out paperwork, consulted with detectives. He seemed so capable and strong as he hefted a crime scene investigator's camera bag and tripod, carrying it through the dining area, past the steps, and into the kitchen. Several times he looked up and they locked eyes—his were hazel, she remembered now, with long lashes—and she pretended to be talking to Maya or Billy, or looking at her phone, scared to be caught staring. A few moments later, without her conscious permission, her eyes wandered back up again to linger on him. Once when she'd looked back at him, she was surprised to see him looking at her, lips pressed together in an expression of comfort and concern. As the detectives and crime scene investigators filed around the room, heading into the kitchen and back to the street, the officer disappeared, then popped back up a few minutes later with an ice pack from his first-aid kit. "Thought you could use this," he said to Jen. "Just bend it like this and it will get cold." She'd thanked him, and then Billy had plucked it from her hands and activated the cold pack. When she looked back up, the officer had resumed his stance by the front door.

Mexican Max's had quieted down now that it was close to one a.m. Normally Friday nights were louder and more boisterous, but tonight was sedate. Even the music seemed to be at a lower-than-usual volume. She thought for a moment, unable to slow the thoughts from fluttering around in her head. "You know what else was strange? Giselle, who is Bess's assistant, *never showed up* to the party. The girl is like a puppy. Wherever Bess is, Giselle is not far behind. She's surly, but really reliable. I told the detective that. I'm actually worried about her. Where could she be? Bess's husband, David, was late, Maya was late, but the reporters showed up super early. *Everything* seemed off."

"What?" Elizabeth gasped theatrically. She gripped the bar with both hands and looked around, like a scene from a bad *Lifetime* movie. "You don't think— What if—" She let the anticipation build. "Could it be they didn't show up because they were busy conspiring and killing Bess?"

Jen slapped her lightly on the arm. "Stop! It's not funny."

Bess could have died of natural causes, Jen thought. She was a workaholic, and under a lot of stress. Maybe she had some condition. Even though she kept a trim figure, she consumed a lot of butter and sugar. Or at least her recipes suggested that she did, though Jen knew for a fact that she ate a maximum of one bite per *Bess's Bakery* episode, and as soon as the cameras cut she tossed the remaining batch in the garbage. Once Jen had suggested they leave them out, but Bess had looked at her as if she were an idiot. "Don't you think everyone around here has had enough sweets?" Bess said to Jen, eyebrows raised with meaning.

With a shrug, Elizabeth said, "Well, something killed Bess Brantwood. Or *someone*." A distressing silence settled over them as they considered the simple truth of Elizabeth's statement.

They all jumped when Jen's phone started blaring Michael Jackson's "Thriller."

Gabby laid her hand over her heart. "*That's* your ringtone?" Jen scrambled in her clutch to pull out her phone.

"That song really dates you," Elizabeth said. "I have Ke$ha on my phone." Jen narrowed her eyes at both friends and held up a finger to her lips to shush them. She could feel the margaritas now as she clumsily jabbed at the "answer" button. She didn't recognize the number, but any call at this time of night must be important. Or a booty call, but Jen wasn't expecting any of those, considering that she had absolutely zero romantic prospects at this point in time. Her mind wandered back to the police officer at the party tonight, but she shook the thought from her head.

"Hello?" she asked, putting a finger in her other ear to block out the noise in the bar.

"Jen Stevens?" a man's voice asked.

"Yes? Who is this?" Her friends were watching with obvious curiosity.

"This is Detective Phil Franklin. Hope I'm not waking you up tonight. I thought I'd leave you a message. We were hoping you could come to the station tomorrow to talk with us about what happened tonight."

"Oh." Jen was surprised they'd called so soon—and so late. "Yeah, sure. No, you're not waking me." She hoped the detective wouldn't hear the noise of the restaurant or the drinks in her voice. It seemed morally reprehensible to be drinking after the untimely death of a coworker. She struggled to remember which of the detectives was Phil Franklin. There was a big dark-skinned man, wide and tall, with a tan trench coat, she remembered, and a shorter, muscular detective wearing jeans and a sweater.

"Good." His authoritative response was clipped and impersonal. "Can you be at the Ninth Precinct's

Fifth Street location at the intersection of Third Avenue at eleven a.m.? Tell the receptionist you're here to see me."

"Detective Franklin," Jen repeated. "Fifth Street and Third Avenue. Yes, sure. I'll see you at eleven a.m."

She said good-bye and hung up the phone, and looked from Gabby to Elizabeth. "I've got to go to bed," Jen announced, suddenly exhausted.

Jen felt her anxiety rising. "Wait, what do you think they'll ask me? God, I didn't even like Bess. What am I going to say? What if they think I did it?" She wiped a tear away from her eye.

"Don't worry. It will be fine. I'm coming with you," Elizabeth said. "That's final."

Jen felt a wave of gratitude for her friends crash over her. She slipped off the barstool and back into her heels. She felt light-headed for a moment, but Gabby stood quickly, bracing her, and said, "Let's get you in a cab. Come on. You need to rest before your date with the law tomorrow."

chapter three

The next morning shook Jen from a fitful slumber, and with the morning sunlight came a crushing, but not unfamiliar, guilt for what she'd eaten the night before. She was still wearing her black dress, and it felt tighter than ever. Basically she'd ingested the number of calories that a man twice her size training for a triathlon should consume. To Jen, the guilt of what she ate was more painful than the headache and churning stomach of her hangover. In her mind's eye, she always imagined herself politely refusing nachos and simply being satisfied popping a piece of cinnamon gum in her mouth. She imagined herself feeling good this morning after only a single margarita, stretching, looking in the mirror and liking what she saw. What if she pulled on her stretchy black pants to take a run, instead of forgoing pants entirely to sit on her couch watching the worst reality shows she could find?

Jen devoted her Saturday morning to TV shows that promised to numb the shame of her total pig-out and keep her mind off of Bess and her sad demise. After a few minutes of brainless programming she couldn't resist clicking over to the Yummy Channel to see how they were handling the news of Bess's death. Nothing had changed in the lineup. Not yet, anyway. An inspiring Weight Watchers commercial featuring a young pop star who lost a lot of weight recently was just ending. Jen could probably lose thirty pounds too if someone was paying her a couple million dollars to do it. The next commercial was for a diet drug that was supposed to reduce tummy fat with some breakthrough formula from the rain forest.

Jen hated these commercials as much as she hated the XyloSlim ads—she hated the principle. Attract a bunch of people who love to eat with food programming, and then sell skinny pills to them in between shows about the best way to prepare bacon? It just seemed mean. When a viewer was enjoying a show about delicious food, why do they need a woman in a lab coat asking if he had "twenty pounds of fat, or more, to lose," or if she's tried "everything to lose weight, but nothing's worked"? Because chances are, the answer was *yes*!

Overweight and underhappy, an advertiser's dream. Jen studied the before-and-after images, sometimes even rewinding and fast-forwarding to see the transformation again and again. A woman in a muumuu juxtaposed with her skinny mirror image in a bikini, holding up the muumuu like a piece of roadside garbage. A man with a barrel belly standing out of place and out of time, next to his muscled, flexing future self.

Watching the diet commercial had put Jen into an even deeper funk. Sudden death did wonders to put things in perspective, and she did not want to go on the way she was. She kept thinking of Bess in her last moments. What had she been thinking? What had she been feeling? Had her death hurt? Did she regret being so nasty to her colleagues in her last moments? The questions swarmed in Jen's head, depriving her of any real rest.

Jen thought about her own legacy as well. She was approaching a place where she felt professionally successful after climbing the ranks of the Yummy Channel publicity department to become the events manager. Hopefully her colleagues would remember her as pleasant and fair, smart and energetic. Personally, though, she felt like that was another story. She knew Gabby and Elizabeth would miss her if she died suddenly, but if they took the last year or so out of context, they'd probably remember her as pretty pathetic. She complained about not having dates but refused to join a dating website like the one Elizabeth belonged to. She said she wanted to lose weight but stopped herself before she even began actually taking steps to do it. If it were her lying next to the Mini Cooper instead of Bess, what would she think about in her last few moments?

Jen agonized. She really did want to *do* something about her problems, not just complain about them. She just didn't know what, exactly. Every Yummy Channel show gave her decadent recipes and suggested that if she wanted to be the perfect friend, wife, or hostess, she'd memorize them all. Then every commercial break told her she's too fat and offered a quick-fix solution.

I'd stop eating entirely, she thought, *but I don't have the self-control.* She'd order XyloSlim but strange chemicals scared her. She could do *The 17 Day Diet,* but it seemed like too long of a commitment. She'd get bariatric surgery, but she wasn't quite fat enough. She could do DASH or detox or Dukan; fruit flush; grapefruit; glycemic index; Jenny Craig; or Weight Watchers. Jen hugged herself and pulled a blanket up around her, wondering how easy it was to get institutionalized. Then she'd be served a ration of food and water each day and would lose weight without making any decisions.

"Billie Jean" began playing, muffled, in Jen's tote bag. "Billie Jean" was her mom's ringtone. Jen should have called her last night. Her mom, Vera, must be so worried after watching the news. Jen scrambled for the phone. Her mother lived on Long Island, a forty-minute train ride away, but may as well have been her only daughter's roommate considering how involved she was in Jen's life. With equal parts resentment and relief, Jen answered and listened to her mother worry herself into a frenzy on the phone. Jen could picture her, pacing in her patterned linoleum-tile kitchen, eating a mix of nuts and chocolate chips from a decades-old chipped porcelain bowl with yellow flowers.

After multiple assurances from Jen that she was fine, Vera seemed a few degrees more relaxed. "I just worry about you in the big city. There's still crime. People think there's no crime, but people are mugged and murdered all the time." Vera's voice went up at the end of her sentence, reaching a desperate pitch.

"Mom, please. It's fine."

"Okay, okay, what do I know? Did you see the article in the *Weekly World News*?" she asked, her accent instantly transporting Jen back to the clapboard houses and strip malls of her youth. Vera loved gossip magazines and tabloids, and referenced them like scripture without even a trace of the skepticism Jen had developed studying liberal arts in New York City.

"According to the article I read this morning on the TMZ-dot-com, the late Bess Brantwood was *cheating* on her husband," Vera said, letting her voice drop to a husky whisper. Her mother still had a landline with a cord, probably the last one in America, and Jen knew she'd be spooling and unspooling it around her fingers.

"Mom," Jen whined, her headache from last night's booze ramping back up to full strength. "I've told you before, you can't trust that junk. It's completely made up."

Vera protested, "But they have photos. You can't fake photos. Just think, I was so proud of you working with this star, and she turns out to be nothing but a floozy."

"Yes, Mom, you absolutely can fake photos. Have you ever heard of Photoshop?"

"You should see it, they have pictures of Bess with four different men. Four! Can you believe it. Not to speak ill of the dead, but that's kind of hussy behavior. God rest her soul." Jen guessed her mom was crossing herself. Spectacles, testicles, wallet, watch, the neighborhood kids used to say.

Jen grabbed her laptop and brought up the site. Her jaw dropped slightly when she saw that one of the men pictured on the home page, under the headline "Bess Brantwood: Quadruple-Timing?" was Yummy Channel CEO Tommy Wegman.

"You don't know what people do behind closed doors, Jenny. You said yourself that you didn't know her personal life that well," Vera countered. "She could have been up to her ears in man-trouble."

"How could she have enough time to date four

different men?" Jen asked skeptically. "And do her show and oversee her bakery?"

"Look here, it says that she was cheating on her husband David Brantwood, with a young B-list actor Benji Gordon; Thomas Wegman, Yummy Channel president; and Will Riley, her costar."

"Hold on a second, Mom." Vera ignored Jen's comment and went on talking about the lack of respect women had for marriage in this day and age. Jen scanned the article and with quivering fingers clicked through to read more. There was Tommy Wegman, looking very cozy with Bess. She was feeding him something, and his eyes were half-closed. It didn't look airbrushed. A photo of Bess looking flirtatious with Will Riley was below that, and as she scrolled down, a picture of Bess and Benji holding hands filled the screen.

"It just seems like a shame, her with these four men, and you with none," Vera said quietly, ending a monologue that had extended the duration of Jen's Internet search.

"Oh, Mom," Jen said, letting her voice taper off. "Don't say that." Ordinarily she'd allow herself to get sucked into a long conversation with her mother about how she didn't need a man to be happy, but today she was too distracted. Her mind was spinning, considering that Bess may have been involved with Tommy. She couldn't think about it anymore. She was nervous enough about her trip to the police station, which she certainly wasn't going to tell her mother about. She'd never hear the end of it. She needed to change the subject.

"Can we talk about something else, Mom? I'm thinking of starting a diet," Jen said.

"You are?" Vera asked, "Why? Your curves are cute. You just need to spruce yourself up a little. Try a new shade of lipstick." Jen could hear her munching on the trail mix in the background. Her mother had the same shape that Jen did, but for some reason Vera seemed blissful to have round arms and legs, ample breasts, curves. To both of her parents, food was the same as comfort. Her mother's lasagna was the cure to every ailment, and to her dad, there was nothing a chocolate chip cookie and a glass of milk couldn't fix.

"I have to. I can barely fit in my clothes. And I can't afford to buy new ones. I wish I could never eat again." Jen let out a big breath that she didn't realize she'd been holding.

"Never eating again is not very realistic, sweetie." Vera chuckled, crunching on another bite of sweet and salty snacks. "There are two types of people, Jen. People who eat to live, and people who live to eat. Sorry to say that you are the latter. So am I, so was your father. My mother before me. In fact, you come from a long line of live-to-eaters."

Jen shrugged. She had moved to her tiny kitchen

and was scouring her fridge for a soothing cookie. Anything other than the limp, preportioned sticks of celery she'd prepared for herself a couple of weeks ago.

Who was she to fight genetics? If her fate was to get plumper and plumper, pudging out of increasingly larger pants sizes, she might as well enjoy it. Maybe a laziness gene prevented her from going to the gym and a junk food gene made her crave salt, butter, and sugar? Her fate was sealed. That was that.

"Oh, honey, it's not that you're fat," Vera insisted. "When you meet the right man, he will see in you what I see: a beautiful, kind, smart woman." Jen smiled on the other end of the phone, grateful for the compliments even if they were exaggerated. Her mother could be annoying, but she loved Jen completely. "And maybe put on a little lipstick before you go out, really. I just found the nicest shade. They mentioned it in this article I read called 'The Top Ten Ways to Land a Man When You're Over Thirty.' I'll send it to you."

"Mom, I've got to go," Jen said. "I'll call you later."

"Okay, I'm sending the article now. Love y—" Vera said, her voice cutting out as Jen hit the "end" button on her phone. She thought about ordering a pizza or running to the grocery store to buy a bag of M&M's or a candy bar. Didn't she deserve a special treat, putting up with her mom's helpful phone calls and the stress of Bess's death? The gravitational pull of low spirits returned her to the couch, though.

She had a few more minutes before she had to get up and get in the shower, so she kept reading online. She stopped by Gabby's blog, Gab & Grub, and read Gabby's tribute to Bess's cupcakes. Jen was relieved to see that she could count on Gabby not to post about Bess's workplace disputes, even though Jen hadn't remembered to tell her it was off the record. She saw that she had quite a few messages waiting in her in-box. Friends from college were checking in after hearing the news from last night. Jen clicked on a message from Elizabeth and found a link to a video site.

Jen clicked the link, and there she was, standing on the podium in Bess's Bakery in her black dress with a slightly aggravated expression on her face. The video had five thousand views already.

Oh no. She didn't want to click "play," fearing what she would see. She sat up and straightened the cushions on the couch, then clicked it anyway.

She watched herself as her face crumpled into horror, and then she saw herself begin to sway back and forth. She must have swayed for ten full seconds, and it seemed like an eternity watching it here on this screen. She didn't remember it happening. Jen could see her stomach heaving as she tried to take breaths and saw herself reaching for the podium, but missing. Then she was falling forward and to the side, her arms flailing to try to stop herself, a strange smile on her face. Her body looked so thick, her rear so bulbous as she fell that she hit "pause" to regain her composure. *The camera adds five pounds,* she said, remembering Haley's comment. She hit "play" and finished the video, watching herself smash into the wire cupcake display, cushioned by only the cakes and her own pudge. She rolled from on top of the tower to beside it, and then three people rushed to her side to help her. She didn't move. A few seconds later, the police officer entered, clearing everyone away, and wiping her face. In the video she sat up blinking, and the officer rushed off.

Jen closed the laptop tightly and stood up, crossing her arms over her chest. She cursed out loud, feeling humiliated. She was annoyed at Elizabeth for sending her the link, but it's not like Elizabeth was the one who posted it. Most of all she felt fired up. Jen knew for sure that she didn't want to spend precious time not liking herself. *What the hell,* Jen thought. She needed to get ahead of this charging bull that was her weight, grab the reins of this runaway steed that was her relationship with food. She needed to go on a diet. Jen stood up and dusted off the crumbs from the box of cereal she'd been munching from all morning. She was saying good-bye to bingeing and feeling guilty. Standing in her living room, she stretched her arms toward the ceiling, an epic gesture for this epic moment. She was going on a diet. But first she had to take a shower.

chapter four

Elizabeth was waiting outside Jen's apartment building at 10:00 a.m. sharp, as promised. Her big black Gucci sunglasses were pulled down over her eyes. She wore a baby blue sundress and a cardigan that fit her like a wet suit. Her tawny hair was pulled back from her face in one of those messy buns that took an hour to arrange. "Good morning, star witness. You look better than you did last night. Are you feeling any better?"

They swung into the coffee shop on Jen's corner and joined the short line to place their order. "Well, thanks to seeing myself in that video you sent this morning, I've finally decided to go on a diet," Jen said. "I keep thinking about Bess just dropping dead. Life's just too short not to go for your goals."

"You're preaching to the choir," Elizabeth agreed. "That's what I tell all my clients." Jen had always been secretly curious about what a paid session with Elizabeth would be like. Jen should probably feel lucky about getting all her friend's advice for free.

"Anyway, I'm excited about the diet. It's really happening this time," Jen pledged.

"Oh really?" Elizabeth asked. Jen thought she detected a hint of skepticism. "What diet are you going on?"

Jen looked over at Elizabeth. "I'm going carb-free!" She squeezed her hand into a fist. "I think that's the diet Maya went on. It obviously works."

Elizabeth wrinkled her nose. "Sounds hard. Why don't you just come to the gym with me sometime?" Elizabeth had been trying to drag Jen along to various workout initiatives since college and still hadn't let up. Then it was kickboxing and Tae Bo. Now, Zumba and weight-lifting boot camps. "Or you could just show some moderation once in a while with the cupcakes and nachos," Elizabeth added, and placed her order with the barista. She ordered a nonfat cappuccino, light on the foam. Jen ordered a large black coffee. The barista handed Jen a cup and gestured for them to wait for the cappuccino at the end of the counter.

"I might take you up on the gym. But I have to choose a diet. I think I only have two modes: diet or splurge. I am not a very moderate person," Jen said. She slid a cardboard sleeve over the cup

Elizabeth watched as the barista prepared her

drink, pulling levers and lowering nozzles with practiced hands. "I really don't think low-carb is very healthy, Jen. Didn't the low-carb diet guy die of a heart attack a few years ago? That's not exactly a great advertisement for the long-term health benefits of the diet." She thanked the barista, and the two walked back out onto the sidewalk.

Jen felt her cheeks get red and tried to keep her voice from going all whiny. "Who are you, the healthy diet police?" Besides, thought Jen, it seemed to have worked for Maya. "It might not be the diet you would choose, but it's the one I'm doing. Support me!"

Elizabeth pulled her sunglasses down and looked at Jen, a nagging frown tugging at the corner of her mouth. "I do support you. I do. I adore you."

"Thank you." Jen flashed a grateful smile at her friend. "Now we can talk about more important things, like how nervous I am about the police station. I keep going over the events in my mind, but what if I'm leaving something out."

"Like what?" Elizabeth asked.

"I don't know. What if Bess said something about taking drugs, but I didn't pay attention because I resent her so much? Or what if she was so mean all the time because she was in emotional pain, and instead of helping her, I just thought she didn't like me?"

Elizabeth shrugged and sipped her drink. "I really doubt her bitchiness was a symptom of some sort of terminal heart disease, if that's the connection you're trying to make." Jen knew Elizabeth was probably right. She thought of the time Bess had made her stay at the office until nearly midnight the night before last Thanksgiving in order to redo the entire scheme of the Yummy Channel holiday party. Then there was the time that Bess had torn up Jen's seating chart for a press dinner in the middle of a meeting with all their colleagues. Not to mention the countless times Bess muttered snide comments under her breath when they were together. She said disparaging things about all her colleagues, especially Will Riley and Maya Khan, and regularly embarrassed Giselle in public by calling her thoughtless, careless, incompetent, and worse.

Elizabeth and Jen walked from the coffee shop on the West Side of Manhattan across the city, along the NYU campus where they'd first met, and into the East Village. Even on Saturday morning, students were already out in Washington Square enjoying the sunshine and warmth of late spring. Elizabeth told Jen about a date she'd had last week, and Jen tried to concentrate, but Bess was staring out from every newsstand and corner store they passed, her face plastered on the cover of the folded newspapers. The effect was eerie, as though Bess were watching their progress toward the police station. Jen thought about Monday, and what the office dynamics would be like without Bess's overpowering presence. "And then I got back into the limo, and said, 'Aren't you the lucky one? Not everyone gets to ride one of those.'" Jen gave Elizabeth a courtesy laugh, but her mind was elsewhere.

They turned the corner and started down Fifth Street, and the police cars parked diagonally in front of the stone building looked cautionary. She'd never been on the wrong side of the law, not really, but got a nauseated feeling when police strutted around flaunting their authority. They were still a couple of minutes early as they approached, but the walk had taken longer than Jen thought it would, so there was no cushion of time for Jen to walk around the block and summon up her nerve to enter the building. She just had to plunge in. Her stomach growled, reminding her that she hadn't eaten yet that morning. She planned to stop by the bookstore for a diet manual, then the grocery store on her way home to the right kind of food. Suddenly she realized that she had no idea how long a police interrogation would take. This could make for a very uncomfortable start to her new healthy and carb-free lifestyle. Jen had the sudden urge to turn and run toward the closest fast-food restaurant. She had nothing really to be nervous about but couldn't shake the feeling that she was going to say the wrong thing in the police station.

Elizabeth sensed her discomfort and put an arm around her back. "Stop worrying. It's going to be fine," she promised. "I'll be waiting for you the whole time."

Jen smiled ruefully and pushed open the doors. Fluorescent lights lined the hallway and the women's footsteps echoed around them in the near-empty hallway. The flat, overdeodorized, vaguely sweaty smell stuck in her nose. She followed directions and put her tote bag on the moving belt of an X-ray machine. Elizabeth tucked her Prada bag neatly into a bin instead of placing it directly on the belt. Jen stepped through the metal detector, nodding at the uniformed officer overseeing the entrance. She tossed her nearly empty paper coffee cup in the giant gray can against the wall and walked into the station.

The uniformed officer sitting at the front desk looked up from her uneven mounds of paperwork. The officer smiled, perfunctory but pleasant all the same. "Can I help you?" she asked, looking at Jen and Elizabeth. Her light purple nails clicking up and down on the end of her pen, extending and withdrawing the writing tip, were the only thing that gave away her desire to wrap up this conversation and return to her paperwork as soon as possible.

"I'm Jen Stevens. I'm here to meet with Detective Franklin."

"Just a moment," the officer said, consulting a dry erase board affixed to the desk. She trailed one of her nails down a column and stopped, tracing backward along the row. "Okay, he's asked that you wait for him in Investigation Room D. I'll take you there." She

pushed up from the desk, and Jen saw the solid-look-
ing black gun tucked into its holster. Being so near a
deadly weapon in real life made her breath catch a
tiny bit, and did not make her feel safer. She swallowed when she thought of how many guns must be
in this building, under this roof.

"I'm going to sit out here, next to that dapper gen-
tleman," Elizabeth said, and pointed to a bench where
a dirty wild-maned man with torn, soiled sweatpants
and shoes with duct tape instead of laces sat. He
seemed to be sleeping, with his chin to his chest and
lolling to the side. Jen grimaced and shrugged at her
friend. She mouthed, "Thanks," and took a couple of
quick steps to catch up with the officer, who was several paces ahead of her.

The officer strode down the scuffed cream-colored
hallway, still clicking the pen. The noise was bringing
back remnants of Jen's hangover headache, and she
wished that the woman would stop clicking or stop
walking so fast, or both. They arrived at a battleship
gray door, and she rapped on it, looked through the
tall, rectangular window above the doorknob, and
then inserted a key to unlock it. The room looked
grim, lined with unpainted cinder blocks and only the
necessary furnishings, a small table and three black
cushioned office chairs.

"You can wait right in here," the officer said, pointing to the chair. "I'm going to close this door, but it's

unlocked, okay? If you need anything, you can come back down the hall and find me at the front desk. The detective will be in momentarily." Jen nodded and walked into the tiny room and heard the door click behind her. All of the interrogation scenes she'd ever seen on television came flooding back, and she again wished that she had eaten some breakfast to provide her the comfort of a full belly. She and Elizabeth had passed a few restaurants serving brunch on the way over, and the smell of French toast, Belgian waffles, and pancakes still danced in her nose. But those foods were in her past. When she finished with this interview, she was going straight to find some low-carb fare. Every time her nerve faltered and she wanted to give up before she even started, she remembered herself in the video, thick arms flailing and thighs jiggling for all the world to see.

The door swung open, and one of the detectives that Jen recognized from last night eased backward through the door and into the room. His wide body took up the entire doorframe, and when he turned to her, she saw that his arms were full to the brim. He clutched a coffee cup in each hand, and balanced on top of his big arms and against his protruding belly were a couple of thick file folders and a notebook. A pen rolled precariously back and forth on top, threatening to undo the delicate balance of the arrangement. From his wrist hung a plastic bag from Dunkin'

Donuts. He smiled as he turned. "A little help?" he asked, waving one of the coffee cups in her direction. She stood and took the cup. With his newly free hand, he trapped the pen and set the pile on the table. He put the second coffee cup down and unthreaded his wrist from the plastic bag, revealing a box that Jen immediately recognized as a dozen donuts.

"Thanks," Detective Franklin said, setting the closed box on the table. Jen eyed it with a sinking heart. "That coffee's for you, do you drink coffee?" Jen nodded thankfully. He continued, "There's cream and sugar in the bag." He settled himself into the chair and ran his thick black fingers through his short-cropped, gray speckled hair. He wore a maroon short-sleeve button-up shirt with a chest pocket. It must have been a size XL or even XXL, and the waistline of his black slacks was probably the same circumference as a giant, floppy New-York-style pizza pie, which just happened to be the first analogy that came to mind when she considered it. His size seemed deceptive though. He wasn't jiggly, exactly, just a solid rock of a man.

"No thanks, I like it black," she said, feeling diminutive in size but growing comfortable in his presence. "Thanks for the coffee. This hits the spot. I don't know what I was expecting when I came down here, but I certainly didn't expect Dunkin' Donuts."

"Well, I needed a pick-me-up," the detective explained. "A person gets hungry when he's working through the night, and I thought I might as well get enough to share."

It was probably too nice. Jen wondered if this was an interrogation technique. "Are you going to collect my fingerprints from this coffee cup or something?" she asked.

The detective looked up from arranging his notebook, his jaw set firmly. "Is there a reason we should be taking your fingerprints?" He suddenly looked like every criminal's worst nightmare, and Jen's fear began to return. The detective held her gaze for several beats, and then he broke into a smile. "Just giving you a hard time. I'll tell you, if we wanted your prints, we would just ask you before doing some sting operation." He reached over and opened the box of donuts. Jen's stomach growled audibly. Detective Franklin reached into the box and grabbed a chocolate glazed donut. The aroma filled Jen's nostrils and made her mouth fill with saliva and her jaw gave a slight pang. She gulped at her coffee to keep her hands busy.

"So, first thing's first, I'd like to ask you if you mind if this conversation is recorded. Running that tape recorder is much easier than trying to remember with my aging mind all the things I talk to people about."

"Sure, yes, that's fine with me," Jen agreed.

"Great, I appreciate that." Detective Franklin scanned the table and lifted the paperwork. "Now where did I put that tape recorder? Damn things have gotten so small that I lose it all the time. Good thing is that I can just plug them right into the computer and *boom!* There it is. In the old days we had to transcribe everything. That took forever. I don't know if you've ever transcribed something . . ." He trailed off and patted his shirt pocket and then his pants. He heaved himself up from the chair using the armrests and thrust a hand into his pants pocket. "Ha! Gotcha." He set it on the table and hit "record."

"Okay," he started. "I'm Detective Philip Franklin and I am investigating the death of Bess Brantwood. It is Saturday, May fifth, at"—he looked at his watch—"precisely eleven oh seven in the morning. We are in Interview Room D as in dog of New York City's Ninth Precinct at three-two-one Fifth Street."

The detective shifted in his seat and Jen took a sip of her coffee. He reached for the file folder and pulled out a form. "I am with Ms. Jennifer Stevens of the city of Manhattan, New York." He read her address aloud. "Miss Stevens, can you verify that this is your correct address?"

"Yes. Apartment 15B." Detective Franklin nodded and wrote her apartment number down on the form he held.

"And Ms. Jen Stevens, can you state your occupation?"

"I work at the Yummy Channel. It's a cooking network. My title is *event manager*. I work with the publicity team and the TV personalities to set up events, parties, charity events, you know . . ." she trailed off.

"Thank you. And one last thing: you are aware that we are going to be talking about Bess Brantwood and recording this conversation, and you can confirm that I have your permission to record, correct?"

"Yup," she agreed.

"Perfect." He smiled at her and reached for a second donut. She caught a whiff of cologne as he shifted in his seat. "You sure you don't want one?"

"No, thank you." She fiddled with her buttons and eyed the box. There was one with bright pink frosting and sprinkles, and another cruller-style with glazed ridges and crunchy layers. At any other time over the past six months, she would have had one. Maybe two or three, actually. But today, she just wasn't going to do it. Something had clicked. She had entered the diet zone. She snapped back to attention and watched the detective take a bite, nostalgic but not jealous. "What happened to Bess?" she asked. "Do you know how she died yet?"

"That's a good question," he said, his voice lingering for a moment, the bite of donut tucked into his cheek. "We are not sure yet." He chewed his donut slowly and swallowed, then reached for his coffee. "Simply stated it was a cardiac arrest, and we should know a lot more when some other tests come back.

We're not sure that it was natural causes. We're not sure it wasn't. Right now I'm hoping to learn a little more about Bess and the party. It seems like a really unfortunate moment to drop dead, you know, right outside a party in your honor. My condolences, by the way. I'm sorry for your loss. You were friends, right?"

Jen thought for a moment, about how exactly to answer this. "I'd say we were more *colleagues* than friends, exactly."

Detective Franklin nodded. "Okay," he said, accepting her statement without pushing further. "So can you tell me a little bit about your job? I'm not sure exactly what an event planner does. It sounds like you know everybody who came in and out of there."

"Sure, you could say that." Jen thought about how to explain her job. "Well, basically we host events for publicity purposes, and when someone has an event in mind, from an awards dinner to a blogger cocktail party or a big party like last night's, I handle the details. I help with some of the shows too, like when the *Hot Chef* program coordinates with charities, and they prepare a dinner for a homeless shelter or school lunch, you know?"

Detective Franklin nodded. "I know that show. My wife watches it all the time." He lowered his voice and leaned in. "Then she tried one of the crazy recipes at home and ended up setting our kitchen on fire." He leaned back out and wove his thick fingers together.

"Okay, so you started planning this event. Whose idea was it?"

"It's not unusual for television networks to celebrate the hundredth episode of a series. We started planning it last season, actually. If you get to a hundred episodes, you've either made it big or you should call it quits. Bess had made it big."

The detective flipped through some of his papers. "How big?" he asked.

"Really big," Jen said. "Her show had the highest viewership on the network, but I'm not sure by how much. Her bakery was—er, is, I guess, still, maybe—really popular."

"And she was really popular with her coworkers too?" Detective Franklin asked.

Again, Jen considered her answer. "Bess wasn't the warmest person to work with. It was just her personality. She was very driven and didn't really like to hear ideas that were different from her own plan, you know?"

"Ah, got it. So no one liked her at work."

Jen screwed up her face. "That sounds harsh. Everyone *respected* her. I don't think anyone hung out with her outside of work, though. I mean, not that I knew of." Jen remembered the TMZ article her mother had found with pictures of Jen with *Deep Fried and Spicy* star Will Riley, and the network president Tommy Wegman. She wondered if Detective Franklin had seen that story.

"I see. There's people like that who work here too." The detective gave her an empathetic nod. "The captain, for example, is not invited to a lot of cocktail parties. What time did you get to Bess's Bakery last night? And did you come right from your office, or from your house?"

"From the office—"

"Sorry to interrupt, hold on one second. That's the office at 1240 Avenue of the Americas, right?"

"Yes," she confirmed.

"And how long have you worked there?"

Jen squinted and looked up, mentally counting. "Three and a half years," she said. "Two years in the publicity department, and a year and a half in my current position."

"Okay," said the detective. "Let's hear about what happened on the night you got to the bakery."

"So Charlie Rosen, the bakery manager, drove his car over to the Yummy Channel in the afternoon. He helped me load up everything for the party—all the decorations, and some glasses, plates, centerpieces. Oh, and the gift bags. And then I got dressed and did my hair in my office, and Charlie went and got something to eat in the neighborhood. Then we drove over to the bakery. Charlie pulled his car around to the back, and he and Billy Davidsen unloaded the stuff. Then I worked alone in the dining area—Billy helped me with a few things—but basically I got everything

set up by seven. That's what time Bess was supposed
to arrive, so that she could move anything around, or
adjust anything if she wanted. She always wanted to
be there when the first guests arrived."

"Aha, okay." Detective Franklin scribbled in his
notebook. "So she was supposed to be there at seven.
Do you know approximately what time Mr. Rosen
finished unloading his car?"

Jen thought. She remembered him coming in right
after she'd tried her first caramel cupcake. "Much earlier than seven. We must have gotten to the bakery
after six, so . . . six-fifteen? Six-thirty?"

"Okay." The detective nodded. "We're creating a
window, you see? So we know that Bess made her way
to the alley between six-fifteen and eight o'clock. So
we're trying to narrow that down, if we can. Any idea
on how she got there, by the way? Plane, train, auto-
mobile?"

"I think so," Jen said, feeling somewhat more useful. "Well, I don't actually know for sure, but I know
that Bess usually uses a car service. I might have their
card. A lot of people at the Yummy Channel use them.
And, actually, now that I think about it, on Friday
afternoon I heard Bess yelling at her assistant earlier
this week for not renting a limo," Jen explained. "I'm
pretty sure they were talking about the usual car service. They rent us limos too sometimes."

Detective Franklin waited, with his eyebrows

raised, while Jen dug in her purse. A hairbrush, chewing gum wrappers from some long-ago empty pack of gum, an engraved tea candle from a wedding she'd attended, and, of course, her little black book of business cards. She pulled it out and flipped through, then handed him the card. "This is it," she said, pointing. "Delancey Car Service."

"Could you hold on a minute?" he asked. He pulled the walkie-talkie from his belt and radioed to someone to please come to Interview Room D. The person responded with a static-y *Ten-four.* The detective looked back to Jen. "I'm just going to go ahead and get on the phone with these guys now. We don't want to waste any time." Jen began flipping through her black book, wondering if there were any more useful cards that she could hand over. The smell of donuts was driving her crazy, and she considered pinching off a taste. Not a whole donut, just a small chunk to tide her over. But she knew herself. A small chunk would turn into two, and then she'd have the whole thing, and still be hungry, and reach for another.

There was a rap on the heavy metal door, and Jen looked up to see the door swinging open and the uniformed police officer that had pulled her from the cupcake mess last night standing on the other side. She sat up straight, and sucked in her stomach.

His hazel eyes shimmered and he gave her a half smile. "Hello," he said.

Jen was speechless for a minute, then smiled. "Hello! I was hoping that I might see you here. I wanted to thank you for being so kind last night. I—I'll return your handkerchief. It's in the wash."

Detective Franklin's eyes followed Jen's, and he raised his eyebrows again. "Oh, so you met Officer Alex D'Alby last night?"

"Not exactly, I mean, not officially," Jen said. "I had fallen and he helped me up. Sorry I was such a mess."

"You have nothing to apologize for. You were unconscious when I arrived," Officer D'Alby said, his voice earnest and concerned. "Then you sat up and you were fine. What a recovery. You're tough. How are you feeling today? Rested up and, um, cleaned up?" Jen blushed, remembering her awful state last night.

"Yes, thank you."

"Okay, well, that's great," Detective Franklin said, clearly trying to wrap up their moment. "D'Alby, can you please give these guys a call and see if they took Ms. Bess Brantwood to her event last night? Ms. Stevens and I are going to finish up in here."

"Please, call me Jen. Both of you should call me Jen." She smiled again at Officer D'Alby. She wasn't flirting. That would be inappropriate, given the circumstances, and anyway, she didn't go for guys like this. He was too handsome, too clean-cut. She wondered what he did when he was off the clock, when he wasn't protecting and serving the city of New York.

There's no way he would be into a girl like her. He probably dated super-fit women with gym memberships, and Jen felt as bloated as a parade balloon.

"Okay, Jen," Officer D'Alby said.

"Okay, Officer," the detective said, shooing him out. After he left, the detective stood. "I'm just going to stretch my legs. I want to ask you a little bit about some of the people you work with."

"Sure." Resolve spread over Jen, despite the grave circumstances of their meeting and this encounter. Officer D'Alby said she was *tough*.

The detective seemed less enchanted by the interruption, though still friendly, and began speaking again. "First, we can't seem to get ahold of Giselle Martin. We understand that she was Bess's assistant, is that correct?"

"Yes," she said. "Actually, I was going to bring that up. Giselle didn't show up at the party, and that is just highly unusual. When I realized that she wasn't there and hadn't called, I don't know. I started to worry. Giselle's very reliable."

"Were you two friends outside of work?"

"No. Not at all. Giselle and I are very different." Jen thought, *Giselle was anorexic and I am on a see food diet: see food and eat it.* Giselle was obsessed with calories, with fat grams, with burning off every single morsel that passed her lips. She wasn't easy to work with in a food-centric place with her constrictive diet and judgmental stares. The detective was staring at her. "Actually, the only person I am friends with outside of work is Maya Khan."

"Ah, got it. So where could Giselle have been? Family emergency? Suddenly sick?"

Jen shrugged. "I really don't have any idea. I can't remember the last time she took a sick day. She seemed to pride herself on putting up with all of Bess's tirades. She was almost a martyr."

"Okay," the detective said. "Got it." He leaned over to scratch in his notebook. "And you said you're friends with Maya Khan? What's her relationship with Bess like?"

Jen's forehead wrinkled. She wasn't sure what he meant. "They have a slight rivalry," Jen said. "Slight. Professional. Totally normal."

"Well," the detective said, sitting back down and releasing a groan of protest from the office chair. He rifled through the manila folder and extracted a black-and-white printout, and Jen immediately recognized the headline and the four male faces all with the pretty redhead from the gossip website she and her mother had looked at earlier that morning. Of course he must know about this article. A bright red line circled the photos of Tommy Wegman, and Will Riley. The detective laid the page flat on the table between them and slid it over to Jen. "Do you know anything about this? Any truth to it? We're trying to figure out what's true and what's gossip, and once we get that, we've got to figure out what of it is even relevant." His thick fingers counted off these steps one at a time.

"I don't," Jen stated plainly, shifting her eyes from the sheet and meeting the detective's gaze. She thought back to the night before after Bess's body had been whisked away in the wailing ambulance. David had hovered by the police and crime scene investigators. He had stayed with the law enforcement officers most of the evening and hadn't talked to anyone. Tommy had been off by himself too, staring mournfully into his BlackBerry, making a point of ignoring Haley Parnell, who buzzed around him trying to plan for the impact of Bess's death on the network. Will Riley had seemed agitated, almost hyper. He'd brought a friend, the owner of a new restaurant in the neighborhood. They both seemed anxious to leave and get on with their night, and exasperated with the police proceedings. Jen spoke up, "Honestly, I can't even speak to that. It's not that I am naive and think workplace affairs don't happen, it's just that I didn't see anything that would make me think it was going on. Everyone seemed professional."

The detective pressed his lips together and scratched at his temple. Jen thought he might push the issue, but he just jotted down a note and moved on. "One more question for today, although I hope you'll let me call you if I have some follow-up questions."

"Of course." On the one hand Jen wanted to get out of there as soon as possible. Talking about Bess's death scared her, but on the other hand she would really like to see Officer D'Alby again if he happened to come back into the interview room to report his findings with the car service. Something about his presence made her feel calmer, and she could look into his hazel eyes all day. He looked so handsome in his uniform, the badge shining brightly against the deep navy blue.

"I want to know about Billy Davidsen," continued Detective Franklin. "The staff at the bakery mentioned you two dated?"

Jen brought her hand to her forehead. Of course Billy had told his coworkers they'd dated. In some ways she liked how Billy seemed to still adore her after all these years, but in other ways she just wanted to cut the tie that bound them together. She released a breath. "We dated like more than five years ago. I still consider him to be a friend."

"Well then I was wondering if you knew where he might be now. He had an appointment here this morning, but we haven't heard from him."

Jen felt a rush of nerves. Billy! She wanted to grab him by the shoulders and shake him. "I haven't seen him since last night, or talked to him. To be honest he's—well, he can be a little unreliable—hence the *ex* status—but I'll call him and see if I can get him to call you back. I'm sorry about that." She felt lame apologizing for Billy.

"That would be helpful," Detective Franklin said. His face was a stern mask, and he held Jen's stare a second longer than she found comfortable. He continued, "And tell him to hurry up, if you please. We're waiting for him. It's not too often that a person finds their boss's body and then just—poof!—disappears on us. We are really looking forward to getting him in here." The detective reached over and closed the box of donuts, the pleasant demeanor he'd had during the interview seemed to have evaporated. He wove his fingers together again and turned them over, cracking them loudly. The sound made Jen cringe.

Jen wasn't sure if Detective Franklin meant what he said about Billy to sound intimidating, but as she walked out of the interrogation room and down the hall she could hear her pulse rushing in her ears. With each thud of her heart, she cursed Billy for getting her twisted up in his infuriatingly unintentional turmoil.

chapter five

Jen's stomach was now physically aching with hunger, and her nerves were shot. What was Billy thinking? She would have hoped he could grow up a little bit, but he never seemed to mature. Not showing up to a police interview was serious and worry nagged at her. He better be okay. As Jen emerged from the hallway, a teenager of Asian descent with a big black eye and a scowl on his face sat on the bench, probably waiting for a set of seething parents to pick him up. Where was Elizabeth? She looked toward the security guard station and X-ray machine, and didn't see her. Jen looked over her shoulder to make sure Elizabeth hadn't gone down the hall for the restroom when a man barreled out from an adjoining hallway and brushed against her shoulder, knocking her off balance. "Sorry," she said, out of habit. The man hadn't even slowed down. She had to remember to stop apologizing when it wasn't her fault.

She looked up but the man was too far away for her to effectively squeeze in an ineffectual but therapeutic "Watch it, buddy." She recognized him. It was none other than David Brantwood. Bess's husband, or widower, Jen mentally corrected herself. *Widower* seemed formal and old-fashioned for the handsome man who had just pushed past her, still wearing the clothes he'd worn when he walked into the party the night before. The smell of his suede jacket and cologne, the most masculine of all scent combinations, lingered behind him in the hallway. David's presence always left Jen flummoxed. Her conversations with David had always been short, polite, and logistical. When Jen was just starting at the Yummy Channel, the rumor mill had filled her in: before Bess had made it big, David had been her agent. Bess had been one of David's first clients. After their wedding made the front page of *People* magazine, Bess had found new representation to minimize any conflicts of interest.

Watching David walk out the door of the precinct station and cross the street, Jen wondered what he'd do, now that Bess was dead. She had no idea if his agency was thriving or not, but guessed that most of the money that he spent on a day-to-day basis was Bess's. Just a guess. Whatever he was heading toward, he certainly seemed in a hurry as he whisked by her.

Jen let her eyes adjust to the midday sunlight after pushing through the precinct doors. She spotted Elizabeth sitting primly on a bench directly across the street, legs crossed at the ankle. Elizabeth saw Jen at the same moment and raised her hand. Jen crossed the street and narrowed her eyes as she saw what was on Elizabeth's lap. A big, round bagel sandwich, spread thick with cream cheese with a triangle of bright pink lox poking out. Great. Carbs. Jen had to get something to eat or she would break down and attack the next hot dog cart she saw. Her hour-long showdown with donuts in the interview room had left her cranky, hungry, and sad.

"You were right," Elizabeth said when Jen got within earshot.

"About what?" Jen asked, trying to keep the annoyance out of her voice as she watched Elizabeth lick some of the cream cheese off the edge of the bagel. First donuts and now bagels? Was she being tested? Being this close to baked goods was torture.

"You were right about Maya," Elizabeth clarified. "She does look great."

Jen wrinkled her brow. "Is she here? Where?"

"She is." Elizabeth pointed over to a bench to her left. "She came out of the precinct about fifteen minutes ago. I barely recognized her until I looked closely. She didn't seem to see me, but we've only met a couple of times. She had black streaks down her face like she'd been crying. She sat there alone, sniffling and messing with her phone, until just this moment." Elizabeth lifted her eyes meaningfully and Jen followed her gaze.

Jen spotted David Brantwood helping Maya to her feet, a hand secure under her elbow. Jen tried to read their body language as they spoke to each other. Maya seemed relieved, Jen guessed

"Hmm." Jen was surprised they knew each other well enough since Maya despised Bess, and couldn't imagine them being social acquaintances.

"Are you thinking what I'm thinking?" Elizabeth asked.

Jen's stomach rumbled, and she looked at the bagel. It was all she could think about. "I don't think so."

"Let's follow them," Elizabeth blurted. "I have a weird feeling they're more than friends. I have a sixth sense about things like this. There's something about it that seems off."

"I have to get something to eat," Jen protested, but Elizabeth was already up and tugging Jen's arm after her down the sidewalk. "I'm so hungry," Jen whined.

"Eat my bagel," Elizabeth offered. "It's so big, I could never finish it in a million years."

"I don't think I've ever said that sentence in my entire life," Jen mused, trying to remember the last time she hadn't been able to finish a meal. She willed her stout legs to move as fast as Elizabeth's lithe ones. David and Maya were walking quickly, but Jen and Elizabeth closed the gap and hurried across the street, only twenty feet or so behind them. Jen was practically jogging to keep pace. The streets were busy with throngs of shoppers that allowed them to get close to Maya and David without them noticing.

Maya wore a green wrap dress that fit her new figure perfectly, and the hourglass of her body created the ideal spot for David to rest his hand on her hip. When he laid his hand there, Elizabeth gave Jen a look that said, *I told you so.* After a few steps, Maya put her hand around his waist too, and they walked curved around each other. Maya was speaking to him, turning her face toward his occasionally, but Jen and Elizabeth weren't close enough to hear what they were saying. She leaned her head onto his shoulder and brought her left hand up to her face.

Elizabeth wrinkled her nose, like she smelled something rancid. "They look cozy. I'm all for public displays of affection, but this is in seriously poor taste. It stinks of tacky!"

David suddenly stopped, grabbed Maya's face with both hands, and kissed her square on the lips. Jen and Elizabeth stumbled over themselves, and ducked behind a newsstand to remain unnoticed. They stood facing the papers, with their backs to Maya and David. There was Bess, again, staring out at them, her red curls shining and the dimples in her cheeks teasing them. The headline on the paper read "Death of America's Sweetheart." She couldn't believe here in plain day on the sidewalk behind them, the Sweet-heart's Husband was having a lover's quarrel with her friend.

Jen's jaw dropped. She thought back to a conversation she'd had with Maya about how all the good men were either married or gay. David pulled away, his hand lingering to caress Maya's face. The sound of traffic drowned out much of what he was saying, but a few snippets of the conversation floated back to Jen.

"—to the funeral parlor . . . alone . . . I *have* to," David said. His voice dropped to a whisper but raised in urgency. "My *wife* . . ." Jen caught the syllable as it sliced through the clear day.

"—coming with you," Maya whined, high pitched and unnaturally young-sounding. She stamped her foot. Jen and Elizabeth looked at each other. Jen couldn't believe Maya was behaving this way.

"—just need some space right now," he said. Maya pulled away from him, stopped in her tracks. Passersby walked around them, clearing the line of vision between Maya and Jen. Jen saw a big, fat tear slide down Maya's cheek and disappear into the trendy scarf wrapped around her neck. Shiny earrings hung from her lobes. Even her smudged makeup couldn't hide that she looked like a whole new woman. It wasn't just that her figure had changed. Everything had changed. The old Maya refused to put on makeup unless she was doing a studio shoot. The old Maya would crack jokes with Jen about the fashion-obsessed interns. Each Yummy Channel star had their own dressing room, and while Bess's had been stocked with little bottles of makeup, fancy jewelry, and so many clothes that they spilled out of her closet and she had to store them in her studio, Maya had kept hers relatively modest, with just a few essentials. Now she looked made up and painted like a Real Housewife of New York.

"David's walking away," Elizabeth said. "Where is he going?" She stood up on her tippy-toes and looked across the crowded sidewalk. Jen's focus was on Maya, who stood in the center of the sidewalk making a spectacle of herself, sobbing into her hands. Without more than a moment's consideration, Jen walked over to her.

"Maya," Jen said. "Hey." Maya looked up, blinking, confused and weeping. Jen wrapped her arms around her friend and pulled her close. "It's okay," Jen said. "It's going to be okay."

For a moment Maya melted into the hug, letting Jen support her. Then she pulled away abruptly, pushing Jen off balance. "What are you doing here?" Maya asked, her voice full of anger.

Jen didn't want to admit that they'd followed her, but a lie seemed too complicated. "We were just coming from the police station," she explained. "We saw you here. On the sidewalk. Just now." All of it was true, though Jen had left out the middle part about following them.

"Did you see—" Maya stopped midsentence, letting the question drift off into a hypothetical.

"Are you sleeping with David Brantwood?" Elizabeth asked bluntly. Jen covered her mouth with a hand.

"Keep your voice down," Maya said.

"We just saw you kissing him on the street in broad daylight, and you're telling *us* to be quiet?" Elizabeth asked, incredulous.

Maya blushed. "I wasn't thinking when he kissed me. I guess I thought we'd blend in on the street. It was stupid to think someone who looks like *him* would just blend in anywhere."

"Who cares what David looks like? His *wife* just died mysteriously *yesterday*." Jen looked at her friend. "It's been less than twenty-four hours. Don't you understand how this looks?"

"We're in love. He was going to leave Bess," Maya said, looking down toward her pointed-toe shoes. "We haven't done anything illegal. We just love each other."

"I don't understand, Maya. When—where and when did all this start?" Questions were compounding themselves in Jen's brain.

"The last time I was in New York, we all went to that foodie blogger dinner. Remember? Bess completely ditched David to go off somewhere else—

probably with her *boyfriend,* because she was cheating on him too. Did you know that? It's true." Maya nodded, her eyes wide, trying desperately to convince Jen and Elizabeth that she wasn't alone in her wrongdoing.

"I don't know *anything,* apparently," Jen said, surprised at what exciting sex lives her colleagues had. How had she missed all this drama, resentment, and sabotage? Jen hadn't had a good date in almost a year, and here were all these people with lovers and secret boyfriends. It was aggravating. "So, what, you guys started going *out*?"

"We spent some time together," Maya said, a hint of suggestion lingered beneath her words. "We had fun. I called him afterward, but he didn't return my call. He said he got busy, which I totally understand because he's an amazing agent. Anyway, when he was in Nashville in March, he called me at the hotel. I'd lost about ten pounds at that point, and he just kept saying how great I looked. That was sort of the beginning of it all." Maya was talking so fast, running her sentences together. Her voice went up an octave. "And now, now that my tour is over and we're finally back in the city and can finally be together. Now *this* happens. We're both devastated by this whole thing. It really complicates our relationship."

"What? Do you mean his wife's sudden cardiac arrest resulting in *death*?" Elizabeth hurled the last word at Maya. "Well, that should work in your favor shouldn't it? Now you get him all to yourself." Elizabeth was not masking her disgust.

Maya's face went pale, and she shook her head back and forth. The tears started coming again, and for a moment, Jen saw through the makeup and fancy clothes to the earnest girl who used to pig out with her on Little Italy's best cannolis and Chinatown's famous dim sum. "Please," Maya said. "Don't make it sound like that. That's not the way it is. Bess's death was just very upsetting for everyone, and I just—" She broke into another round of sobs. Elizabeth made a face and a thumbs-down sign when Jen went to comfort her with a hug.

"David just said he needed space," Maya said, hiccupping, pushing Jen away. "He basically broke it off with me. Can you believe that? The police don't think Bess just had a heart attack and died. They told David that it looked like she'd overdosed on something. They asked him all these questions about her drug habits. But she doesn't have any drug habits. Get it?" Maya was fuming now, her eyes narrow slits boring into Jen. "Don't you *get it?*"

"Take it easy, Maya," Elizabeth said. "Jen didn't do anything to you."

Maya went on, "Bess. *America's Sweetheart.* She doesn't use drugs, doesn't even smoke cigarettes, and she just drops dead out of the blue. No way. David just told me that the investigators are testing all the food Bess ate and everything she drank the whole day. *For poison.*"

Jen wrapped her arms around herself, understanding the situation from a new perspective. "They think that Bess was murdered." Until that moment, Jen felt like the unnatural causes surrounding Bess's death all could have been a misunderstanding somehow, or an accident.

"I know that the police are going to come knocking at my door, asking me about it. Wouldn't you ask the *other woman*?" Maya found a tissue in her purse and blew her nose. Jen noticed that her purse was a monogrammed Louis Vuitton. Apparently haute coture purses were a new interest for Maya as well. Maya blurted, "They should be asking the *other men* Bess was seeing. David told me all about her infidelity."

"Did you do anything to Bess?" Elizabeth asked point-blank. She had her hands on her hips in full-on confrontation mode. "If you didn't do anything to her, you shouldn't be worrying."

"Of course not. I've got to go," Maya said, suddenly turning on her heel and walking away quickly in the opposite direction that David had walked. Jen called after her but didn't have the energy to chase her down again. Jen and Elizabeth turned to look at each other. Elizabeth's hands were in fists by her sides.

"Are you okay?" Jen asked. "Relax."

Elizabeth exhaled a long, slow breath. Then she inhaled and breathed out again. Jen recognized the cleansing breath routine. When Elizabeth was ready to speak, her voice sounded chipper. "Women like that disgust me."

"It takes two to tango," Jen said, shrugging. She'd never been a moral absolutist when it came to relationships, though she would never personally date a married man.

"Oh, I don't care about them having an affair. It's just so pathetic and whiny when someone is so bent out of perspective. She can't even see that much bigger things are going on than her own ego."

Elizabeth was right. Maya had been acting like a diva, but she hadn't always been like that. What had changed while Maya was out of town to make her behave like the world should revolve around her? Jen's stomach issued a huge growl and she pressed her hand against it.

"Excuse my stomach for changing the topic. I've got to get something to eat. I'm going there." Jen pointed at the first restaurant she saw, a small East Village spot that didn't seem mobbed given the brunch crowd. "Want to come?"

"Sure, I'll go wherever. We need to talk more about this. Do you think Maya was right? Was Bess really murdered? I always knew it couldn't be a natural death, you know. I said that right after it happened. I can't believe Maya started seeing David."

"Hold that thought," Jen said, walking up to the restaurant and peering at the menu posted on the outside door. She pulled out her smartphone and typed into it, clicking until she found a food that she could eat on a low-carb diet.

"Caesar salad with New York strip steak," she said victoriously, proud of herself and her determination in the face of a very stressful situation and full access to fried dough pastries. "No croutons," she said as an aside to Elizabeth. They walked into Alexa, and only after Jen had ordered and taken the first bite of the cool crisp lettuce with warm juicy steak, only after she had washed it down with a bubbly sip of seltzer water with just a splash of lemon—only then did the very strong possibility that Bess Brantwood had been murdered really begin to click.

Elizabeth sat with Jen for half an hour. While Jen ate, they analyzed Bess, Maya, David, Billy, and after a brief update on Officer D'Alby's name and verification of his hotness, Elizabeth left to go meet a client. Jen finished her lunch and paid the bill. She walked a meandering route in the general direction of her apartment, passing by countless restaurants, bars, and dessert spots. She turned when she got to Broadway and walked up toward Union Square. The park was crowded with teenagers and people getting on and off the subway, and vendors with little artsy crafts, T-shirts, and jewelry to sell. Jen made her way through and walked into the big bookstore. She wove in, through the bestsellers in the front, back into the food and diet section. For a moment she wasn't sure whether to turn left into the *I Feel Bad About Myself and Want to Feel Better* "Self Help" section, or turn right, into the *I Feel Bad About Myself and Want to Change* "Diet" section. She turned right.

There were plenty to choose from. Jen picked up one low-carb diet book and started flipping through it. She put it back and grabbed another, then another. They all seemed so dense and scientific. So many words, all composing the same brutal truths: no bread, no sugar, no booze. Follow this yellow brick road and your waistline will shrink. The end. Jen ignored distracting titles like *The Cookie Diet*, and *The Lemonade Diet* because she had to see this low-carb effort through. Jen finally decided on one with a red burst that bragged "Over a Million Copies Sold!," a two-inch-thick paperback. She skimmed the back. *No more than twenty grams of carbohydrates each day. All carbohydrates should be in the form of vegetables, preferably leafy greens.* It sounded doable.

Billy was weighing on Jen's mind. Each scruffy guy she saw wandering around the bookstore reminded her of him. Peter Pans, all of them. Clinging to their Converse sneakers, their funky hats, and sloganed T-shirts. She couldn't believe that Billy had pulled a disappearing act. She pulled her phone out of her purse on the spot and it went right to voice mail. She left him a message. A twinge of concern pricked at her, but she knew that he was probably just hanging out in his sister's backyard birdwatching or rolling joints—or both. She scrolled through her phone, considering who else she could call. Billy's sister Robin's phone number was still saved in her phone after all these years, synced from one cell phone to the next over the years. She wondered if it would still work. She might as well try.

She hit "dial" and listened to it ring. Robin's voice came over the voice mail—the number hadn't changed, apparently. Jen tried to leave a coherent message without alarming his sister too much. "Robin, hi, this is, um, Jen Stevens. I used to know Billy—I mean, I still know him. Anyway, I'm actually trying to get ahold of Billy. If you see him, would you have him call me? It's kind of urgent." She left her number and hung up. All around her couples were browsing the bookstore, holding hands, and here Jen was leaving a message on her ex's sister's phone and shopping for diet books. She felt intensely lonely and tried to shake the feeling away.

Jen walked through the stacks to the cookbook section. The kitchen was the real challenge for Jen: making food that was anywhere near as appetizing as a slice of pizza from the corner shop. Delicious foods popped off the cover of glossy hardcovers, promising simple, easy, delicious, low fat. Recipes for diabetics, for hosting parties, for picky toddlers. A shining red flash of hair caught Jen's eye, and there was the Bess's Bakery cookbook.

Bess's hair was swept up, her blue eyes sparkling, and a smattering of freckles so sweet and girl-next-door pretty, that Jen couldn't help but feel a tug of despair. In the cover photo, Bess held a cupcake in the palm of her hand, like Eve offering an unholy apple. Directly next to Bess's cookbook, Jen saw Will Riley's latest publication, *Deep Fried in the South*. On the cover, his fleshy face stayed frozen in an expression of ecstatic celebration and awe as he gazed at a deep fried corn dog. The two Yummy Channel stars had been at each other's throats for the entire time Jen worked with them. They constantly interrupted each other in meetings, one-upping each other, or suggesting to Haley Parnell, who planned and scheduled each season, that the other's program time get switched or cut. It was exhausting to be in a room with them together. Jen wondered if two colleagues had ever been more adversarial as she found the diet cookbooks. She chose a low-carb title with a lot of glossy photographs and paid the cashier while trying not to notice the mouthwatering display of Godiva chocolate by the cash register. Leaving the bookstore, she walked farther west toward the new all-organic grocery store in her neighborhood before heading home. She walked slowly up and down the narrow aisles with her new glossy cookbook open over the cart's child seat.

She located a recipe that sounded easy enough to make and delicious enough to get her through her first night on the diet. She put chicken cutlets, fresh mozzarella, Parmesan, garlic, a bunch of basil, and a bottle of olive oil into her cart, and then added a dozen eggs and a package of Oscar Mayer thick-cut bacon. She pushed up to the cashier and eyed the person's cart in front of hers. Frozen pizza, ice cream, a bakery pie, boxed cookies, cookie dough, and a single organic vine-ripened tomato. Jen had to pinch herself to make sure she wasn't just hallucinating all these forbidden foods. She averted her eyes and gazed at the magazine headlines.

Most of the covers were graced by famous celebrities airbrushed, polished, hair blown back by a sexy breeze. The headlines varied from "8 Foods to Make You More Attractive" to "Get Your Best Beach Bod in Twenty Minutes a Day." From experience, Jen knew that articles titled "What Men Want" always quoted guys who, among other predictable predilections, were looking for a girl who "actually ate when they went on a dinner date." But also someone who looked great in a bikini. Someone who drank beers with the guys and could climb the corporate ladder with one hand tied behind her back. The best German chocolate cake recipe shared space with reviews of the newest diet books, herbs found only in the rain forest that could help you drop ten pounds in a weekend, and all the celebrities' top diet secrets. An urge to rip the magazines from cover to cover, throw them up in the air, and then dance in a shower of mixed-message confetti crossed her mind. Instead she flipped through a *Cosmo* and tossed it in her cart.

On the walk home, she called her mom. "Hey, Mom, what are you doing? I'm just checking in."

"Just watching a rerun of *Wheel of Fortune*, baby, nothing. Wait, hold on, they're buying a vowel." A second passed and Jen heard the canned applause and then Pat Sajak's voice uttering a disappointing grumble. "Of course there's not an *O*," her mom muttered.

"Mom?" Jen asked. "Is this a bad time?"

"No, no." Jen described the details of her day, her interview with the police and her run-in with Maya and David. Vera was shocked and sucked in a staccato breath of air. "Listen, Jenny, I've been watching the cold case show on Lifetime. Whenever there's a mysterious death, it almost *always* ends up that someone emotionally close to the victim killed them. Everything is normal, until one day they just snap and bash somebody's head in. Why don't you come here tomorrow? I could make Fettuccini Alfredo, your favorite."

Jen took a deep breath. Her mother was nothing if not dramatic. "I can't, Mom. Things are crazy here and work on Monday will be so strange with Bess gone." She paused, and then confessed, "I just keep thinking that if Bess was murdered—if someone slipped her something, it could have been *anyone*."

"Did you smell almonds on Friday night? Cyanide smells like almonds."

"No, Mom, I didn't."

"I can feel it in my bones. Bess was hurt by someone close to her," Vera announced. Jen could hear a commercial in the background, a little sound bite that looped over and over again. She put her key in the door and walked upstairs.

After she said good-bye, leaving her mom to commune with Pat Sajak, Jen slowly unpacked her groceries. She prepared her ingredients and studied the recipe in her brand-new cookbook. Jen dug through her cabinets for kitchen equipment and rinsed off the grimy dust that had accumulated in the months they'd remained stashed away and unused. She added the basil and blended the low-carb pesto, then spread it over the chicken breasts. The sharp, earthy smell of the herbs wafted through the kitchen. It smelled so fresh, so healthful and full of life. She refused to think of Bess, concentrating only on the preparation of her dinner.

She sliced mozzarella over the pesto and then rolled the chicken breasts up. They baked for forty minutes at 350 degrees. While they were in the oven, Jen got markers and two pieces of paper out of her printer. She wrote at the top: OKAY TO EAT. She listed meat/protein, cheese, and veggies and drew some attempted illustrations to accompany the rules. The creative work was therapeutic but not particularly inspired. She hung it on the fridge, the magnet making a satisfying thunk as it stuck the page to the door. After consulting her book again, she drew a line dividing the other page in half. On the upper half she wrote: DON'T EVEN THINK ABOUT IT! She listed every carb-laden food she could summon: cupcakes, soda, apples, oranges, raisins, candy, bread, muffins, tortillas, and pies. With a tear in her eye, she added wine, beer, margaritas, and gin and tonics. As she hung it up next to the first, the timer sounded, and she dug in to her dinner. The chicken was slightly dry, but otherwise it was perfect.

She'd officially gotten through her first full day of low-carb eating. Also, her first police station visit, and a shocking run-in with Maya. Her belly full, Jen rinsed her dishes and then summoned the conviction to toss out the microwave popcorn, a half-eaten gourmet chocolate bar, and leftover pizza and Chinese food that she'd ordered last week. She pulled open her freezer and ran hot water over her mint chocolate chip ice cream, watching it run down the drain in lime green rivulets that were still mildly appetizing. Good riddance. She gazed at her reflection in the microwave. She moved her neck around, angling it to find the most flattering angle. If she wasn't mistaken, her clavicles looked thinner already.

chapter six

In the morning, an incessant chirp alerted Jen to a text message. *Mom, it's too early*, she thought. Blinking to adjust to the light, she spotted her cell phone across the room and climbed out from under her comforter to grab it. As she moved around, she realized she felt a tiny bit hungover. Of course alcohol wasn't allowed on her diet—which she was rocking—so she knew that wasn't the problem. She'd read in her low-carb diet book that people often experience a withdrawal from carbs. Great. Feeling hungover without even having the pleasure of embarrassing herself properly the night before was irritating.

The phone was in her bag where she usually dumped it, on a small, cheap wooden table by the front door. A little alcove separated the door from the kitchen and living room. Jen's bedroom was down the hall on the right, sharing a wall with the kitchen. A small second bedroom—which was so small it may as well have been a closet—was next to the bathroom on the other side of the hallway. Jen always imagined setting the room up as a home office, but hadn't even taken the IKEA desk she'd ordered out of the box yet. She put this into the category of things that would happen when and if she ever settled down with a serious boyfriend. They could have his-and-her work areas. Anyway, her apartment was comfortable and decorated just as she liked it and furnished with compact, self-assembled pieces that were made just for city dwelling. A few framed photos hung on the wall of her hallway, and two large paintings that she'd inherited from Gabby hung in the living room.

She was surprised to see Elizabeth's name instead of "Mom" when she checked her text message. It cryptically read: "U, NYSC-48th, Noon. We r n self dfnse." Rather than responding by text and falling down a high-tech rabbit hole, Jen decided to do it the old-fashioned way. She called Elizabeth. It rang once before Elizabeth answered.

"Good morning, sunshine! I have a client coming in five minutes, so I can't talk. Must get in coach mode."

Jen squinted at the clock. "At nine a.m. on Sunday morning?"

"Whenever and wherever I am needed," Elizabeth answered somberly.

"Okay. What does your text mean? Please interpret," Jen asked.

"I think it was crystal clear. I signed us up for a self-defense class at my gym today! I just kept thinking that if Bess's death really was murder—well, I know I can't do anything if someone puts something in my dinner, but I could tone up my ass-kicking skills."

Jen looked at her tummy flab and felt her face grow hot. "Elizabeth, I do not like straining myself physically in public," she said, though she was scared too. She was anxious to get back to the office, to see everyone she worked with and get some answers. Was Tommy actually seeing Bess romantically? And would Giselle just show up on Monday morning like nothing had happened?

Elizabeth continued, not letting Jen back out. "I'll bring cute workout clothes for you. Meet me at the New York Sports Club on Forty-eighth in Midtown just before noon. See you there, bye—"

"Self-defense, huh," Jen said into the disconnected phone. She threw the phone down on her soft blue cotton comforter and walked to the bathroom for the morning ritual of weighing her worth. The scale had the power to make or break her day. Not wanting to be disappointed or heartbroken, she hadn't weighed herself regularly until yesterday, when she'd decided to start the diet. The number on the scale had seemed impossibly high and had fueled her determination all day. She couldn't wait to see the difference a day made.

She slipped off all her clothes and pulled her scale out from underneath the small bookshelf she used for storage in her tiny bathroom, wiping a thin layer of dust from it. She slid it across the tiles and set the numbers to zero by tapping it with her toe. Then she took a deep breath, held in her stomach, and stood on the scale. The numbers blinked for an excruciating five seconds, then settled on a number. She felt an instant lift in her spirits. The diet worked! *Carb free worked.* She was down a pound. Now she only had to lose nineteen pounds in the next three hours so she could exercise in public with Elizabeth.

Jen gazed into her fridge and contemplated her breakfast possibilities. Pancakes. Waffles. Hash browns. *Not allowed.* So much was off-limits, but thanks to her trip to the grocery store last night, her refrigerator was full of the foods she could eat. She chopped green onions and mushrooms, broke eggs into a bowl and whisked them with a fork. She heated a pan, poured in the eggs, then the veggies, and stirred them around in the pan. After a quick calculation she realized she'd used her kitchen more in the past twelve hours than she had in the five years she'd lived in this apartment.

As the eggs got firmer, she congratulated herself on her newfound cooking prowess and thought about taking a picture to post online. Her friends would be pretty impressed, except for the foodie snobs—but there was no pleasing them anyway. She put out a plate, and just as she was taking her rarely used spatula out of the drawer she smelled something burning. Jumping toward the pan, she shut off the burner and scooted the pan to another one. Jen dug under the eggs with the spatula. They didn't move. She dug harder. No movement, only the increasingly strong smell of burnt omelet. Jen frowned and pushed the spatula down harder. Eggs popped up, spewing out of the pan onto the floor, along with dark brown flecks of char from the bottom of the pan. She stamped in frustration. How did people like Bess, Will, and Maya cook so effortlessly, and why hadn't their skill rubbed off on her after working so closely together? It didn't seem fair.

Jen wiped up the egg with a kitchen towel and considered her options. The middle of her omelet was fine, in fact it looked delicious. Only the bottom was ruined. She shrugged, abandoned the plate she'd set on the table, and dug her fork straight into the center of the pan. Not bad, if she ignored the charcoal on the bottom. She poured some dish soap and hot water into the pan and vowed not to look at the mess for at least twenty-four hours.

Stomach full, Jen opened her laptop to check the latest news. She started with the less reputable sources, which featured some pretty far-fetched theories about Bess's demise. Jen flipped through them, rolling her eyes and shaking her head at some of them, particularly the alien abduction and the vigilante vegan who protested the amount of butter she used in her recipes. It felt strange to be reading all this online about someone she'd actually known in real life. She didn't feel like she was mourning the right way. She tried to remember good moments with Bess, but it felt insincere. The truth was, she hadn't liked Bess very much, and that made her feel terribly guilty.

Along the side of the gossip website she'd clicked into, Jen focused on a bright pink advertisement for XyloSlim. It flashed the promise "Lose 30 Pounds in 30 Days!" A little animation showed an apple-shaped stick figure slimming down to an hourglass over and over again. Jen watched it loop a few times before clicking off the page. Should she learn to cook, or learn to diet? Why was society so confusing about eating and weight? Was being slim feminist or antifeminist? She couldn't worry about it. If networks like the Yummy Channel were involved in the diet pill industry and trying their best to keep the confusion alive so they could reap the financial benefits, Americans didn't have a chance of combating it. Jen had a burst of rebellious pride knowing that she didn't need the XyloSlim. What she was doing was actually working. She was one pound down!

Jen felt antsy and didn't know what to do with her energy before heading uptown toward her first exercise class in many, many months. Should she save her strength? Or get warmed up? After thinking about it for a few minutes she realized that if she waited any longer she would be late, so she left her apartment in a hurry.

She huffed up the gum-spotted subway stairs to the street and walked a couple of blocks to the gym. Through the front window she could see about a dozen hyperfit men and a scattering of tight-bodied women jogging, climbing, and riding stationary machines. She waited outside for Elizabeth, not able to get past the jacked, sweaty guys working the front counter.

Exactly four minutes later, Elizabeth tore around the corner, walking faster in heels than anyone had a right to. A flock of city birds flapped away from the bread crumbs they were eating, clearing a path. Elizabeth looked fantastic in a fitted red jumpsuit and Jen told her so. "I'd never be able to pull that off."

"Why would you? This is me. That's you. You look very nice in your little dress." Jen smiled and stood up straighter.

"Thanks!" She enjoyed the flutter of the sundress around her knees. "Flattery will get you everywhere." They walked in the airy, breezy gym, and Jen tried to look like she belonged there after Elizabeth ushered her in using a guest pass.

In the dressing room, women mingled around in various states of undress. Jen leaned over to Elizabeth. "Is it just me or is the pattern of nudity in here directly opposed to every women's magazine out there? The older, um, bigger women just walk around, letting it all hang out. The younger rib-thin girls are all changing in the bathroom stalls!"

Elizabeth laughed. "It must be a confidence that comes with middle-age wisdom, or rolls, or wrinkles. *I'm not hiding my body just because* you *don't think I'm beautiful.*"

"Someday, when I get old, I want to wear purple. And walk around naked in the dressing room."

"Here, here!" Elizabeth agreed. "Here," she said again, handing a duffel bag to Jen. Jen slid the zipper open and dug in.

"My old jogging sneakers!" Jen squealed, pulling them out of the bag and putting them next to her on the wooden bench.

"You left them at my house after we did that breast cancer walk last year," Elizabeth said.

Jen cringed. She hadn't even missed the shoes. Next she pulled out neon pink stretch pants and a thin cotton tank top. She held up the pants. "Where's the rest of the outfit?"

"Trust me," Elizabeth said. "I picked those out especially for you. There's a special slimming panel. Just try them on." In that moment, holding that outfit, Jen knew that Elizabeth was evil. Really, truly evil. She'd pulled the spandex over everyone's eyes. "Trust me," Elizabeth said again, clearly not affected by the death ray Jen was glaring into her.

Jen had no choice. She had made the mistake of trusting Elizabeth to actually bring clothes that fit her. She sat on the bench facing the corner of the locker room and quickly pulled down her pants. She pulled on the pink pants and then in one swift movement yanked her shirt off and bra. She slid on the black sports bra Elizabeth had included, getting momentarily tangled in the arm loops. Like a dolphin stuck in a net, she flailed around for a moment and slid the bra down over her chest. Then the white tank top. Finally, she pulled her hair into a tight ponytail on top of her head then walked the dead man's walk over to the full-length mirror.

Her jaw dropped. She'd only lost one pound on her diet, but she looked ten pounds lighter in Elizabeth's workout clothes. The panel in the front of the pink pants flattened her tummy bulge, and the bra and tank top worked together to make her chest look compact but full at the same time. Jen turned to the side. Then she grabbed her sneakers and, grinning, laced them up.

"I did good!" Elizabeth said. "You look great."

"Thanks, I lost a pound on my diet." Jen sucked in her cheeks and put her hands on her hips, jutting her shoulders out to look thinner.

"Well, that's great and all, but I take full credit with that outfit." Elizabeth patted Jen once on the behind. They walked out of the dressing room together.

Jen felt attractive in the outfit, but she couldn't help but fidget. She was not used to clothes this tight. She tugged the neckline of the top up to cover her chest. "Jen, you look great, but pull those pants down a little bit," Elizabeth cooed from the corner of her mouth as they walked from the dressing room to the workshop studio. "You don't want a, um, front wedgie situation." Elizabeth's eyes scanned down Jen's legs. "Also, anything you can do to cover up those socks would be a good thing."

Jen hiked the tight capris down, but no matter how hard she tugged they fell a couple of inches above where the sneakers ended. "Ugh. I would never have worn these socks if you'd told me you'd be bringing flood pants." Jen looked down at the snowflakes and reindeer decorating her socks. *So embarrassing,* especially in May. *Laundry day socks.* She fidgeted more.

Elizabeth noticed Jen's squirming. "Stop freaking out. We're hot!" Jen tried to smile. Elizabeth raised an eyebrow. "Seriously, look at you . . . you're beautiful. Just relax and enjoy yourself. Exercise should feel *good.*" Jen crossed her arms over her chest to hide her stomach and looked around at some of the other women in the gym. Elizabeth grabbed Jen's shoulder and stopped her. Elizabeth's green eyes peered into

Jen's blue ones. "It's not a competition. It's not a punishment, or penance for calories consumed. It's just exercise. Come on!"

Jen told herself to loosen up as they climbed up a short flight of stairs toward the classroom studio space. Elizabeth was right. There's no reason she couldn't just enjoy this at the same time that she learned how to protect herself. She wouldn't be kicked off the island if she took a misstep or failed to perfect a move on the first try. Plus, it's not like there was anyone here that she cared about impressing. "Okay, okay. I can do this."

"Yes. You *can* do this. Plus, I have a surprise for you."

Jen grinned. "A surprise? Tell me, what is it? It can't possibly be inside these two-sizes-too-small workout pants you've kindly brought me. There is not a bit of room for a surprise here." She turned a half-turn, gesturing to her posterior, laughing.

Then she saw it. Taped to the studio door was a flyer promoting a self-defense class with an active NYPD officer. A familiar face grinned at her, standing in front of a group of women posing with their biceps flexed in a display of she-power. Officer Alex D'Alby. She looked over at Elizabeth, who had a gleam in her eye. Elizabeth winked at her.

"Can you believe it?" Elizabeth said. "I saw it last night when I came to spinning class."

"Elizabeth!" Jen squeaked, spinning around to run back down the stairs toward the door. "No!" Jen suddenly felt like a clumsy hippo shoved into a tutu in Elizabeth's workout clothes.

"Jen, get with it." Elizabeth's voice revealed her frustration. She tugged her to the closest mirror. "I don't think you see yourself the way the rest of the world sees you. There's actually a term for it. Body dysmorphia. Some of my clients have it. Sure, you could firm up your thighs. Yes, your underarms could use some work, and maybe some of the fat on your backside, and maybe—"

"Is this supposed to be a pep talk?"

"Right. Sorry. I just mean that physically, you're fine. So you're a little chubby." Jen shot her a look in the mirror. "The bottom line is you are you, and everyone else likes you, so you should too. Do you think that if Bess Brantwood had another day on this planet, she'd waste it being self-conscious? No. She'd strut her stuff like she was a supermodel. YOLO! You only live once." With that, Elizabeth turned and walked into the studio bumping her hips back and forth like a sexy cartoon character. Jen watched her go. She breathed in, and then out. She stretched her arms above her head, then touched her toes. She thought of Officer D'Alby's chin cleft. Then she just froze, planted outside the door of the studio, unsure of whether to go inside, hide in the locker room, or hightail it out of the gym.

"Jen Stevens? Three days in a row." His voice cut through the whirring of gym machines, the clanking of weights, and Jen's constant and all-consuming inner monologue.

"Officer D'Alby." A cold sweat broke out on Jen's hands. Jen could see the form of his muscles underneath his T-shirt. He looked even better than he did in uniform. "I'm coming to your class," she explained, sucking in her stomach. "Self-defense."

"Cool," he said. He looked at her earnestly. "I volunteer to teach these things, but they still make me a little nervous. You'd think after working a shift as a NYPD cop, public speaking would be a non-issue." He flexed his neck back and forth.

"You'll be fine," Jen said, smiling, saying it to herself as much as she was saying it to him. "This is nothing, Officer D'Alby."

"How about just Alex when I'm not in uniform?" he suggested.

"Anyway, I'm glad to see you here," he said, his eyes lingering another moment. She followed him into the studio. Alex's voice rose above the women's chatter.

"Hi, hello. I'm Officer Alex D'Alby of the NYPD. I'm here to teach you a few self-defense moves that could save your life." His face was a mask of sobriety, and he slowed his words down to deepen their impact. "A violent crime occurs every five seconds. And I want *you* to be one less victim. Thank you for being here today." Jen loved the way his voice sounded so serious, so polished and rehearsed, with a shake that betrayed his nerves. "Please form a line against the mirrored wall. And can I have one volunteer from the audience?"

Several women's hands shot up. Jen walked through the room and stood next to Elizabeth.

"Jen? Could you come up and help me out?" A nervous giggle escaped her mouth. Now Alex, and the entire class full of women, would have a front-row seat to her clumsy lack of physical fitness. He smiled encouragingly and she let his smile draw her toward him. She took the few steps to join him, drawn in by his smile like a tractor beam, and turned around to face the class. She saw Elizabeth biting down a self-satisfied grin.

Jen refused to reveal how nervous she was. She pasted a huge smile on her face as she looked back at the women standing against the dance barre. Seconds ago she was one of them, but now she stood at the head of the class. Teacher's pet was a sweet spot to be in, and there was no doubt that she was happy to be Officer D'Alby's pet.

"The first thing I want to do is familiarize you with the 'soft spots' on your attacker." He used finger quotes. "Jen, any ideas what those might be on the average male attacker?"

Jen was caught off guard by the question and sucked in air too fast and coughed violently. She grabbed her water bottle and sucked on the end. "Just a second," she said, when she regained use of her lungs. She looked at the other women as their bemused smiles stared back.

She replaced the water bottle and pressed her lips together. She could handle this. She was an adult. "Well, Officer D'Alby, I mean, Alex—" She looked around to see if the other women noticed how intimately she was addressing their instructor. "I guess there's the face. Maybe the eyes, specifically. And, well, then there's the—well, I think the medical term is the *groinal area*." She used finger quotes and bit back the smile that was trying to escape. From teacher's pet to class clown, she could play the role.

A smile cracked Alex's serious demeanor, and he nodded. "I'm not sure that's the correct term, but let's just be imprecise and call it *balls*. Sorry, ladies, sorry to be crude, but if your attacker is a man, and they usually are, one of the most effective ways to defend yourself is to get him where it hurts. The balls. I'm using this language for a reason, ladies. You cannot be *shy* or *appropriate* or *polite* when it comes to defending yourself. I've heard *cream puffs, nuts, rocks*, whatever." The ice was officially broken in the classroom and Alex seemed more at ease in front of the class.

Alex continued, unfazed. "And let's not forget the face, eyes, nose, throat, as Jen correctly pointed out. And I'll show you a few moves that will get you safe *fast*." The class regained its composure and listened raptly as

Alex demonstrated several self-defense techniques, and explained that the voice was a powerful self-defense tool as well. "You should be yelling *No* throughout. Make a fuss. Make a stink. Don't be *polite*," he said again, and paused for emphasis. And you may have heard this, but don't yell *Help*. Calling *Fire* will get more people's attention than calling *Help*." He asked if there were any questions before they tried some moves.

"Jen, pretend you're walking down a dark street with an armful of groceries. Someone's walking behind you, a little too close for comfort. The second you feel uncomfortable, confirm your discomfort. The second you feel uncomfortable, *Act*. I've said it before, but don't worry about being polite." Jen spun around so that she was facing her attacker—her very good looking attacker. She stopped walking. When he took another step toward her, she dropped her fake groceries and raised her arms in the protective stance.

"Good. Then," Alex continued, "your attacker grabs your shoulders. What do you do?" Jen turned her body to slip out of his hold, though every cell in her body wanted to push back against his muscled chest.

"And if your attacker grabs your waist?" Alex's hands wrapped around Jen's waist, and she simultaneously felt intensely attracted to him, and horribly self-conscious of her love handles. She squirmed away from him. "Try that again," Alex said, and put his hands back on her waist. She executed the move as he'd instructed, plunging her arm upward to disrupt his grasp. "Good," Alex said, his eyes sparkling.

She felt his breath before she felt his hands. His arm snaked around her neck, and he begin narrating his assault. His voice was gravelly and warm in her ear. "And if an attacker grabs you from behind, and you're not prepared, remember that your first line of attack is your voice. Shout! *No!*"

Jen shouted, "No! No!" even though her whole body was pulsing, "Yes!"

"And then, your next move is to get yourself out of the choke hold." Jen followed directions to free her airway. "Now use your elbows to hit hard. Once. Twice." Jen did the movements. "Jen, you can hit me harder. I can take it." Jen smiled and pushed her elbow back hard into his strong chest "That's more like it," he joked. "Ouch."

With Alex still directly behind her, she tried one of the moves that he'd told them about. She spun around and pushed with both hands. She knocked him off balance, and he stumbled backward, landing on the hardwood floor. "Umph," he said.

"I'm sorry!" Jen cried. "I thought you were ready."

Alex grinned up at her. "You did exactly the right thing, and disabled your attacker. Don't apologize."

"Now what?" she asked, offering her hand to help him up. He slapped her five instead. They were flirting openly, in front of all these other women. She was overcome with a sense of guilt. She'd gone fifteen minutes without thinking of Bess. It was disturbing how fast she could just fall back into her life.

As Jen smoothed her smile down to contain it, Alex grinned even wider. "This is when you go for the soft spot." He paused. "Right in the—"

"—cupcakes," Jen finished. She blushed scarlet as her mind went immediately to Bess. Why had she said *cupcakes*? It had just popped out. If Alex noticed her gaffe, he didn't react. Had Alex's team made any progress finding Billy or Giselle? Were they any closer to learning exactly what had made Bess's heart stop? Jen retreated back and sipped from her water bottle, suddenly introverted, standing in the exercise studio with all these other people.

After class let out, Jen told Elizabeth she'd catch up later. She waited for Alex by the door and watched the other women flock around him, asking him advice on some of the more intimate physical moves. He answered their questions, and started for the door. "Where are you headed now?" Alex asked Jen as they walked down the steps. He matched her stride and turned toward the door. She had to ask him about the investigation.

"Oh, well, I just wanted to tell you that I really liked the class. I really do feel safer now." Jen gave a tight smile, preoccupied with the questions bouncing around in her head.

Alex smiled, his hazel eyes, brown around the rim and green near the center, gleamed as they walked toward the exit. They were light spots in the center of his tan face. A few wrinkles around the corner of his eyes unfolded as his smile faded. His hair was close-cropped, and everything about him looked determined.

"Did you always want to be a cop?" Jen asked, not sure how to bring up her questions about the investigation.

He stopped as they neared the exit, and looked at her. "Yeah, actually. My father was a cop. Retired now. I don't want to be a cop forever, though. I want to be a detective. I'm putting in overtime on Bess's case and learning a lot working with Detective Franklin and his partner."

"Detective Franklin seems very smart," Jen agreed.

"He is," Alex said. A moment passed. Alex looked toward the door and then back at Jen. A moment passed.

"Can I ask what happened with Delancey? The car service that Bess used? I've got all these questions. Have you found Giselle?" Jen asked.

Alex hesitated, then cleared his throat and answered. "Off the record, the car service said that a woman called and canceled the car a little over an hour before they were supposed to pick up Bess at the Yummy Channel office. We have our people trying to trace the call now. It didn't come from her cell phone. Any idea why someone would do that?" he asked.

Jen frowned. If Giselle had made the original reservation, had she also canceled it? Or could Bess have canceled it herself from a different number? "If she didn't take the car, how did she get to the party? Who took her to the bakery?" It seemed highly unlikely that Bess would walk forty-something blocks in her usual five-inch heels, and the thought of Bess on the subway was implausible.

"If you have any theories, Detective Franklin would love to hear them," Alex said. "No additional information on Giselle so far. Nothing on Billy Davidsen, either. I've got to run to get to the station." He pulled a pen and business card out of the tiny pocket on his duffel bag. "Here's my cell number. You could call me if you ever needed anything. Anytime, whenever." He handed her the card. She looked down. His printing was legible, but not neat.

"Okay," Jen said. "I will." She walked back into the gym, toward the locker room, thinking about why someone would have canceled Bess's car service right before Friday night's event. It didn't make sense. She was so deep in thought that she barely let herself feel slightly giddy to have a handsome cop's personal cell phone number in her hand.

chapter seven

Billy Davidsen put one foot in front of the other, climbing the flight of stairs to Jen's apartment. She'd moved in here the last year they dated, he remembered. In fact, he remembered lugging her big-ass couch up these stairs like it was yesterday. She'd yelled at him for breaking the banister, but it hadn't been installed right anyway. *Damn.* His eyes fell on the loose hardware holding the thing in place. *They still haven't fixed it?* Jen was probably too busy to call the super about it.

He slowed down as Jen's door came into sight. Maybe it was a mistake, coming here and bugging her. Billy got the feeling that Jen thought he wanted her back. He didn't. She was cute and all, and part of him would always love her, you know, because of who she was inside. But he didn't want to go out with her again. He was seeing somebody else. Well, he was sleeping with someone else, anyway. *Not the point.*

The truth was, Jen was too intense now that she was, like, Ms. Business and everything. Basically he just wanted to be *cool* with her. He wanted to be able to *talk* to her about his life and stuff, without feeling like he was annoying her. In fact, Jen was the only one that Billy wanted to talk to about finding Bess's diary. Sure, he had friends, but they mainly talked about music and craft beers. Not death and diaries. He scuffed the toe of his worn-out Converse along the frayed carpet on the corner of the stair, in the place where people stepped and wore the carpet down a millimeter at a time.

That's how he felt. Worn down. A millimeter at a time, although seeing Bess's dead body had worn him down, like, a foot all at once. He kept jumping at noises, and feeling sick to his stomach. He felt like the neurons in his brain weren't connecting right, whatever that meant. Yesterday he lay in his bed all day and only got up a couple of times to pee. Once to smoke and once to eat. The rest of the time he just lay in bed flipping channels, but avoiding the Yummy Channel. He didn't want to take the risk of seeing Bess's face again.

And this book. This fucking diary that he picked up the night Bess died was freaking him out. Bess Brantwood's diary. It was in his backpack and it pulled on his back like it weighed a literal ton. His back ached under its weight. Why had he picked it up in the first place? After the cops arrived he'd been so out of it. He'd stuffed his weed and all the shit in his pockets, whatever was in his pants, into his backpack in the biggest rush of his life. The last thing he needed was to get busted for weed when all he'd been trying to do was save somebody's life. The whole time he sat with Jen after she'd face-planted into a stack of cupcakes, he kept worrying that the cops would search his stuff and find the weed. He almost ralphed at the bakery while he was sitting there next to Jen, no joke. Jen pretty much acted like he wasn't even there. He'd been sick when he got home that night. He just thought of Bess's skin, her hair, her pale face. He went straight to bed without even washing the cold sweat off his skin.

He did not even remember that he had the book until the next day, Saturday, yesterday, when he went to his backpack for his stash. Right before he was supposed to go to the cops. He didn't go—he couldn't. He just sat on his bed, flipping through this book, reading about what Bess Brantwood, his dead boss, wrote about her life. He didn't even know that grown ladies kept diaries. She had schedule stuff, to-do lists, and then long passages about her feelings. Like *"Tell Giselle to pick up dry cleaning," "Try new peanut-butter-scotch cupcake recipe variation," "Get blouse for Thursday's filming—Prada."* The longer notes seemed sad. She wrote about how she didn't think her husband loved her anymore. Some of it seemed nuts, like two pages of jealous ranting about her assistant's skinny bod. There were pages and pages about the people Bess worked with. They were all *useless*—she used that word over and over again. She had a couple of paragraphs about Jen in there, and some stuff about Charlie too. While he was reading it, Billy felt a cloud gather around him, like a lot of negativity entering his headspace. *Bad vibes.*

After more than twenty-four hours of barely leaving his room, Billy decided he did not want this book in his life anymore. It was bringing him down in a big way. Jen was the only person he could think of to give it to. She'd know what to do, so on Sunday afternoon he went over to her place. Someone was leaving the building just as he walked up, so he slipped into the front door and rapped softly on her apartment door. After knocking for a minute he realized she wasn't home. Damn. He sat down on the stairs, turned his baseball hat around, and put his head in his hands, rubbing over the stubble he'd allowed to form on his chin and cheeks since Friday. Someone came in, and he stood up, hoping it was Jen, but it was just an old lady coming upstairs with her groceries. After she'd passed him, huffing and puffing up the stairs, he realized he was a creep for not helping her with the bags up the stairs. *Too late now,* he thought as an apartment door on the next level slammed shut with a judgmental wham. He just hadn't been himself since Friday night.

He didn't bother looking at his watch because he didn't have anywhere else to be on Sunday. The bakery was closed at least through next week. Daisy texted him after she'd talked to Charlie yesterday. Billy hadn't texted her back. He also hadn't called the girl he was seeing even though she'd been texting nonstop. And, worst of all, he hadn't returned the four voice mails that the detectives left, calling to reschedule his interview. The thing was, he just felt too miserable to answer a bunch of questions. He didn't know what to say. A woman was dead and Billy hadn't been able to save her. She was dead and now Billy knew all her secrets, too many secrets to know about another person.

Sitting in Jen's stairwell, Billy unzipped his backpack and put his hand on the book. The dimpled leather cover felt cool to the touch, even though the outside of the backpack and its other contents were warm from the afternoon sun. Was May always this warm? He couldn't remember. The book was around the same size as a frozen dinner, but a little thicker. Not as thick as a novel, though. The pages were uneven and feathered to look old on purpose. Billy ran the ball of his thumb over their edges. Just knowing what Bess had written inside made the thing feel contagious.

Some of the stuff he read in this journal was going to hurt Jen's feelings. Probably a lot. He would tell her not to read it, but he knew her well enough—she wouldn't be able to help herself. As soon as he told her what it was, she'd crack it open and read it all, probably before even yelling at him for accidentally taking it home with him Friday night. The last thing he wanted to do was hurt Jen's feelings, but he just couldn't deal with this by himself.

After what seemed like an eternity of waiting and feeling generally disgusted with himself for being unable to come up with a better plan, Billy finally heard Jen's voice carry in through the door. The front door slammed shut and Jen's voice became clear and audible as she walked through the hallway and started up the stairs. He could tell she was talking with her mother just by her tone. "I don't think it's something in the water," she said. "No, it's not!" Her voice went up at the end. When she came into sight, he saw she wore a flowery dress that looked nice on her. She held her phone trapped between her shoulder and ear, juggling her tote bag and a bag full of groceries. She noticed him when she got halfway up the stairs. He met her gaze. She looked annoyed. He waved a hand in equal parts apology and greeting. "Ma? I've got to go. Now. Billy is here, waiting outside my door." After a moment's pause, she said, "Fine. Bye."

She looked at Billy, unsmiling. Her cheeks were

flushed a pretty pink, and her hair was down, forming a wild mane around her face. "My mother says hello," she said, walking past where Billy sat on the stairs.

"Oh, cool," Billy said, twisting to look at Jen. "How is Ms. Vera?"

Jen shrugged. Billy thought she might be on the verge of blowing her top at him, but she just sighed. "She's . . . Vera. The same as always." She put her key in her apartment's dead bolt. "What's up? Do you want to come in?" She pushed it open and deposited her bags up on the table by the door, catching the door with her foot and gesturing to him.

Billy pushed the journal back inside his backpack and scrambled to his feet. A queasy feeling in his stomach started again. Seeing Jen hadn't exactly made him feel instantly better like he was hoping. He probably shouldn't be here, he thought. He should just go home and crawl back in bed, pull his fluffy comforter up over his head and go back to sleep. Instead, he walked in after Jen. She moved her foot and let the door swing shut behind him.

"Billy, can I ask you something?" He bobbed his head up and down, dropping his backpack on the floor. Then he picked it up again by its strap to retrieve the journal. He heard Jen sigh. Then she did that thing she always did, that little smacking noise of disapproval. He waited, knowing what was coming. She unleashed. "What the *hell* is wrong with you? Like, what is *wrong* with your mind? You're a grown man. Why are you acting like a teenager?"

His stomach lurched and his eyes filled with tears. He was so dumb to come here. Jen wasn't his friend. "Oh god, Jen. Don't yell at me. I know I'm an idiot, okay. I'm just going to go."

Jen screwed her face up, with her eyes in glittering little slits, and glared at him. She tapped a foot. "I could probably get in trouble for harboring a fugitive."

"Jeez, I'm not a fugitive. I'm just a—"

"If you're avoiding the cops, I think by *definition* you're a fugitive."

"Really?" Billy thought about this for a second. He knew he was going to get shit for not showing up to meet with Detective Franklin, but he never really considered it running from the law. More like not showing up to a job interview.

"Listen, I'm sure this will come out in the news if it hasn't already, but Bess Brantwood did not die of natural causes. The police are just waiting on test results to figure out what exactly it was. This is a big deal. Get it?" Jen addressed him like a child, standing with her hands on her hips by the fridge. She looked proud of herself for knowing the inside scoop. She always had liked being the center of everything.

Billy took a breath and stepped back into the apartment, toward Jen. He clutched the backpack tighter, determined to reveal its contents. "Yeah, I get it. Look, the reason I haven't gone is— Well, I don't know if it's the real reason, or if it's just—the thing is—"

"Billy, please. Get to the point," Jen said. "And then let's go to the station. I'll take you over there, if you want. We can call first to see if Detective Franklin or his partner is there, but they probably are. It's only a twenty-minute walk from here." Billy wondered why she was so eager to go to the station with him.

"The thing is—" he continued. "The thing is that I took something on Friday night." There. He'd said it. He pulled his backpack up and unzipped it, pulling out the journal. "I took this. It's—well, I think it's Bess's personal diary."

He watched the blood drain from Jen's face as she saw what he held in his hand. He could practically see the gears turning in her mind. "Why did you take her *diary*?" Jen asked, her voice raising dangerously high. "That's evidence. Or at the very least it's someone else's most personal, intimate thoughts and feelings. Let me see it!" Jen stepped toward him, and he let her take it from his hands. He moved past her to the couch and sat down.

"It's not very nice, Jen," he said. He knew that before too long, she'd see something about herself and be hurt. He wished she had thicker skin. "I don't think she was a very happy woman."

"What the hell?" Jen cursed, still overwhelmed as

she flipped through the pages. "Why did you take this? It's like looking into her whole inner life."

"Honestly, I didn't mean to," Billy said, placing his hand over his heart. "Seriously. I found it out back before I found her. Right by the door. I picked it up before I even saw her, before I called 911, and I stuck it in my pants. I was, you know, trying to help her. Trying to bring her back to life. Then I called the ambulance, I came back in. I didn't want the cops to find my weed, so I put everything in my backpack. I didn't even find it until yesterday morning."

"Oh, Billy," Jen exhaled. She looked back down and seemed to get absorbed in the pages. A few times she lifted her hand to her mouth. He felt the rock return to the center of his belly. He put his arms behind his head, leaned back on her couch, and closed his eyes. He wondered if she'd gotten to the part where Bess had written that Jen resembled a hungry, hungry hippo.

"Jen, maybe you shouldn't read—"

"Too late, Billy," Jen said. "I'm already reading it."

He exhaled but didn't make a move to stop her. "Do you have something to eat?" he asked, not wanting to sit still.

"Help yourself," she responded, still staring down at the journal. "That *bitch*," she murmured as she flipped the pages.

Billy made his way to the fridge and noticed the signs Jen had posted. She must be on a diet. He read the lists of foods she could and couldn't eat. With the exception of pizza, most of the stuff he ate every day was on the approved list. *Not bad.* He opened the fridge and saw a block of cheese. There was some deli meat in the drawer. He looked around for bread so he could make himself a sandwich, but there wasn't any on account of the diet. When he looked in the cupboard, there was nothing there other than a package of beef jerky, a few plastic bottles with dried flakes of spices, and a bag of something called kale chips. He took the jerky and sat down on the couch.

"Can I watch TV?" he asked Jen, ripping open the bag and gnawing on a piece of jerky.

Without looking up she leaned over to pick the remote up off an end table. She chucked it at him a little too aggressively for his taste. Thankfully he caught it without dropping his snack. He turned on the TV, and of course it went right to the Yummy Channel. The *Deep Fried and Spicy* show was on, Billy liked to watch it sometimes—the host was kind of a badass. On Friday night he'd been so psyched to see the host of this show at Bess's Bakery. He'd come back into the kitchen early, before—well, before. The guy, with his bleached, spiky hair and his crazy shirt, had just looked around, then gone back to the dining room. Billy remembered talking to Daisy about it, neither one wanting to admit that it was cool as hell to have a bunch of celebrities in the house.

He watched the show for a few minutes, watching the host bread and fry a bunch of different stuff like jalapeños and pickles. He wondered what it would be like to deep fry jerky. *Weird,* he thought. Jen finally stopped pacing with the journal and sat down on a chair across from him. Occasionally she'd sigh or sniffle. He heard the pages turn every so often. He looked up when he finally heard the snap of the cover closing. Jen cleared her throat and looked at him.

"Get your stuff," Jen said. "You're coming with me."

"Where are we going?" Billy asked.

"To the police station, Billy. You have to tell them what you did. There's so much in here. She had so many issues with other people, and with herself. They need to see this."

Billy's heart jumped up into his stomach. "I thought you were going to help me," he cried, jumping to his feet.

She stood too, putting her hands up to calm him. "I am going to help you," she said, clearly trying to calm him down. "Billy, I'll talk to them with you, if they'll let me. I'll explain how you are, that you just got nervous and didn't know what to do." Jen's voice sounded confident, and for a split second he thought maybe she was right.

"Um—" he said, feeling trapped. He had made a huge mistake. "You should go, and talk to them for me. They're going to arrest me."

"No they won't, don't be stupid," Jen said. "Get your backpack."

He hesitantly walked toward the door, picked up his backpack, and kept walking. He just turned the doorknob, stepped into the hall, walked down the stairs, and out into the street. Jen called his name and it echoed through the hallway. He didn't plan to bail, but as his feet hit the pavement he was glad he'd left. He'd call the detective tomorrow. Maybe the next day. He slid his backpack on his shoulders and felt the weightlessness of it. Jen could take care of it from here.

chapter eight

The smell of garlic, basil, and tomato sauce was over-powering and mouthwatering as Jen walked into Gabby's apartment. She pressed her tote bag close to her body, Bess Brantwood's diary wrapped up inside. When Billy ran out of her apartment, leaving her holding Bess's diary, Jen knew she had to turn this evidence in to the police but didn't know what to say just yet. She didn't want to rat on Billy for taking it, and above all else, she did not want Officer Alex D'Alby reading the derogatory things that Bess had written about her in the diary, even though she knew that was selfish. She needed time to think. She needed her friends. Jen jumped on the train, switched at Grand Central, and arrived in East Harlem fifteen minutes later. Gabby opened the door and handed Jen a glass of wine.

"Drink. Talk," Gabby directed, wrapping her arms around Jen as she walked in. "Tell me everything." Though the air-conditioning was working to cool down the steamy room, working in the kitchen had warmed Gabby's skin and hair, and Jen absorbed the comfort as she pressed her face against Gabby's cheek. Hugging Gabby felt like home. After college they'd shared an apartment, and they'd been inseparable for a long time. Gabby moved in with her fiancé Marco in January, only a few months ago. Sometimes Jen forgot how much she missed Gabby. The quilts, Gabby's stained apron, the kitchen appliances that filled the counters, everything reminded her of those great years of being roommates.

Jen talked but didn't drink the wine—it was not allowed on her diet. She put it on the table and nudged it out of reach as she filled Gabby in on yesterday's interview, what she ate on her new diet, the self-defense class with Officer D'Alby—Alex—and Billy's visit. Gabby sat across from her in Marco's leather recliner and listened attentively. Finally, Jen brought the diary out of her tote bag and held it, her hands fidgeting over the edges, taking a deep breath and fighting the desire to lunge for the wine and chug the whole glass.

"This is too much," Gabby said, wringing her hands together. "I don't believe it!"

"I know," Jen agreed. "Isn't it crazy?"

"No, *you're* crazy!" Gabby said. "I can't believe you started a low-carb diet. How are you going to give up bread, pasta, sweets, and wine?"

Jen laughed, despite her nerves and the horrible mood *"That's* the part of the story you don't believe? How about we put that on the back burner? By the way, *please* tell me you have something carb-free on your back burner? It smells delicious in here."

"Pasta? Not carb-free, right?" Jen shook her head sadly, and Gabby threw up her hands then took a deep sip of her own wine. After a moment of thought she said, "Why do you think Billy hid the diary for two days? You don't think he could have had anything to do with Bess's death, right?"

"Honestly, no way," Jen said. "He's just— I don't know. He's just a kid in a man's body. Always has been. He got scared and instead of doing the right thing, he avoided it."

"Yeah." Gabby considered. "Seems like him, I guess."

"Do I smell garlic butter?" Jen asked, momentarily distracted as the smell wafted to her nose. "Because I can eat that."

"You can eat butter but not bread?" Gabby asked, incredulous.

"It works. I have already lost one pound," Jen said. "Don't worry about feeding me. I'll get something later. Anyway, believe it or not, the diet is the least of my concerns. If I show you this, will you promise not to blog about it until after I turn it in to the police?" Gabby had already blogged about Bess's death and the investigation on Gab & Grub, and her posts were being shared virally all over the web.

Gabby nodded. "Of course! I promise."

Jen knew she could trust Gabby. "Look at this," she said, holding the book up. "There are, like, no entries between March first and March twenty-second. None. Not even notes or to-do lists. Do you think someone could have removed pages?" Jen showed Gabby the spine of the diary. The binding was dense, and if pages had been removed, there were no torn stubs or obvious evidence.

"Jen, should we even be touching these? Isn't this evidence? I mean, that is proof that she was cheating on her husband. Here." Gabby reached into a drawer and pulled out a box of plastic bags. She waved the box at Jen. "Take one of these. Don't tamper with it."

"It's already been tampered with, Gabby. Remember? Billy was carrying it around in his backpack for a day and a half. I have to turn it in. I think I have to tell the police about Maya and David too. They might already know. It doesn't sound like either was hiding the affair particularly well."

Gabby gave her a sympathetic look. "Are you sure you don't want wine?"

"Yeah, no. I mean yes, but no thanks." Jen opened the diary to distract herself so she didn't change her mind. "Here, I'm going to read this to you." She turned a few pages until she got to the page she was looking for.

"January 8th. To-do list.

1. Call theater linguist for southern accent. (Al Goldman 555-9342.) Note: Want cute drawl, not ugly swamp sound.
2. Pack for trip to Las Vegas awards ceremony. (Giselle)
3. Cancel XS meeting with Haley Parnell.
4. Cookbook signing Friday at 2 p.m."

"Whoa," Gabby stopped Jen. "Do you think her accent was fake?"

Jen raised her hands palm up in question. "I never heard her speak without an accent. Could she have faked it all the time?"

Gabby exhaled. "You have to be careful with that book. She's dead and gone, but if that comes out it could ruin her whole brand—her whole reputation. It sounds so devious to fake an accent."

"Gabby, there's so much more. This diary even has stuff about me in it. After the self-defense class, I actually feel like there's a connection between Alex—

Officer D'Alby—and me. I'd hate to blow it by letting him read about the time I ate nine cupcakes in a meeting."

"She wrote about that?" Gabby said. "I remember you telling me that. You had just gotten the promotion to event planner, right?"

"Right. I was super nervous in the meeting, and the cupcakes were so good." Jen recalled the feeling she'd had walking out of the conference room after that first meeting. The problem was, she went for sweets when she felt emotions of any kind: happiness, sadness, nerves, and excitement. It seemed fitting that all emotions should be processed with cake. "They were mini cupcakes, you know. And I hadn't had lunch."

Jen sighed. She flipped open the diary. "Listen to this one," she said, and started reading.

"February 18th. Is it feeding time at the zoo? It seems like it. Everyone around here pigs out all the time. It's like a nonstop horse trough buffet around here. I was in a meeting today when a total of twenty thousand calories must have been consumed between the executives, Maya and Will, and the event planner. It was like a fat fest. The event planner girl wore pants that were a little too tight and muffin-topped all over the top of her pants. God help me if my gut ever looks like that.

Speaking of which, I hired a personal trainer to come by the house to train David and me three times a week—note to self: Have G quit the gym for me."

Jen looked at Gabby. "See why I don't want a man I may be romantically interested in to read this? It's pretty unflattering."

Gabby cringed on Jen's behalf. "G must be Giselle, right? That's Bess's assistant?"

"She's still missing too, as far as I know. To me, Giselle being mysteriously gone is even more suspicious than David's affair with Maya. Bess was always a total bitch to Giselle around the office, and the things she wrote in her diary are venomous. Listen to this." She flipped through and started reading from the diary.

"February 11th. Today my idiot assistant tried to get out of doing her job. I told her, it is your JOB to try the recipe, and taste it, before I use it on-air. Oh, and whenever I ask her to go to the bakery to run an errand it's all these deep sighs, like being around food is going to magically expand her skinny ass to normal proportions. I don't care if she has to go throw up after she leaves work each day (Why doesn't she, by the way? *Everyone* else does.) but she's going to pull her weight, even if that means consuming more calories than she can work off with a spin class."

"Ooooph," Gabby said. "That is brutal. Their relationship sounds awful." A large pot of water on the stove began to boil and Gabby salted the water, then poured in a box of penne. Jen imagined eating it, stabbing big, delicious forkfuls and stuffing them in her mouth. The texture of pasta was so unique and impossible to replicate with carb-free substitutes. She couldn't even have the tomato sauce that filled the apartment with the lush, rich scent of Italian cooking.

"The worst part of the diary, though, is that you can tell toward the end she was going through a lot—even the handwriting changes and looks wilder. She kind of unraveled and started sounding like an angsty teenager instead of a successful millionaire celebrity star with her own bakery and show. There are a few entries about Charlie Rosen, the manager at the bakery. She thought he was stalking her." Jen looked back down at the book.

"March 24th. Charlie showed up again, out of the blue. He was outside our building, and pretended to be on a run with his dog but he was just waiting for me. As soon as I gave him a glance he pounced all over me, asking me to fix the payroll glitch so he'd get a check. I told him my accountant is

getting around to it. Note: Call accountant about
that. Now I don't even want to go to the bakery
anymore for fear of Charlie bugging me to death."

Gabby looked at Jen "Wow. Do you think he had
anything to do with—"

"I mean, who knows?" Jen said. "This diary is a
Who's-Who of people who might want to hurt Bess
Brantwood."

"She must have been miserable. Anyone who
would think such nasty things about other people
must be miserable themselves," Gabby said.

Jen's eyes filled in earnest, and she pressed her lips
together. "I know. Right after Bess died, the last thing
I wanted was to get involved. I didn't even like her,
not really. But now I'm involved, whether I want to
be or not. I'm going to help the cops catch whoever
did this. What time is it?" Jen asked.

"Close to five," Gabby said.

"Want to hear one more before I go forth in the
name of justice?" Jen asked.

"Of course."

Jen flipped toward the end of the book.

"April 4th. I'm going to slaughter David. He
thinks that I don't know about him and that slut
Maya Khan. She can't even cook—her nasty cakes
taste like bricks. She actually thinks she can

compete with me. I smelled her all over him when he came home last night. They think they can make a fool out of me? I'll show them who the fool is."

"I can't believe Bess knew about the affair," Gabby murmured thoughtfully. "Last month—that's a long time. I don't remember reading anything about a sep- aration, and I blog about all the food-world news." She thought for another moment. "I can't believe they kept this under wraps."

Jen stood up. "I could sit here all night and try to put together the mystery of the decade, but I've got to go to the police station before I get arrested for withholding evidence. Thank you so much for letting me come here to get myself together."

"Please," Gabby said. "Don't thank me. You didn't even let me feed you. Promise me you'll get something to eat tonight?"

"I promise," Jen agreed. "Wish me luck." Gabby did, and Jen left, stepping out into the late afternoon. She started walking, but when she got to the subway station closest to Gabby and Marco's house, she wasn't quite ready to get on the train yet. The fresh air felt so nice, and while she knew that she couldn't put off her trip to the precinct any longer, she simply didn't want to rush there. Unable to think of a more creative dinner solution, she stopped by a burger place where she and Gabby ate a few months ago. She studied the menu and ordered a burger with no bun and no tomatoes, onions, or ketchup to go. She held it in the wrapper and chomped it while walking down Lexington. A few blocks later, full and ready for whatever pastries the precinct might have in store this time around, she headed down the subway stairs, down to the platform, and downtown to the precinct.

She exited the train at Astor Place and walked quickly toward the station, emboldened with each step forward to turn over the diary and help with the investigation any way she could. Giselle was foremost on her mind as she walked toward the precinct, and the way Bess described their relationship in the diary was quite alarming. Jen had never fully trusted Giselle. Upon a moment's reflection, Jen realized that she didn't really trust anyone who didn't eat. Giselle had earned a nickname at the Yummy Channel. The Food Freak. The rail-thin assistant looked like she hadn't eaten a proper meal in years, and tended to get unhinged around food. She'd go office to office, huffing and tsking, counting calories, bemoaning how long she'd have to work out to burn off each bite. She stalked by any shared food left around the office, walking slowly over and over again past gift boxes of chocolate, leftover pizza, popcorn tins, or homemade cookies. It was unnerving, and Jen could definitely imagine Giselle snapping and doing something to hurt Bess.

Jen's stomach twinged, and she let out a small burp as she picked up her pace and turned onto Fifth Street. The city was as busy as usual on Sunday evening, with people out on errands, or just enjoying the afternoon, but no one seemed to have heard her body's outburst. She knew that stomach troubles could bother her for a few days after starting the low-carb diet, but her book promised that after a few days she'd be feeling as good as new. Her biggest concern was her odor. Everything she'd read about a carb-free diet warned that the chemicals her body released when it burned fat would make her breath smell. The inside of her mouth had a metallic, grimy feeling all day. In fact, now that she reflected on it, she'd noticed Gabby turn away quickly from her earlier at an odd point in their conversation. Call it paranoia, but Jen thought it was her breath.

The worst part was that she couldn't even chew gum or eat mints: even the sugarless variety had too many carbs. She pulled the bottle of water from her bag and took a swig. On this diet, you could tell you were doing the right things by your breath smelling bad. It was the opposite of a bakery, where someone as experienced as Bess could tell by the scents wafting out of a hot oven whether or not she'd gotten a recipe right. Maybe bad breath was in the nose of the besmeller—what smelled like mouth funk to others smelled like success to Jen. When she reached into her bag to put her water bottle in, her hand brushed Bess's diary. In an instant, her bad breath seemed trivial. At least she was breathing.

Jen approached the Ninth Precinct on Fifth Street and could see about twenty people out front. Even from a couple of blocks away, it was immediately recognizable as a protest. A few cameras were on tripods capturing the action, and Jen could see the NBC and ABC logos, along with the umistakable blond hair of Callie Rogers. Of course she'd be here. Jen squinted to read the sign that one of the women was holding up. POLICE: GIVE US YOUR BESST, NOT YOUR WORST it read. *A stretch*, Jen thought. Someone else hoisted a sign that said JUSTICE FOR BESS BRANTWOOD. Jen rushed faster toward the building to see what was going on.

Jen made eye contact with one of the protesters and walked toward her. She was a slim woman with bifocals and gray, greasy hair pulled back into a ponytail. "Hey," Jen said. "What's going on here?"

"You're the woman from the YouTube video," the woman exclaimed. Jen cringed. She'd almost forgotten about the embarrassing video of her falling into the cupcakes on Friday night. The woman's eyes were red and puffy, and she blinked a few times. "Anyway, thank god you're here," she said. "I thought no one from the Yummy Channel was going to show up." Jen looked around. She didn't recognize any of these people.

A very short woman walked up, with a head sprouting red curls that looked surprisingly like Bess's locks. "Did you bring your own picket sign?" the woman asked. "Welcome, we're glad you're here."

Jen shook her head, attempting diplomacy. "I'm just here to—"

"You didn't come to join us?" The greasy-haired woman tugged at her ponytail, tightening and adjusting it. "So no one who was actually *there* is going to be here today?" Her disappointment was palpable.

Jen shook her head. "I'm sorry. I just came to talk to the detectives."

The woman narrowed her eyes, and began pulling harder at her hair. "Why are you going in to talk to the detectives? What do you know?" The hair pulling must be a nervous tic, and with the rigor she was going after her own scalp, this woman must be very nervous. Jen took a step backward and reflexively fluffed up her own hair.

"Mary," the redhead said. "Cool it." The redhead angled her body ever so slightly, just enough to exclude Mary from their conversation. "I'm Janine Herring. I'm the president of the New York chapter of the Bess Brantwood fan club."

"Oh." Jen looked more closely at the women gathered in front of the police station. "I see." Janine wore a long-sleeved yellow dress with a wide belt at the waist. It flared out around the hips, just like something

June Cleaver would wear, except the proportions were all off. Janine was small on the top and heavy on the bottom, so the dress made her look like a bell instead of an hourglass. She wore a backpack and its nylon straps confused the vintage look. On her feet, she sported a pair of flat-soled riding-style boots.

"We're protesting here today because the police are not releasing information about Bess Brantwood's death to the public. Her fans—her friends—need to know what happened. We are heartbroken." Janine paused for effect. "Heart. Broken," she repeated earnestly, her eyes filling with tears.

Jen touched her arm, and she could tell how crushed Janine truly was. Bess really had touched people, no matter how difficult she'd been to work with. Janine continued, "Bess was a wonderful, incredible, kind genius and her death is a tragedy." Jen could see the passion burning in Janine's eyes, and stepped back, intimidated by the intensity. Janine continued, "Bess was a woman we could all aspire to be. I feel—we all feel—that Bess Brantwood's values carried through the television, through her recipes, and into our cooking. We could literally taste the love when we watched her show and followed her recipes."

Jen pressed her lips together and held her tote bag tighter. She could only imagine Janine Herring's reaction to some of the excerpts in Bess Brantwood's diary. What would she think if she knew her idol was really calculating, cheating, and manipulative and not the Southern domestic goddess they'd seen on TV?

"The police need to do their job. They're withholding information—either that or they're completely incompetent," Janine said, raising her voice. A few of the women around her let loose sounds of approval. Callie Rogers stepped forward and tilted her microphone toward Jen and Janine. "They need to let us in on what is going on in there." Janine shook her fist and hoisted her sign to her shoulder.

"Right," Jen said, not knowing what else to say. She paused a moment, unsure of how to extricate herself from the conversation and avoid providing another embarrassing clip for the news to post online and humiliate her with. "Good luck."

"Good luck to you too," Janine said. She looked Jen in the eyes and tilted her chin up and out, toward the police station. "You'll need it if you're going in *there*."

Jen walked in the door of the Ninth Precinct office. Before she'd taken three steps, a uniformed officer had his hand up, bidding her to stop. He said, "Ma'am, you're going to wait outside like we told you. An officer or detective will be out to talk with your group when they get a chance."

Jen shook her head. "No, I'm not with them. I have information for Detective Franklin, actually." The cop looked dubious. "See," she dug in her bag. "See? I have his card and I had an interview yesterday morning. I worked with Bess Brantwood at the Yummy Channel. I'm not a protester."

"Is he expecting you?"

"No, he's not. I have some information for him. I could talk to Officer D'Alby too, if he's around." She tried to sound offhand when she mentioned Officer D'Alby's name. She loved the way it rolled off the tip of her tongue.

The cop took a moment to weigh her legitimacy, looking closely for any sign of affiliation to the Bess Brantwood fan club. "Go on through. Stop at the front desk to check in, and they'll call back to see who's here. I think Detective Franklin might be gone for the night, but D'Alby's probably still in. He's been working around the clock on this one."

Damn. Jen knew that Alex would probably see or hear about the diary eventually, but she did not want to physically hand him a book that detailed her grossest eating habits. She didn't have a choice now. Besides, maybe the information in the diary would actually help them solve the murder and if Alex could do that it would be good for his career too. She put her tote bag on the X-ray machine and retrieved it on the other side, walked down the now familiar hallway to the front desk.

"Hi," Jen said to the uniformed officer behind the desk, her eyes widening at his size. "I'm Jen Stevens. I need to speak to Detective Franklin if he's here." The man was enormous. Standing above where he sat, Jen could see his rear spilling over both sides of the chair. His uniform barely fit, and the buttons of his shirt were tugging and threatening to pop off. He did not wear a gun belt around his waist. Jen spotted it on the corner of the desk.

"Detective Franklin's gone for the night, ma'am," the man said, shaking his head. The flesh under his chin shimmied back and forth, an echo. Jen furrowed her brow. A *ma'am* instead of a *miss*? The mountainous cop looked at her. "Do you want me to get another detective for you?"

Jen thought a moment, but after her conversation with Alex earlier at the gym, she knew how invested in the case he really was. He was the person she needed to talk to, even if it meant he'd see what Bess wrote sooner instead of later. "Officer D'Alby? Is he here?"

The large officer nodded, again sending his flesh aquiver. He picked up the phone and punched at the numbers. "D'Alby? A woman here to see you." He paused, then hung up. "Wait over there," he said, gesturing at the bench. Jen sat down and tried not to stare while she waited for Alex. Though she scolded herself for being judgmental, Jen wondered how this man could even function as a police officer. What if someone came in and threatened disorder? How would the man prevent him from acting? What if a fugitive escaped from one of the interview rooms? There was no way this man could chase them down and return them to their interrogation.

"Jen?" Alex's voice surprised her. She tore her eyes away from the man's elephant-size thighs to look up at him. Alex followed her gaze and looked quizzically at her. "Why don't you come with me to the interview room?" She stood up and followed him down the hall, this time trying not to stare at his fit bottom as she remembered their flirty interchange earlier in the self-defense class.

"What's up?" he asked, as he gestured toward a chair for her to sit.

She exhaled and reached into her tote bag to pull out the diary. "I actually have a lot to tell you. First, I saw Billy Davidsen this afternoon. Right after I got back from the self-defense class—he was in my building waiting for me." She trailed off, trying to think of something she could add to make sure Alex knew Billy didn't come over and wait for her often. Despite the seriousness of what she had to share with the officer, she couldn't deny the attraction she felt to him here in this room. She wondered if the sexual tension she felt was one-sided.

"Did he hurt you?" Alex asked, setting his jaw. His instant protectiveness made Jen feel safe. Why did this man elicit such fluttery feelings in her? He made it hard to concentrate on what was really important, the diary and solving the mystery of Bess's death.

"No, not at all," Jen said. "It wasn't like that. He was just scared. I told him he should come here to the office, but he—well, he couldn't for some reason."

"Did he say where he was going?"

"No, unfortunately. But he did say why. This is Bess Brantwood's journal and planner." Alex's eyes got wide. Jen continued. "Billy apparently picked it up without knowing what it was right before he found Bess's body. He put it in with his own stuff in his backpack and forgot about it until Saturday."

"Are you sure it's her diary? How long have you had this?" He peppered her with questions, one after the next, and she felt off guard.

"Well, he left it at my house around two-thirty this afternoon, I guess. Yeah, right around then."

"Jen," Alex stated, looking down at the black digital watch around his wrist. "It's almost six p.m. Why didn't you call us when this happened?"

"I just—I don't know. I had to go meet with a friend, so—"

"Wait. You see someone who just a few minutes previous I reminded you we were looking for . . ." Jen thought back to the gym. Her face felt hot, and she felt a lump form in the back of her throat. "And then he gives you vital evidence . . . and then you go see a friend instead of calling us?"

"I just didn't think a few minutes would make a difference."

"In an active investigation? Of course it makes a difference. The first hours are vital for gathering information. Did you show the friend the evidence?" he asked. He was drumming his fingers lightly on the table, and the movement made Jen nervous.

"Well, yes, but she promised she wouldn't write about it."

"Write about it?"

Each question was making Jen more defensive. She plunged her shovel in again, digging a deeper hole. "She's a blogger, but she promised—"

"You showed a blogger evidence before turning it in?"

"I'm sorry," she said finally, looking down at the diary in her hands. "I didn't think—"

"Huh," Alex said, cutting her off. "Hold on a second. Hold that thought." He stood up and opened the door, calling down the hall. "Joe?" He stepped farther in the hall and called again. A moment later Alex walked back in the room with another man, a few years older than Alex with a receding hairline and a thick gray mustache. Jen recognized him from Bess's Bakery on Friday night. "This is my partner, Officer Joe Romano. This is Jen Stevens." Officer Romano had a black plastic case in his hand. He laid it on the table and unsnapped the plastic latch. He pulled out a printed pad of paper and handed it to Alex. Then he extracted a pair of plastic gloves and a clear plastic bag with a gray square on it. He put on one of the gloves and took the diary from Jen. He opened it and flipped through it.

"Jen, Officer Romano is processing this as evidence. I need you to tell me again how it came into your possession. I'm going to be writing this down so we can submit it."

This wasn't going at all how she'd imagined. She stumbled over her words as she told them about it. "I wanted to tell you about some of the entries—" Jen tried. "I read them, and they are really crazy. After reading it, I just think Giselle is obviously—"

"We're working on finding Giselle Martin," Officer Romano stated flatly.

Alex took a breath. "We're also working to find Billy Davidsen. As you know."

"He didn't *do* anything," Jen said. "Really. He's just immature."

"With all due respect, Ms. Stevens," Alex said, "we'll be the judge of that." Jen crossed her arms over her chest. She had not missed Alex's formality when addressing her.

After she'd finished answering their questions about the diary, Alex began packing up the case. Officer Romano, quiet except for a few short questions and responses, tucked the labeled plastic bag and the form he'd filled out under his arm.

"Hey, Romano, do you have a piece of gum?" Alex asked. Romano used one hand to dig in his pocket for a bright green pack of spearmint-flavored gum. He held it out to Alex. Alex grabbed the whole pack. "Thanks."

Romano grabbed the black case and left the interrogation room with a polite nod to Jen. Alex took out a piece of gum and laid the rest on the table in front of Jen. "Help yourself, if you want a piece," he said, looking away.

She was mortified. A hot red blush flooded her face and neck. Alex's not-so-subtle comment on her breath came through loud and clear. Could she be paranoid and misreading his generosity? Unlikely. She considered her options and reached begrudgingly for the gum. She had more to tell this man, and whether or not he respected her when she was finished, she would not continue to disgust him with her bad diet breath. She comforted herself knowing that bad breath meant she was continuing to burn fat.

"I've got something else to tell you," Jen said. Her mouth felt dry despite the gum she was chewing, and she could hear her heartbeat in her ears, but she pushed forward. "If you're mad at me about the diary, you might be even more irritated about this. David Brantwood has been seeing Maya Khan, the star of another Yummy Channel show, for a few months. I just found out yesterday when I saw them together." She let the words flow out of her mouth as quickly as she could, without looking at Alex's face. She fidgeted with the hem of her blue flowered dress, wrapping it around her finger. He was silent. After a few moments he cleared his throat, and Jen looked up.

"Are you smiling?" she asked, bringing her hands palm up.

"No," he said, tucking the corners of his mouth back down, removing any levity from his expression.

"What?"

"Nothing." Alex's face returned to neutral. "Nothing," he repeated. "You just said that whole thing so fast. It was—" He stopped himself. "It's nothing."

"I just thought you needed to know that the *husband* of the dead person is dating her professional rival."

Alex's thick eyebrows raised at Jen's tone, making his forehead wrinkle a bit. "We appreciate that. We actually were aware of their relationship. David told Detective Franklin during their initial interrogation."

"Oh." She'd been preempted. She sucked on her gum and laid her hands flat on the table. "Great. Okay, then. I guess I'll be going."

"Jen?" Alex said. His eyes, more green than brown, flickered in the fluorescent lighting of the interview room. She marveled at his ability to look handsome even in this lighting.

"Yes, Alex," she said. They were back on a first-name basis, apparently.

He looked at her a long moment, his head cocked to the side. One elbow was across his knee, and his other arm was on the table close to hers. She stared at their hands, thinking about what it would feel like if he moved his just an inch over to touch hers. "Thanks for coming in tonight. If you see Billy again, just call us. You have my number. You have Detective Franklin's number. Just call, okay? We'll take care of the rest."

"Got it," she assured him. "I just—I do want to help, but there's something that I wasn't completely honest about with Detective Franklin." Alex crossed his hands over his chest and narrowed his eyes. "I mean, it's not that I wasn't honest. I just didn't paint the whole picture. The women protesting outside, you know, they love Bess Brantwood so much, and I know that the whole world thinks she's amazing, but I have to tell you that the people who interacted with her on a personal level—not just me, but others as well—we felt bullied by her. Intimidated and bullied, and that's why I think it's so important that you get in touch with Giselle if you think Bess's death was—"

"Jen, rest assured that Giselle is on the detectives' radar. There are other leads too that I can't discuss at this time. We have already been to the Yummy Channel and we will be back there tomorrow to ask more questions and learn as much as we can. Trust us, we will get to the bottom of Bess Brantwood's homicide."

"Homicide." Jen let the word settle in the room. "That's the first time I've heard it officially referred to as a homicide and not a suspicious death."

"Don't go telling the blogger, okay? It will be released publicly by the captain at a press conference tomorrow morning."

Jen pressed her hand to her mouth. "Oh my god." The confirmation of her suspicions made her stomach churn even more than it already had. "Did you ever find out how she got to the bakery from the office?"

"We think she arrived in a yellow cab, but we're waiting on confirmation. If she'd used her credit card it would be easier to trace, but she must have used cash." He stood up. "Now I've got to go call Detective Franklin and interrupt his Sunday dinner to read that diary. We'll call you if we have any questions."

Jen thought of Bess in her final moments, her heart racing, walking toward her bakery, safety in sight. Had she even known what hit her? If her death was anything like her life, Bess had tried to be fully in control of her situation until the very last second. She shook hands with Alex and stepped into the evening air, now nearly dark. Jen felt a chilly breeze rattle the leaves lining the block, cutting through the warm, still night as she exited the precinct. The temperature had dropped. She rubbed her arms for warmth. Bess had been murdered. She had a feeling that all the fragmented pieces of Bess's life must fit to form a cohesive explanation of her death, but here on the sidewalk, Jen simply couldn't figure out how.

chapter nine

Jen jolted awake, sitting upright, knocking her pillow off the bed. The clock read five o'clock in the morning. Monday morning. The taste of one of Bess Brantwood's famous red velvet cupcakes lingered in her mouth, and the sensation of biting still vibrated freshly on her tongue. She cursed herself for having accidentally broken her diet until she realized that her indiscretion had been subconscious. The dream that startled her awake came back in flashes.

She had been in the Yummy Channel studio where Bess filmed her show, sitting in the studio audience, watching Bess Brantwood mix together ingredients in a recipe. Giselle and Maya were in the audience as well. Jen knew they were there; she could sense their presence, but she couldn't see them. She looked all over, but every time she thought she saw them, they disappeared. The audience clapped suddenly, and Jen clapped along, although she wasn't sure why. She looked up at the stage, and Bess was lying dead on the prep counter. She looked beautiful, her red curls neat around her face, her makeup perfect, lilies clutched tightly to her chest. Callie Rogers had a news crew that zoomed way in on Bess's face. "What do you think of your murder?" she asked Bess, holding the microphone toward Bess's frozen face. The audience clapped, hooting and hollering, stomping their feet. Jen looked around, horrified, and the crowd seemed to be reveling in Bess's demise. She knew she heard Will Riley's raucous laugh, thick and phlegmy, from behind her in the crowd.

Then, suddenly, moving without moving, Jen was at a wake. She looked around for anyone to talk to, someone to whom she could pay polite condolences, but there was no one in sight. She walked from a foyer into a large living room. On the table in the living room were bowls of chips, pretzels, popcorn, and candy. Jen reached for them but remembered her diet. She was incredibly hungry, her stomach growling and sending waves of discomfort through her body. She called out, "Hello, is anyone here?" She wandered into a dining room where a large, ornately framed portrait of Bess monopolized an entire wall. In the painting, Bess was painted with a halo, but the sneer on her face looked demonic.

On the dining room table, which stretched on and

on longer than Jen could see, there was a huge variety of food. A bowl of pasta salad, a long loaf of browned garlic bread, bubbling macaroni and cheese, all the foods that Jen couldn't touch. She looked for poultry, fish or meat, eggs, or vegetables, even a cheese platter, but there was nothing that didn't have any rice, breading, pasta, or flour. As she walked the length of the table, it continued to expand, stretching longer and longer. She walked faster, then started running, her stomach cramping with hunger pains. She slowed down as she reached the desserts. Cobblers, donuts, sparkling sugar cookies, all piled over the table, overlapping and begging to be eaten.

Jen, succumbing to her hunger, giving in to the temptation, reached for the best-looking dessert on the table, one of Bess's red velvet cupcakes. She bit into it, letting the frosting melt over her tongue, the moist cake coat her mouth as she savored it. As she looked to her hand to take a second bite, she saw red pouring out of the center of the cupcake. It flowed down from her fingertips and palm, pooling on the floor beneath her feet. Blood. Jen looked up, and Bess's portrait was shaking a finger at her, scolding her for breaking her diet.

The sweat on Jen's brow made her feel even hotter as she sat in her twisted sheets. Her hands felt dirty. It was far too early to get up, but her heart was pounding so hard she didn't think she could go back to sleep. She had to leave for work in three and a half hours.

She wondered what returning to the Yummy Channel would be like that morning. Would there be people crying in the halls and bathrooms, or would it be business as usual, with tapings, meetings, budgets, and events? Either possibility seemed unfathomable. The last time she'd been at the office, Friday morning, seemed like a million years ago. She'd avoided even logging in to her work e-mail account over the weekend, a rarity for Jen. She had three events in various stages of planning, and she had no idea what might happen with them. Haley Parnell and Tommy Wegman would have to figure out the right direction for the company in the wake of Bess's death. Jen threw on her soft downy robe and walked to the kitchen to pour a tall glass of water, gulping it down, trying to wash away her discomfort.

She was hungry, and she could see in the clarity she felt at this predawn hour that before she started the diet her *weight* problem wasn't just about weight. It was a *life* problem. It affected her friendships, her social life, her work life, her romantic life—or lack thereof. Her struggle with food had its fingers in every conscious aspect of Jen's life, and clearly the unconscious ones too. When she'd started the diet on Saturday morning, the scale blinked the cold, hard truth that she was twenty-five pounds over her

prescribed ideal weight at five feet and four inches
tall.

No, she wasn't so obese that she couldn't walk or
climb stairs or run to catch the train. She wasn't even
so obese that she couldn't, with the help of empire-waist
garments and strategic layers, camouflage the full
extent of her bulges and look at least slightly sexy for
a night on the town. But it didn't matter. She was sick
of hiding the weight. Sick of trying on her clothes
that didn't fit, and then shoving them back in the
closet, or worse, wearing them and feeling awful all
day. Most of all, she was sick of wondering if people
around her were judging her as a weak person for
being overweight. Reading Bess's diary hadn't helped
her push those thoughts out of her mind. Weight
seemed inexorably linked to morality, and Jen wanted
so badly to be *good, well-behaved, controlled, and thin*
instead of *sloppy, unhinged, bad and fat.*

Jen put a pot on to boil to make a cup of chamo-
mile tea. Thankfully that was still allowed on her low-
carb diet. When it whistled, Jen poured the steaming
water into her cup and added the tea bag, holding the
string and dunking it a few times, then letting it steep.
Ordinarily she'd pour in a little bit of milk and sugar
for maximum comfort, but of course her diet prohib-
ited it. The tea didn't quench her hunger, though, and
she opened her fridge and looked inside.

Jen had a theory that each food group had one

special member, one food that stood out among the rest: the candy of that particular food group. Fruit has berries, for example. Bread has biscuits. Even the candy group has its own candy—chocolate, of course. The candy of the protein group is bacon, and it was completely acceptable at this stage of her low-carb diet.

Staring into the cool light of the refrigerator, with the creeping dawn beginning to shine in through the blinds, Jen decided that she would make herself a grilled cheese and bacon sandwich—sans bread. She thought for a moment about how exactly to accomplish this. One of the many great qualities of cheese was that it browned up nicely when cooked slightly past the point of melting. She decided to try to crumble cooked bacon into melting cheese, and cook it until the cheese was crisp enough to be picked up and eaten. Very good for her diet. She shushed the part of her consciousness that added, *but very bad for your health!*

After the bacon cooked to perfection, she put the strips on paper towels to cool and began the experimental cheese melting. She placed a small handful of shredded cheddar in the center of the pan and watched as it spread out on all sides. She sprinkled Parmesan into the bubbling cheese. When the cheeses swirled and melted together, and the edges started to brown, she crumbled in a strip of the bacon. Then she turned up the heat under the pan. The sizzling got more intense, and she watched carefully as the edges of the cheese began to dry out and curl up a little bit. Perfect. Jen cut the heat and waited a minute for everything to cool down a bit. Then she used a spatula to pick up the cheese and place it on the paper towels. It was every bit as delicious as she'd hoped. With a full belly she went back to bed as the morning light began creeping through her blinds. She rested and tried to clear her mind, though in the end she could not force herself to fall asleep.

When she got up for the day a few hours later she turned on the television after showering and blow-drying her hair. Callie Rogers's face greeted her. She was at the same place Jen had last seen her, in front of the Ninth Precinct station house. Jen rifled through her closets to find her dark suit jacket and matching slacks that may or may not fit her. She turned up the volume on the television to hear what Callie said and made her ritual trip to the scale. She couldn't believe her eyes—she was down two more pounds. She'd lost three pounds after two days on the low-carb diet. The slacks were a little tight but zipped up and looked good on her, especially from behind. She wore a flowy blouse under a blazer, and a big, chunky necklace.

Callie's voice carried through Jen's apartment, and Jen walked from the bathroom with her toothbrush sticking out of her mouth. Behind a podium set up outside the Ninth Precinct building was the police captain. Standing next to him was the familiar face of Detective Franklin, and officers Romano and D'Alby were also visible. David Brantwood also stood erect, tall, and dry-eyed in the frame. His face was frozen in a stoic mask, not revealing any emotion.

"We're going live now," Callie said from the screen, "to a press conference at the Ninth Precinct for new information about Yummy Channel superstar Bess Brantwood's death." Jen's mouthful of toothpaste would have to wait. She sat down, hovering on the edge of her love seat, and raptly watching the screen. The camera cut to the police captain's stern face. He spoke, "It's been confirmed that Bess Brantwood died when a medication that she was given—most likely against her will—interacted with a prescription medication. That combination led to the cardiac arrest." Jen felt ill. She went to the bathroom and rinsed her mouth out and walked back into her living room. The police captain was still speaking.

The captain finished his thought and tapped his notes on the podium. Before he could speak again, reporters began firing questions at him. "What evidence do you have that Bess took the medication against her will?" Callie asked loudly.

"I'll take a few questions," the captain said, tipping the brim of his hat forward slightly. "Someone up here just asked what evidence we have that Ms. Brantwood did not willfully take the substance that caused her death. Well, we have an excellent team of forensic scientists here, and they have gathered some detailed information about Ms. Brantwood's history of medication. Paired with extensive interviews with her husband and medical professionals, we have no reason to believe Bess Brantwood would disregard the possible effects of mixing the two chemicals to which the medical examiner attributes the cardiac arrest." A murmur went through the crowd gathered at the police station, audible through the television.

The captain answered a few other questions and then continued, "It is vital for us to gather all the information from the parties we've contacted for questioning. We are very saddened by this case and know that Ms. Brantwood was not only a celebrity but also a staple in our community. Our entire department sends our condolences." After answering two other questions, the captain said, "We are going to get back to work now. We will share more information from the toxicology reports and our interviews as soon as we can." He stepped back, and the detectives, officers, and David Brantwood followed him inside the doors of the precinct. Her phone rang from her tote bag and she answered it, more than a little bit grateful to hear her mother's voice. With her phone on her ear, she locked her apartment door behind her, completely unsure of what waited for her at the office.

Closing in on seventy-two hours on her diet it hit her for the first time how many places there were in her neighborhood to buy a bagel, croissant, English muffin, Danish, or donut—and how very much she was craving them. More than wanting the flavor of those foods, she wanted the comfort they provided. She took the subway uptown, and walked toward the front doors of the skyscraper where the Yummy Channel offices were, directly across from Rockefeller Center. No matter how many times Jen walked by the center's tall art deco buildings as an adult, childhood nostalgia crept in and whisked her back to her eight-year-old self, holding her father's hand and looking at the statue of Atlas shouldering the globe. Her dad had worked in the flagship building, way up in the clouds on the thirty-first floor. Then it was known as the RCA Building; now it was 30 Rock.

Jen remembered visiting her father's office as a little girl. Each time she visited, they would go out to lunch at a nearby diner. She'd perch, blond pigtails among tall men in suits, and order a burger, fries, and a milk shake. That meal: it still tasted like adulthood and childhood, all at once. Then, after the boy behind the counter cleared the dishes away and her dad paid the bill, they'd take the elevator up to his floor—Jen got to push the button—and they'd walk through a maze of offices, greeting everyone along the way. "This is my daughter Jen," he'd say. "I'm so proud of her."

Her father had never cared if she was chubby, she reflected with a warm rush of love and loss.

She pushed through the doors early that morning. At a quarter to nine in the morning, she ascended up to the twelfth floor. A uniformed policeman stood by the door. It was no one Jen recognized from the station over the weekend. All the Yummy Channel employees Jen saw arriving seemed to be moving in slow motion, like they were wading through mud. The bright white of the walls, along with the fluorescent lights of the office area seemed too bright and anesthetic. She passed the familiar milestones, the extreme close-up photographs of pasta, the curve of a meatball, the rich color spectrum of a bowl of soup, the raised, alien terrain of a piecrust. Jen never realized how many portraits of Bess decorated the walls. Just like in Jen's dream, her redheaded face grinned down from all sides. It was eerie.

A group of six of Jen's colleagues had gathered in the communal kitchen, along with boxes of donuts, platters of grief-inspired brownies and cookies baked, iced, and decorated over the weekend as a coping mechanism for the complicated emotions packed in with Friday night's tragedy. Jen stepped in, putting in the fridge the grilled chicken breast, cheese squares, and celery sticks she'd packed. She nodded solemnly to the one man and two women she knew, offering the straight-line of a heart-heavy greeting. Everyone was in shock about Bess's death, and apparently eating their feelings. *No carbs,* Jen reminded herself as she watched others mow through baked goods that smelled heavenly. None. Zero. Zip. Not even mourning carbs. She made a cup of green tea—healthier than coffee for dieters—and waited for the questions. All her colleagues must be anxious to grill her, because she was so involved with the tragedy on Friday night. She had a powerful feeling of being on the inside of the investigation, of knowing the inside scoop.

"Jen," a girl so young she must be an intern said, looking down at the floor as she spoke. "I saw you online." Everyone froze midsentence. Clearly everyone in the kitchenette had seen Jen plummet into the cupcake tower on YouTube. Jen sent a wistful prayer out to the Internet gods that the video of her from Friday night would fade away and stop racking up views.

"God, Madeline, what the hell? She must be embarrassed enough—" Another intern scolded the one who had spoken up. Jen cursed herself for not knowing the interns better. She didn't even know what department they worked in. She made a mental note to reach out more at work. She hadn't realized how much she stuck to herself and the people she worked with most regularly. How did it come to her being a lone wolf around the office?

"I meant—I didn't mean—" Madeline tried to backtrack.

"It was a rough night," Jen said simply. Madeline looked up, relieved that Jen's reaction had been tame. "See you later," Jen said, and fled the kitchen, mug in hand.

She stopped by her own office, far down the hall from where the others were gathered. As she often did when she was feeling alone, Jen pulled up Gabby's blog, Gab & Grub. She read Gabby's latest restaurant review, and then scanned her e-mails, mostly vendors sending their condolences and asking how things were going.

An e-mail offer caught her eye. It was promoting a nearby yoga studio and promised a free Intro to Yoga class. Jen clicked on it. Jen had always wanted to get into yoga but had been so busy. With the stress of Bess's death, and the constant reminder that life was short and nothing was for sure, Jen decided she was sick of waiting to start her real life. She needed action. She'd started her diet, and now she was going to take another step toward being the person she wanted to be. She clicked through and signed up for the yoga class. There was one today, and she surprised herself by selecting it. *Why wait?* she asked herself, after reading the small print to make sure she could switch class times last-minute if she needed to.

Jen went back to her e-mails. The most recent message was from Haley Parnell: a mandatory meeting request for the whole staff. Jen felt so ingrained in the investigation, by accident and coincidence. It would be good to talk about it as a group, to hear about the direction that the company would go in now that its most popular star was violently, suddenly gone. Jen's eyes flicked up to the time in the top right corner of her monitor. The meeting was starting only ten minutes from now, at 9:00 a.m.

Unable to concentrate on anything other than the coming meeting, Jen wandered toward the conference room but took a detour around a corner and down the hall toward Giselle's desk. Half of her expected to see Giselle sitting there, pecking at her keyboard with a sneer on her face as always. Of course she wasn't there. The desk was abandoned, dark, and quiet like the rest of the office. Jen looked around for any clues that the police might have missed—she didn't know what she expected to find. Jen doubted that Giselle's disappearance was coincidental, but in reality, Giselle hadn't even missed a full workday. It seemed like she had vanished off the face of the planet though, because so much had happened since the last time Jen had seen her.

Giselle's desk was the last cubicle before a long hallway that led to the studios where the cooking shows were filmed. Each of the stars had their own dressing room as well. The police department had clearly been to the Yummy Channel studios. Yellow crime scene tape stretched across the hallway, blocking entry. Jen could see a light on down the hall, coming from the studio where they filmed Bess's show. Muffled voices carried toward her, and she heard movement and rustling. She walked up to the yellow tape and peered down the hall, trying to make out what was being said—or who was saying it.

"Anything interesting?" a voice said a centimeter from her ear. It was so close she could feel the moisture of lips and the heat of breath. She yelped and jumped, spilling a few drops of her tea on her hands. She wiped them on her slacks as she spun around to face Will Riley.

"Will! What the hell?" she said loudly. "Don't sneak up on people like that."

"Oh, take it easy, Princess," Will said, putting his hands on his chubby hips. "I'm not coming on to you or anything—unless you're into that. Could be fun in a kind of dark way, back here in Bess's studio." Jen's death glare answered his tasteless proposition. "Life goes on, you know."

"Will, I feel it's only fair to let you know I've recently completed a self-defense class in which I learned to kick men really hard in the groinal area."

"*Groinal*, you say? Watch yourself, little lady. That's sexual harassment."

"Get a life, Will," Jen said.

"Whatever," Will said. "I just came back here to drop my stuff off in my dressing room. I'm out of here.

You're literally making me fall asleep standing up. Literally."

Jen wanted to yell a comeback after him, and point out the misuse of the word *literally*, but everything at her workplace was up in the air and she couldn't afford to cause friction. Will shrugged and strutted away. After a moment, Jen followed him down the hall toward the conference room, wondering if she even wanted to work here anymore. Even though she hadn't liked Bess Brantwood personally, would she really be happy working with Will Riley more than she already had to? Maya was a beacon of light but lately she'd only been in the office sporadically. Plus, with all Maya's recent endeavors, Jen didn't really know what to expect from their friendship.

Jen entered the conference room behind Will. She slid into an empty chair near the door. Tommy came in behind her. He looked around and shut the door behind him. The sound made everyone look up. "Mornin'," Tommy said. He looked awful. His cheeks were puffier than normal, dark circles ringed his eyes, and his skin looked blotchy. "Good morning," Haley Parnell said, opening the meeting as soon as Tommy made his way in and settled into a seat at the conference table.

Haley was wearing a snug heather gray suit that made her blond ponytail shine even brighter. As usual, she looked like CEO Barbie. "Thanks for coming this early on Monday morning." She took a sip of water in front of her, leaving a print of lipstick on the glass, and continued, "After the truly shocking and horribly sad events of Friday evening, we have some decisions to make about the Yummy Channel programming, and I wanted to get us all together to discuss the changes that are going to be happening."

Tommy cleared his throat, and Haley looked over. Jen thought she picked up a whiff of impatience but couldn't be sure. Haley nodded to Tommy and he began speaking. "Wait a minute, Haley. Before we get too far into this, I have to pay respects to one of the brightest stars and most brilliant cooks I've had the pleasure of knowing. Let's take a moment of silence and bow our heads for Bess Brantwood."

Jen looked around the room at the cameramen, stylists, the marketing team, production team, and random assistants. It was calm. There was no pandemonium, and Jen didn't see any tear-streaked faces, hysterical crying, commemorative armbands, or swaths of black clothing. No one seemed heartbroken, not like the women from Bess's fan club. All the Yummy Channel employees seemed nervous, though.

Tommy continued, "If anyone has any information about this tragedy, please contact the police officers that are here in the office today. We are supporting them fully in this investigation, and they have full access to anything they need here. We will never be able to replace Bess, though we can try to live up to the standards of excellence she set."

Jen thought his words rang true. Bess's perfectionist attitude had kept everyone running all the time, and because of it her show was always perfect. If it weren't for the diary entries so fresh in Jen's mind, she could have seen only the good in Bess postmortem.

Maya, wearing a crisp white suit, sat immediately to Haley's right in the seat that Bess had traditionally occupied. Maya serenely flipped through food magazines, sipping something hot from a paper cup. Jen tried to catch her eye and make a connection, but Maya didn't look her way. "I have some big ideas about this," Maya said, speaking to Haley and leaning in across the table.

Jen couldn't take her eyes off lean and elegant Maya. She wore her black hair piled in a bun on top of her head, her makeup was fresh, her brows were tweezed. Maya crossed her arms over her body and leaned back in her chair, confidence radiating from her movements. She pounced. "God rest Bess's soul, but this is the perfect time for my show to get more airtime. People are really into craft and art now, and cake decorating is taking off in a big way. I know I can drive ratings better than anyone."

"Right," Haley said, "that's what we're counting on. We're planning to give you and Will both more airtime. Congratulations."

Will Riley blew out a breath and dragged his hand through his bleached hair, clearly unhappy with the conversation. "Shouldn't *Deep Fried and Spicy* get more airtime than the decorating show? Maya's cakes are all show and no flavor. *Normal* people want fried food, not fruity decorations," he whined.

"Riley, get with the times," Maya retorted. "Look at Pinterest. Look at Instagram and Facebook. People are really into art and style. Audiences love learning how to add style to their food. The food-as-art demographic is growing." She looked to Haley for confirmation.

"Both of you please calm down." Haley's tone stopped them in their tracks. She was a monarch no longer amused by the rumblings of the jesters. "May I continue?" Haley cleared her throat. "We are also going to bring some other cooks in to give us some taste tests and screen tests to see if there's any potential for a new show next season." Maya began tapping her fingers against the table to express her annoyance. Will crossed his arms over his barrel of a chest and shifted in his chair. Haley pulled a stack of papers from a file folder and passed it on. Everyone took one and continued passing it.

"I'm passing around a revised schedule for filming. What we're going to do here is cash in on the popularity of reality television programming and do some additional in-studio filming with Maya and Will that we'll edit quickly and get on the air as soon as possible. We're going to play fast and loose with reruns across the board, and some of our up-and-coming faces are going to do a panel show where they discuss their favorite restaurant dishes."

Jen took a sheet and passed it on. She hadn't wanted to succumb to self-interest, but she'd been worried about her job security after Bess's death. As she studied the revised production schedule she realized that she'd be as busy as ever if she stayed on at the Yummy Channel.

"Haley?" Jen asked. "I see my name here next to the XyloSlim Tasting Hour. What is that, exactly?"

"Ah, Jen," Haley said, flashing Jen a smile with her million-watt teeth. "That is our most pressing and ambitious project. Here's the vision: we get a dozen local chefs to share their favorite foods with us here in our studios. We get XyloSlim's advertising team to cosponsor the event, and intermingle before and after success stories with the chef's work."

"I don't understand," Jen said. "Will the chefs be sharing diet recipes?"

"Just the opposite," Haley corrected her. "The point of XyloSlim is that you can continue eating your favorite foods while losing weight."

"Okay." Jen wrinkled her forehead, still not totally getting the concept of how diet pills tied in with local cuisine. She looked over at Tommy, who was staring blankly down at the paper in front of him, glassy eyed. "The question is, Jen, could you spearhead this and put together a local tasting event on Friday right here in our own prep kitchen?"

"This Friday? As in four days from now?" Jen looked at Haley to see if she was joking. She obviously wasn't. Jen thought about what to say. "I'll do my best," she said, her voice cracking. Apparently there would be no mourning time, no downtime for the company to regroup without its masthead.

Was Haley ruthless and money hungry, or was she creating a near-impossible challenge to keep everyone from wallowing in their sorrow? Somehow Jen didn't believe Haley was concerned with anyone's sorrow. Jen had a choice: either stay on board with Haley's vision and step up to the challenge, or step out of the limelight. She told herself that not many people got the opportunity to do what she did, to plan events for the biggest names in the food world. There were a dozen younger, more creative men and women lined up, ready to take Jen's position at the drop of a hat. Jen had to shake the creepy feeling of Bess's ghost watching over them in order to get on with her own career, and her healthy new life.

chapter ten

Jen hadn't jogged in a year, but she found herself running to the yoga class. She almost called and canceled, but her desire to start something healthful outweighed her feeling of being completely overwhelmed by the near-impossible job Haley had tasked her with for once. The staff meeting had gone long, most of it spent on bickering between Will and Maya about who would profit most from Bess's death. Then Jen remembered that she had no workout clothes in her office, and she couldn't wear work clothes to yoga. She'd rushed across the street to buy a yoga mat, stretch pants and a T-shirt at the closest shop that sold them, then back to her office to change. She'd purchased a medium-size pair of pants instead of a large. They were a tad snug, but her future self would certainly need a medium.

The irony of stressing herself out in order to make

it on time to her Zen-inducing lunchtime yoga class was not lost on her. Wind chimes sounded as Jen heaved the doors of the Bend and Blossom studio open with her hip. She sniffed deeply and recognized patchouli. A ceiling fan swirled around another odor that smelled like half peppermint and half sweat, making the patchouli more palatable. She juggled the spanking new yoga mat and never-before-used, earth-friendly water bottle she'd just purchased. Elizabeth would be so proud of her for channeling her inner self and taking care of her body. Maybe she'd even clear her mind enough to put some of the pieces of Bess's death together. How did it all fit?

"Hi, hello?" She fought to catch her breath. "I'm Jen. Jen Stevens. This is my first class. I'm sorry I'm late." The receptionist, an adorable young man sitting behind a bamboo desk, smiled serenely and looked her up on the iPad in front of him. Jen took a second to smooth her tousled blond hair back into a ponytail and wipe the sweat from her upper lip and forehead. "How late am I?"

"Um . . . only about five minutes. They should just be starting, hon, so don't worry too much." The boy tossed his silky black hair. "Okay, it's straight back to your right. Enjoy your first class, and congratulations!" He grinned again. *Was he hitting on her?* He *recognized* her reinvention from ball of stress into a health-conscious, yoga-loving, vibrant spirit. She could do this. She could cut out the negative energy in her life and welcome in only positivity. It started today. She would make her reaction to Bess's death a cathartic one, and channel all the frustration she'd felt with Bess over the past few years into perfect yoga form. Or at least she'd try.

She followed the receptionist's directions to the back studio. On her way she passed what must have been an advanced class. The glass door revealed ten or so svelte, lithe beautiful women who were standing on one leg, with the other tucked up on their thigh. There wasn't a single wobble in the whole classroom— or an ounce of thigh fat. It looked like a commercial for a yoga studio, not a real-life yoga class. These women were beautiful swans, and they scared the hell out of Jen. Her biggest fear about group exercise was that the other women in it would be experienced supermodels and she would be the fat flounder, flopping through the moves.

Jen opened the door to the back classroom, where the women were all crouched in Child's Pose on their mats. An aura of tranquility pulsed in and out as the women filled their bodies with breath, and then slowly exhaled. Jen knew she was in the right place to be mindful of Bess and still be supportive of herself and her life. She nodded a greeting and apology to the instructor, and mouthed "Sorry!" The class politely ignored the sound of Jen's never-before-used yoga mat echoing like the world's loudest Velcro as she unrolled the soft plastic for the first time.

Jen crouched down and mimicked the other women, squatting way down with her arms stretched out on her mat. The teacher instructed the class to breathe in, and breathe out, square their hips. Jen relaxed into the stretch. Her body really was responding to the breathing and the movements, and she felt invigorated after only a few moments. Her mind naturally wandered back to Bess, Billy, Giselle. Her mind wandered to Tommy and his bloodshot eyes and the article that suggested he and Bess had been lovers. She willed herself to empty her thoughts and simply *be* in the moment.

Next, the instructor demonstrated curling her toes under and pushing up into Downward Dog. Jen's calves were tight, and she could feel the stretch working her muscles. It felt great to use her body, and really great that she hadn't waited for Elizabeth to initiate it this time. Since everyone was upside down, she couldn't see her classmates' faces, although she had a clear view of their posteriors. She was happy to notice that there were a variety of body types in the room, unlike the other advanced classroom she had passed on the way in. Wide hips, thick legs, and ample buttocks were aplenty, and she gratefully noticed that she wasn't the biggest girl in the room, or even the least graceful. When her teacher moved in to a lunge-stretch she called Warrior, Jen felt so proficient that thoughts of the murder slipped into a fantasy about her teacher looking over, tapping her on the shoulder, and saying, "You are clearly a natural. I cannot believe this is the first class of your adult life. You should go down the hall to the advanced class."

A few moves later, the teacher instructed everyone to come to a comfortable seated position. Jen flopped down to her mat and reached for her water bottle. The instructor led them in a few breaths with their hands pressed together over their hearts, and then suggested they go around the room and introduce themselves. The lid to Jen's metal bottle slipped from her fingers and made a clanging sound as it rolled off her mat onto the hardwood floor. It rolled out of her reach, and she scrambled up to her knees to grab it, nearly spilling the bottle. Embarrassed, she grabbed the lid and screwed it back on. She'd completely missed what they were supposed to say when they introduced themselves. She mentally prepared a line about needing to channel her energy and unwind after a tough week. She didn't want to wreck the vibe by explaining her sad, depressing inspiration for joining the class.

The first woman was talking, a lovely brunette, and Jen honestly felt bad for her. She said she was two months pregnant with her first child and suffering from constant nausea. What a trooper to make it to yoga class at all, especially in the middle of the day.

The next woman introduced herself and giddily reported recently learning her baby was a girl. Weird that there were two pregnant women in this class, especially when Jen was fairly sure that the studio taught special prenatal yoga classes. But when the third woman rubbed her protruding belly a bolt of realization shot down Jen's spine. Had she walked into the wrong class? No, the hot receptionist had definitely said to go to the back studio. It meant one thing, plain and simple. He thought her slight tummy bulge, smaller even after three days of dieting, was a *baby bump*.

Jen's horror grew as the women continued around the class, speaking about their fetuses and stroking their round bellies. She had no idea what to do and could feel her heart pounding. Her throat went dry. She couldn't speak when it was her turn, and before the next woman stopped talking, Jen had collected her things and left the room. Screw yoga. Who had she been trying to fool? She blinked back embarrassed tears and rushed into the lobby. A few women had gathered in the lobby, waiting for another class to start. The receptionist was nowhere to be seen, lucky for him. Jen was ready to give him the glare of a lifetime. She slipped on the shoes she'd left in the lobby and headed for the door. A tiny woman stood in her way, completely oblivious and messing with her phone. Jen wanted to snap this twig of a girl over her knee.

Jen made eye contact with the woman blocking her path and jumped back. It was Giselle Martin, Bess's assistant.

"What are you doing here?" Jen asked, reaching out and touching the young woman's shoulder lightly. "Where have you been all weekend?" A sense of unease crept over Jen. If Giselle had been the one to slip drugs to Bess, Jen imagined she'd be long gone by now, not in a Monday afternoon yoga class across the street from her office.

"What am *I* doing here?" Giselle repeated. "I'm always here. Every single day. What are you doing here? And are you coming out of the prenatal class? I didn't know you were pregnant."

Jen blushed and shook her head. "No, it was a mix-up, I guess. Do you know the police are looking for you?"

"It's probably those pants," Giselle said disdainfully. "They don't do you any favors. You should have gotten a size bigger."

Jen shrugged and maintained eye contact with Giselle. "Hello? Focus. Police? Your boss? Homicide?"

"Right. They left me a message," Giselle said, looking at her phone. "I quit the Yummy Channel, though. On Friday before all that happened. I told her to fuck off and walked out."

"You know she's dead, right?" Jen was incredulous. Giselle blinked. "I know she's dead." A shudder shook through her frame. She regained her footing and responded with a snarl, "Of course I know. I have a television."

"Why haven't you gone in to speak to the police?" Jen asked.

"Why haven't *you*?" Giselle responded crossing her arms over her chest.

"I have! What are you talking about?" Jen was bewildered by this girl and all the anger that she carried.

"Well, I will. I was going to today after my yoga class. I need it to stay centered."

"Giselle, we should go now. The crime scene guys and an officer are right across the street at the Yummy Channel studios. You could go and talk to them right now."

Giselle shook her head like Jen must be crazy. She made a face like she'd tasted something bad. "Okay, Jen, can you move along now? You're ruining everyone's qi."

"Their what?"

"Their energy. Their life flow? You're just bringing a lot of negativity in here."

Either Giselle had no idea of the seriousness of the situation, or she was insane. "I have to call the police now. I promised that I would if I saw you." Jen shook her head. The only reason she'd even promised Alex that she'd get involved is because she assumed she'd filled her quota of random run-ins with wanted people. Apparently she had some sort of homing device that drew her to flaky people involved in serious wrongdoing. "I have to call them. If you don't come with me, they'll come in here to your class and get you and maybe even put you in handcuffs. It will be very embarrassing and I bet it will really mess with your qi."

Tears filled Giselle's eyes suddenly. Jen guessed she was imagining what the other women in her class would think of her being dragged out in handcuffs. She looked desperate, glancing from side to side, trying to find an exit strategy. For the first time that day, Jen had been grateful for her larger size. She turned around and blocked the door so Giselle couldn't run out.

Giselle began crying big fat tears that trailed down her cheeks. The other women in the lobby stared. Jen didn't know what to do. She reached out a hand to Giselle. Giselle reached out and grabbed her hand, letting her minuscule weight lean against the curves of Jen's body. Jen felt like she could be Giselle's mother, even though they were only a few years apart in age. Jen put an arm around Giselle's shoulders and together they took a step toward the door.

"There's no way I was going to sit there on Friday night and see Bess get another celebration in her honor. It was always Bess, Bess, Bess, with no mention of how everything got done, and no appreciation for everyone else's work. Did you know that the last three recipes she added to the menu at her bakery were *mine*? No, no one knew that. No one cared." Jen squeezed her eyes shut as she led Giselle out the door and toward the street. Was this a confession? She took a deep breath and hugged the girl's bony body closer to her. With her other hand, she reached into her tote bag and pulled out her cell phone and the piece of paper with Alex's number. She dialed with one hand, still patting Giselle with the other.

He picked up on the second ring. "Officer D'Alby."

"Hi, this is Jen Stevens. I—well, I'm with Giselle Martin. She was at my yoga studio."

Giselle sniffed loudly. "You were at *my* yoga studio."

"I was at *her* yoga studio," Jen corrected herself on the phone.

"Where are you now?" Alex asked.

"We're right across from the Yummy Channel. We could walk over there and meet the officers there?" But Jen didn't trust Giselle not to run if they crossed the street. If she did, Jen would have no hope of catching her.

"I'm not going back there. I swore I'd never go back there," Giselle wailed as they made it to the street corner. Taxis, buses, and cars whizzed by. Jen felt her body pull away and tense up.

"I think you should send an officer to the corner

of Forty-seventh and Sixth," Jen said. "As soon as you can. I've got to go." She tossed her phone into her bag and looked back at Giselle.

"Giselle, you had every right to be mad at Bess. She treated you like shit."

Giselle looked up, wide-eyed. "You noticed?"

"Well," Jen continued. "She treated *everyone* like shit, but yeah, of course I noticed. I just didn't want to get involved. It was a mistake. I should have spoken up for you, for myself, and for everyone. She was a bully."

"She was so mean to me. Not just mean, cruel. She had no respect for my spirit."

"She was jealous of you," Jen said. It wasn't just a lie to make Giselle feel better. Jen knew it was true after reading Bess's journal.

"I know. I read her diary too," Giselle said. A siren started down the street, and Giselle jumped at the noise. "I didn't do anything. I didn't kill her. I swear." The siren got closer, and Jen put both hands on Giselle's shoulders to stabilize her.

"They just want to talk to you, okay? No one thinks you hurt her." This time Jen was lying just to make Giselle feel better. The police car pulled up and an officer Jen had never seen jumped out and approached them. She felt a shallow relief that Alex wouldn't see her in pants that made her look pregnant.

"Giselle Martin?" Giselle nodded at the officers,

her eyes looked huge in her head, like a frightened baby animal. "We're going to take you to the station." Giselle allowed herself to be led toward the cruiser.

Jen began walking back toward her office, feeling completely defeated. She looked up to the twelfth-floor windows of the Yummy Channel and wondered if anyone in the offices was watching these events. What would she tell them when she got back upstairs? Jen couldn't decide if she was the hero or the rat in this situation, but relief rushed in because the person she considered most likely to have hurt Bess was now in the hands of the authorities. More than anything, she wished she could just go back in time to being another cog in the wheel of Bess's fame, instead of just stumbling around trying to piece things together, and being in the right place at the right time to help solve her murder.

As the officer helped Giselle into the car, something she'd said snapped into place for Jen. Jen jogged toward the car. "Giselle," she said. "Wait a minute." The officer closed the car door and began walking to the driver's side. She tried to get his attention, but he slid into his seat and talked on his radio. As they eased into traffic, Jen jogged toward the car. It was too late and Jen stood on the corner. "When?" she said quietly, to herself. "*When* had Giselle seen Bess's diary?"

chapter eleven

Jen changed back to her street clothes in her office. She stuffed her barely used workout pants into a drawer and vowed not to look at them until she was five pounds lighter. Confusion overwhelmed her. She had a dozen tasks to do now in order to accomplish Haley's vision for the XyloSlim-sponsored event, but there was no way she could concentrate on work. It's not like Bess was always flashing her journal around; Jen hadn't even known she kept one until Billy brought it by her apartment over the weekend. But Giselle was Bess's assistant and worked much more closely with her than Jen had. It's possible that Giselle read Bess's entries before her death. It's possible that reading the diary was what made Giselle decide to quit. Jen replayed their conversation over and over again, trying to recall anything that would determine if Giselle had read her diary pre- or postmortem.

A text message caught her attention. She squinted down at the screen. "Hey, this is Alex D'Alby. Just wanted to thank you for the call. You did the right thing." She read it again and let the comfort the message provided calm her. She didn't think that texts were standard officer-on-duty procedure, but she didn't know for sure. She wondered if he could have the same warm, fuzzy feelings for her that she had for him. It seemed so unlikely, since she was round enough to get accidentally routed to the pregnancy yoga class. He probably had gorgeous, fit women throwing themselves at him all the time—Jen had seen the women's stares in the self-defense class.

Jen needed to talk to someone with a heart. If she tried to talk to Haley Parnell, Haley would probably be annoyed and question Jen about how her new assignment was going. Maya—well, Maya wasn't even herself anymore. Jen thought about calling Gabby or Elizabeth, but no matter how many details she provided about Giselle and Bess's relationship, or about Will Riley's bad behavior, they'd never understand it like an insider would. Only Tommy seemed like he was genuinely grieving Bess. Jen hesitated. Tommy was the CEO of the whole network. Could she really just pop in to talk about this? As the CEO of the network, though, Jen should tell him what was going on with his employees. He might not even know that Giselle had officially quit, since she hadn't told anyone other than Bess. Jen took a deep breath, trying to remember the calming technique she'd learned in her five minutes of pregnant yoga class, and headed for the corner office.

"Yes, come in," Tommy said from behind the closed door when she knocked.

Jen turned the doorknob and took a step into the exec's plush carpeted office. "Hi." Tommy held up a finger and gestured to his phone pressed to his ear. He looked even more exhausted than he had in the conference room, his face sagging and swollen. For the first time Jen noticed that the executive's head was balding, little pink bits of sunburned scalp showing through. It was a look that not many men could pull off, but Jen thought Tommy wore it with dignity.

Tommy's face was stern as he spoke into the phone. He was quiet but firm as he spoke to a press agent who apparently had asked the wrong question. Jen padded farther into his office, feeling out of place. Her eyes wandered to her own reflection in the mirror. She certainly did *not* look pregnant, at least not in this outfit. Though the yoga class had been a blow to her ego, Jen could tell that her face looked leaner already after sticking to her diet. Tommy raised his voice to the person on the other end of the phone call, clicking around on his computer and ignoring Jen. She subtly shifted to get a better view of her rear while he wasn't paying attention. Not bad. She stood on her tiptoes and sucked in her stomach.

"Unbelievable," Tommy exploded. "Learn some manners. Have some respect." Jen jumped, but quickly realized he was still on the phone. He hung up the phone with a slam. In the same breath, he said, "How are you holding up, Jenny?"

Jen pivoted to face Tommy, wondering if he'd noticed her vanity. "I've been better," she confessed. "How about you?" The rumor of Tommy's involvement with Bess popped into Jen's head and she tried to banish the thought. It couldn't be true. The photograph of Tommy and his wife and children grinning on a snowy ski slope sat earnestly on his desk.

"Well, you know I'm fine. My wife was a little flustered at that picture that went around, and the suggestion that Bess and I were having an affair," he said candidly. "That made for an uncomfortable weekend." He let out a breath—not quite a laugh, but better humored than a sigh.

"I can imagine," Jen said. The unasked question hung in the air. Jen started to change the subject but stumbled over her words.

"I don't know why it's anyone's business," Tommy said, straightening his tie. "The press are monsters. They want every detail of these celebrities, every moment of their life, every single, solitary fact, all in the name of the public good. People are asking me the most personal questions and they're dragging Bess's reputation through the mud. It's bullshit. It's ratings.

There's something wholesome about a channel about food compared to the three-ring circus of the news media. We cook, we talk about it, we film it."

Jen silently nodded at her boss, wondering if Tommy was slightly delusional. His biggest stars all seemed far from wholesome.

"Tommy, I have something I need to tell you," Jen said, moving to close the door behind her. "I'm not trying to gossip, but—"

"A closed-door something?" Tommy asked, furrowing his forehead. He looked to Jen like he couldn't handle any more bad news. "Sit down."

Jen dropped into one of the guest chairs in Tommy's office and began speaking. "I just found Giselle Martin. Well, sort of. I mean, I wasn't trying. She went to the police for questioning. She said she quit on Friday. Did you know that?"

Tommy brought his hand to his chin and frowned deeply. "I did not hear that."

"I don't want to make assumptions, but it seemed like Giselle had both motive and opportunity to give Bess something."

"Jen, I've been through this with the police. All day yesterday, in fact. I don't want to rehash it all here."

Jen was crestfallen. She thought that Tommy would want to discuss this, dissect it with her, look at all the parts. Now she sat in front of her boss feeling like a busybody. Irritation pulsed through her as she looked at Tommy and contemplated his passivity. This was his company to run, and in the wake of his star's death he needed to provide leadership. All the meeting this morning had done was give everyone more work to do while they were mourning. Bess may have been unpleasant to work with, but she was a cornerstone of this office.

"Fine. I thought you'd like to know that Giselle is saying she quit, at least. Since you are, technically, her boss." Tommy looked up, startled at Jen's tone.

She continued, unable to filter her thoughts. "Also, I thought you'd like to know that your *other* star—not Bess, the dead one, or Will, the walking sexual harassment lawsuit—but the one who's supposed to be *nice*, Maya Khan, is schtupping Bess's widower. Just so you can get a full feel for the publicity nightmare this channel will be in for if Giselle starts talking."

Tommy's face darkened. At first Jen thought he was angry at Maya, at the situation, but his glare zeroed in on Jen. He slammed a fist into his desk, a more violent action than Jen had ever seen him take, and stood up fast, letting his chair roll back into the wall behind him with a bang. "So you're the expert? I'll thank you for keeping your mouth shut about this. This is *not* your business. If you so much as open your mouth about this, I'll get you charged with libel." He straightened his tie and tugged on his jacket pocket.

She crossed her arms over her chest, anger forcing

the blood up in her ears. She felt so betrayed and stupid for coming into his office. If Tommy wanted to stay an ostrich with his head in the ground, she should let him. "Tommy, it's not like they're being discreet about it, they were out in public the day after Bess was killed. The police know too. It's not a secret and it's only a matter of time before it's all over the news."

A knock at the door made them both jump. The door opened and Officer Alex D'Alby stood outside, along with Officer Joe Romano and Detective Franklin.

"Are we interrupting?" Alex asked, stepping into the office. His face was a mask of concern.

"Come in," Tommy said, sounding defeated.

"Ms. Stevens," Alex said to Jen, his eyes measuring the situation. "Thanks again for getting in touch earlier." She pulled her mouth tight and lifted her head in a small acknowledgment, blinking back the tears that had filled her eyes earlier. "Would you mind excusing us?" the officer asked, indicating that they wanted to be alone with Tommy.

Jen shook her head, turned, and walked out, trying not to let anyone see how upset she was. When she was in the hallway, she heard the heavy door click shut. She should have gone back to her office, but if Tommy thought she was a busybody, why should she stop now? She positioned herself about two feet from the door, and leaned on the wall, trying to look natural. If anyone asked, which they wouldn't, she'd say she was waiting to go back in and finish her conversation with Tommy.

Detective Franklin spoke first, and Jen could hear him clearly through the thin drywall. "I'm here because we got the results back on the toxicology screen we did on Bess Brantwood this morning. We want to talk with you a minute, share our concerns, and ask your assistance with a few things."

His voice was slow and steady. "Okay. What was the news?"

"The results of the test show that she consumed appetite suppressants, thyroid medication, and a health tea. These interacted with the antianxiety pill that she took before the event. It is clear to us after some interviews with those close to Ms. Brantwood, and a personal record we found of her medication, that she was rigorous about not mixing these prescriptions. The fact that she consumed an excessive quantity of the appetite suppressant, and that it had been dissolved into a beverage before consumption, suggests that it was not an accidental death."

"They released this information yesterday, didn't they?" Tommy asked, growing impatient. "Is there new information?"

"When did you learn that she took antianxiety medication before public speaking, Mr. Wegman?" the detective asked. "I know we talked about a lot of things yesterday, but that didn't come up for some reason."

"It's not polite to talk about other people's health problems. It wasn't mine to tell."

"Usually people don't feel that way about someone who's been murdered," Alex said quietly. Jen had a harder time hearing his voice through the wall and pressed her ear flush against it. "Maybe you didn't tell us because you didn't want it getting out that your big star and your girlfriend was on such serious medication for anxiety."

Jen's jaw dropped. The rumors had been true. She cursed the online tabloids for being right. She really hadn't wanted to believe that Tommy had been involved. She bit her lip and kept listening.

"Thank you, Officer D'Alby," the detective said. "Furthermore, the appetite suppressant was a very unusual compound, and our labs ran the analysis twice against FDA-approved brands of medication, both over-the-counter and prescription. There were only two that matched the formula that we found in Bess Brantwood's stomach. One is sold as a prescription drug in Korea but not legalized in the United States. The other is sold over the counter with the name XyloSlim."

Jen gasped and clapped a hand to her mouth. The Yummy Channel's pet advertiser created the drug used to kill Bess Brantwood.

"Here's the facts," the detective said. Jen could tell he was moving closer to Tommy as his voice got farther away. "One. Bess Brantwood did not take this medication herself. Two. Whoever gave it to her may or may not have known she also was in the habit of taking an antianxiety pill before public speaking, but the person who put this in her drink certainly gave it to her to impair her abilities. This is an active homicide case, for that reason. She was given an amount more than quadruple the size of the recommended dose. Three. Whoever gave her the dose slipped it in her bottle of tea an hour or more before she ingested it, and then she ingested it at least an hour before she passed away. That would place her here when she ingested the substance." Everyone was quiet for a moment. Jen tried to imagine what Tommy's face looked like at that moment.

Tommy finally spoke. "We have security cameras in the hallway. Maybe—"

"Glad you said that," Officer Romano interrupted him, reminding Tommy that they were in charge of this conversation. "This is a warrant for those records, Mr. Wegman. Our original warrant didn't cover electronic surveillance images."

"Of course—" Tommy said. "Can I ask you one question? How do you know what time the XyloSlim was put into her tea? And how do you know it was in her tea?"

"Our forensics guys looked at her stomach contents. They can tell by the amount of saturation. The XyloSlim was over ninety-eight percent saturated in the tea, so we know it was in the liquid more than an hour." A rustle in the hallway made Jen stand up straight. Haley Parnell was walking out of her office with Maya Khan. They walked away from Jen and toward the elevators. Their heads were bent in talking quietly to each other, and they didn't notice Jen.

After a few more moments in the hallway, Jen couldn't hear any more talking coming from the office. She tried to process what she'd just heard when Tommy's door swung open and she stood face-to-face with Detective Franklin. His brown eyes were the color of melted chocolate, and she noticed that the stubble he'd had on his upper lip had filled out a little more over the last few days to form the beginning of a mustache.

"Ms. Stevens. Back again?" She nodded dumbly but couldn't think of words to explain her presence hovering outside Tommy's office. Officers D'Alby and Romano filed out next.

"Hi," she said. "I was just heading—um, just walking by to make a copy." She wasn't carrying anything to copy, unfortunately. "I mean pick up a fax." She knew how lame the lie must sound. "Okay, see you." She stepped toward the elevators, then turned and walked in the opposite direction back toward her office. "Bye," she mumbled again, her face scarlet.

Back in her office, she felt useless. She couldn't think here, the crime scene investigators were still everywhere, and the whole studio and dressing room wing was still not open. Jen sat down at her computer and typed an e-mail to Haley and Tommy, letting them know that she was going home early, and would be working from home tomorrow. She didn't know about the company's policy, and she didn't care. If they wanted her to get any work done on the local tasting event, they'd have to allow it. For Jen, it was impossible to concentrate on work knowing that just down the hall Bess took the sips of tea that killed her, not to mention that the proposed sponsor of the event was the brand of diet drug that killed the channel's biggest star—America's Sweetheart.

It was nice having friends that didn't work traditional office hours. Jen called Gabby before she left the Yummy Channel, and forty-five minutes later they were sitting in a sports bar. Jen talked nonstop about everything that had happened. It felt so good to unload. "I can't believe you're not drinking after your day," Gabby said after the waitress dropped off their glasses. Gabby sipped a glass of white wine and Jen drank a club soda with lime. "You are so serious about this diet. I've never seen you so serious."

Jen bobbed her head up. "I am serious. I don't know what it is, but I'm just *ready* to lose weight and take control of my life."

"Could this have anything to do with Officer Hottie—oops, I mean D'Alby?" Gabby asked, teasing her.

Jen rolled her eyes. "Obviously," she said. "It's more than that, though."

"I can tell." Gabby laughed. "Good for you. I want to be healthy but I really like food." Gabby took a big bite of her cheesy bruschetta. "Does it kill you that I'm eating this?"

"Not at all, seriously," Jen assured her. "Eat away." She smiled at her friend. It felt good to be normal for a few moments, normal girlfriends out on the town.

"Good," Gabby said, her mouth closing in on a big bite and mozzarella stringing between the food and her lips. "Wait," she said, chewing for a moment then washing down her food with a gulp of wine. "Are you totally judging me for eating this?"

"No!" Jen laughed. "Definitely not," she said. But it was a lie. Jen thought about Gabby's lack of self-control each time her friend reached for another slice. She tried to push away the thoughts, but she couldn't help but keep count. She'd already had four slices!

They had so much in common. Like Jen, Gabby had built her professional life around eating and being around other people who love food. Jen reached for a hot wing and dunked it in blue cheese. Hot wings weren't the epitome of health food, Jen knew, so she reached for a piece of celery to ease her conscience.

At least she was losing weight. A moment of silence passed, the only sounds the occasional smack and gulp of a bite and swallow.

Jen once read an article that stated obesity was contagious. As in, fat people hang out with other fat people. In some ways, Jen would rather spend time with Gabby than almost anyone in the world, but as she watched her friend down drinks and junk food, she wondered if Gabby was part of her problem with eating. Either way, there was something strangely motivating about exercising self-control while someone else binged. That must have been how Bess felt about everyone in her life, why she maintained such strict control over everything. Jen shook off the fear that gripped her. She had no idea what was in store for her at the Yummy Channel, but it felt like the only thing she could do was just keep going.

chapter twelve

Working from home on Tuesday went much more smoothly than the office had on Monday. Jen was basically hiding out. She couldn't dispel the funk that had settled over her, despite losing one more pound to round her total up to four and being able to zip up a dress she hadn't worn in at least six months. The weight seemed to be coming off her belly, which was obviously her problem area.

With the TV on and her laptop open on her lap, she began lining up chefs and rounding out the plans for Friday's short-notice event. She carefully worded an e-mail to Haley proposing that, with the recent news, they drop the XyloSlim sponsorship and shift the focus of the event to a memorial for Bess Brantwood. Jen came up with the name Comfort Food, and suggested it to Haley. Haley wrote back a few minutes later agreeing to both suggestions. Haley was no fool when it came to avoiding bad publicity. XyloSlim boasted all-natural ingredients, but Jen had heard people at the Yummy Channel say it may as well be crystal meth, that it made them jittery, nervous, high-strung. Jen thought it wasn't a coincidence that Bess, who apparently had an anxiety problem, had been about to take the stage for her hundredth episode.

Jen let herself watch the news in peace, without forcing herself to multitask and work simultaneously. She knew that she had a few hours before the chefs would begin to call and respond to her e-mails—the restaurant industry was not a nine-to-five gig.

Jen reclined on the couch, feeling emotionally fatigued. She balanced her laptop on her stomach and sent an e-mail to Gabby to see if she could swing a short-notice lunch visit. To Jen's relief, Gabby responded right away that she'd be over in an hour. Jen called two vendors to arrange delivery of flowers and decorations to the Yummy Channel on Friday morning, then jumped in the shower, weighing herself one more time for good measure. She got dressed just as the buzzer let her know that Gabby had arrived.

"I'm so glad you could come over," Jen said, embracing Gabby as soon as she opened the door. "I'm trying to work on this new event—which, by the way, I'd love if you could do a write-up about it on Gab & Grub."

"My blog is your blog," Gabby said. "E-mail me the info?"

"Done," Jen said. "Thanks. We could use some good press right now."

After a few moments of small talk they drifted toward the unavoidable subject of Bess Brantwood. "I've heard," Gabby started, "that the police only detained Giselle for a couple of hours."

Jen looked at Gabby suspiciously. "Do you have a mole? How do you get this information?"

Gabby raised her eyebrows. "I'm a blogger, babe. I have my sources."

Jen narrowed her eyes.

"Okay, it was on Twitter." Gabby shrugged. "I have no idea if it's true. But here's my question: Could Maya have done it?"

"No way." Jen shook her head. Maya prided herself on being a lover, not a fighter. She was an artist, an ultimate pacifist. "Once a cockroach showed up in the Yummy Channel bathroom. Maya refused to squish it—she picked it up in a square of toilet paper and carried it in the elevator down, then let it loose in a planter outside."

"Please. No one does that," Gabby said.

"Maya did." Jen nodded with her eyes wide.

"But slipping a couple of gel tabs in someone's tea is a little different from a violent act like smashing a bug." Jen shrugged, admitting the truth. The problem was that it seemed like a slippery slope. If Maya could have done it, *anyone* could have done it. Jen preferred to keep the list of possible suspects to people she didn't personally like. Not a particularly scientific method of analyzing suspects, Jen admitted to herself.

"Can we change the topic?" she asked Gabby. "I do have one piece of good news." She turned around, showing off her body. "Another pound down since I saw you last night. It's falling off."

"Good work, sister." Gabby gave her a thumbs-up. "Oh, and I wanted to tell you about this place Marco and I ate at the other day. I'm working on the blog entry right now. It was amazing. Buttermilk fried chicken over this thick, crispy waffle. Oh, and the strawberry shortcake!"

"That's great that you just let yourself eat all that deliciousness," Jen said halfheartedly. Gabby cleared her throat.

"Wait, did you just roll your eyes at me?" Jen demanded. They climbed up onto the barstools in Jen's kitchen nook. The kitchen was painted bold orange, and Gabby sat across from Jen at the little two-person table tucked over in the corner, sipping her Pellegrino.

She could tell that Gabby was drifting as Jen fed her details of the carb-free lifestyle, but Jen felt compelled to share it. Her mind just naturally snapped back to carb counts and poundage, like a magnet to the refrigerator.

"No! Tell me more about the diet. It's intriguing.

Tell me again about how the weight is just falling off of you." Gabby spread her arms wide. "Have at it."

"That time you *definitely* rolled your eyes at me. *Sorry* to have bored you with talking about my life."

"Oh stop," Gabby chided. "You're being too sensitive, honey. Yes, I'm rolling my eyes at you a tiny bit. And I'm sorry. Your colleague was murdered, your workplace is full of police and suspicious activity, you have a crush on a very good-looking police officer, and yet all you want to talk about is the diet. Boring! Also, no offense, but your diet is crazy. Remind me why you think eating bacon-wrapped hot wings is going to make you any healthier in the long run."

"The bacon-wrapped hot wings were just an *example* of the type of food I can eat!" Jen exclaimed. "I don't actually eat those . . . um, very often. There are lots of mostly healthful foods I can eat." She pointed to the fridge, where the rules of the diet were posted. No starch, no rice, no sweets. And it was working. She looked better, felt better, fit into her clothes better.

It was more than that, though. Strange things were happening to her. She could wait to eat until a late lunch, for example, without presnacking and grazing at the fridge at 11:00 a.m. She'd somehow become unshackled from the feeling that cake was the answer to all her problems. She wanted to share her feeling of liberation with her best friend.

Jen sucked on her upper lip, considering her

bruised feelings. She started preparing comebacks for the next time Gabby's eyes searched out the ceiling. Jen picked up the serving knife and silently spread soft herbed cheese over a cucumber slice. She made another and handed it to Gabby.

Gabby took the cucumber and looked down at her plate of cheese, cucumber, thin-sliced deli ham, with a scoop of homemade chicken salad. "You just should have told me in advance that this was BYOB. Bring your own bread. All protein and no carbs make Gabby a dull gal . . . or at least a hungry gal."

Jen laughed at Gabby's joke, forcing a light and pleasant sound, but patronizing thoughts started to gather like thunderclouds. *Oh, that Gabby. She sure does love to eat unhealthful food . . . it's like an addiction. Poor thing. She doesn't know any better.* "Oh, Gabby. You knew I was on the diet when you agreed to have lunch with me," Jen argued, smiling through her irritation.

Gabby shrugged. "True. But I didn't think I'd have to go on the diet too just because I came over for lunch." *There.* A definite edge to Gabby's voice. Jen was not imagining it.

"You don't! When you leave here, you can stop at the bakery and eat a whole cake for all I care."

"I might," Gabby said. "Where's the closest bakery?"

"Ha." Jen wondered if she'd actually do it. *Go ahead. Eat all the bread in the world. What do I care if you're fat when I'm thin.*

There was undeniable tension in the kitchen nook. Too much tension. Tension that could be cut with a knife and served over low-carb tofu noodles. Jen looked down at her plate and wondered what had happened to her friendship with Gabby.

A couple of uncomfortable moments went by, and Jen blurted, "Gabby, what's going on here? I feel like it's so hard to talk to you lately. Are you mad at me?" Jen felt like a middle-schooler. Did adult women in mature friendships still get *mad at each other*? Her cards were out on the table, and spiderwebs of doubt began to creep in as the silence continued. Gabby just stared at her. "Oh my god, you are actually mad at me!" Jen exclaimed. "You don't even have to say anything. I can tell. I can tell just by the look in your eyes."

Gabby raised her eyebrows. "Get over yourself, Jen," she said quietly. "Now it's your love handles, but when that's fixed, then what? A nose job? Breast implants? You are a grown woman. Insecurity is no longer cute and endearing in women over twenty-five. You are very beautiful, and your love handles make you look like a hot and sexy woman and not a little girl. Plus you are successful in your career, and you are a genuinely good person. What difference do a few curves make?"

A loud buzz from the intercom interrupted them. Gabby jumped up. Jen stared her down as she walked toward the door and pressed the button to open Jen's building door. Gabby said innocently, "I forgot to tell you—when you started talking low-carb, I invited Elizabeth to join us. It's so funny, you didn't even notice that I was texting." Gabby's tone made it clear that she did not find it very funny.

"Well, thanks for letting me know," Jen responded, throwing her hands up in surrender. "It's like we're still roommates, only I pay all the rent."

"I was going to tell you, but you didn't let me get a word in edgewise," Gabby retorted.

Jen felt her blood pressure rising and a rush of emotion lit her up like a Christmas tree. "Gabby. I never wanted to say this to you, but since you moved in with Marco, you've become really hard to be friends with. All you do is worry about him. What about me? I was your roommate first. And now I'm alone." Gabby's deadpan look lifted, and a look of real pain crossed her face. She knitted her hands together and set them on the table. Jen pushed her hand over her mouth. She had not meant to blurt that out.

Elizabeth knocked at the door and Jen walked past Gabby to open it. Gabby plopped back down in a chair by the kitchen table.

"Hello, hello!" Elizabeth twirled into the room wearing a pale yellow sundress belted in the middle with a hot pink sash. She grinned and danced in.

"I bet you're wondering how I'm free to hang out in the middle of a workday. Well, as you know, I work for myself and today I took an *Elizabeth* day. I advise all my clients to do this and finally took my own advice. Some time off just for me. Lunch with my ladies." Elizabeth laughed. "I just got a mani/pedi. I have a massage scheduled later this evening. Oh, I brought wine." She pulled out a chilled bottle of white dripping with condensation from her purse. "And this morning I caught up on my reading." She pulled a curled-up magazine out and tossed it to Jen.

"*Women's Life?*" Jen asked.

"I stole it from the nail ladies," Elizabeth explained. "Don't tell on me."

Jen unrolled it and looked at the cover. It was damp from pressing against the sweating wine bottle. A very fit, very tan woman in a sports bra and a bikini stood with her chin up and hands on her hips like superman. She looked very proud of herself for all her hard work. The headlines in bright blue and red all had the same underlying message. *You're doing something wrong*: "Undo Your Skin Damage," "Lose 5 Pounds of Ugly Fat," "Stop Poisoning Your Family with Sugar." Jen tapped the magazine against her palm, hesitant to open and face further criticism. Women's day-to-day lives are filled with so many things to worry about. Why would anyone read a hundred reasons why they're not living up to perfection? The headlines could make a sane person batty.

"Do I sense tension? What's going on in here?" Elizabeth asked, looking carefully at Gabby and then at Jen. "Are you guys in a fight?"

"No," Gabby huffed. She grabbed another cucumber. "Come get some rabbit food."

"Jen, there's an article that I think you'll find very interesting in that particular issue of *Women's Life*. It's a real women's weight-loss story written by Ms. Maya Khan, cake baker extraordinaire," Elizabeth pointed. She picked up a cucumber. "I thought you guys were having lunch? Where's the food?"

"Exactly!" Gabby slapped the table.

Jen settled down in the love seat and flipped through the pages until she found the creased corner. A before and after picture of Maya grinned at her, and Jen was amazed at the difference when she saw her friend's transformation in print.

"What?" Jen exclaimed. She read the headline out loud. "I lost thirty-five pounds with XyloSlim?" She skimmed the article then flipped to the cover to check the date. It was the most recent issue. In the article, she claimed to have taken a XyloSlim tablet before each meal and eaten her normal food. *The weight just fell off,* Maya's article claimed. Jen grimaced. It sounded so snide coming from someone else.

Jen stopped reading to catch Elizabeth up on the latest news that she'd learned yesterday. She went back to the article. "Listen to this: 'I ate pancakes for breakfast, pizza for lunch, pasta for dinner. Oh! And, being a Yummy Channel personality, there's no way I could just give up eating desserts, especially cupcakes, my specialty.' That is insane. This was not written by the Maya I used to know."

"Doesn't XyloSlim have the commercial with the siren that says 'Fat Alert, Fat Alert!'?" Elizabeth asked.

"Yes! And after the lady's transformation, they play that cheesy old, 'Who's that girl!' song," Gabby said.

"Those commercials are the worst." Jen crossed her arms over her chest.

"Does anyone actually call 800 numbers and take pills like that?" Elizabeth asked.

"Probably the same people who give up everything with flour and sugar," Gabby offered. "Just kidding."

"Ouch," said Jen, but she considered Gabby's point. "Yeah, I'll admit it. I've tried diet pills in the past. But they never work; not unless you're totally devoted to the diet, like I am now."

"Says the girl who eats mayo spread on slices of ham rolled up with cheese," Elizabeth said, making a face.

"Says the girl who spends three hours a day working out," Jen countered. "Unless they're offering Zumba the same day as High-Intensity Spin. On those days, she spends *four* hours a day working out." Jen glared at Elizabeth. She did not know why her friends couldn't support her.

"You guys are both out of your respective minds," Gabby said, looking through the take-out menus she'd found stuffed in the back of one of Jen's kitchen drawers.

"Why don't you guys go out to lunch?" Jen suggested, an edge to her voice. "I have a lot of work here, and I'm really upset. I'm upset because my best friends are not being very supportive of my diet. I'm upset because my old best friend at work has pulled a total one-eighty and is now apparently a spokesperson for the same drug that killed a colleague. And I'm a little scared, to be honest. Because I think someone I worked with slipped an overdose of diet medication into Bess Brantwood's drink, and whether or not they intended it, they *killed* her. My life could be at risk." She huffed off to get her laptop from the couch and quickly found the link on the *Women's Life* website. She pulled Detective Franklin's card out of her tote bag and e-mailed him the link to the article. She didn't know if the police force subscribed to *Women's Life* or not and figured it would be worth sending.

When she returned, Elizabeth and Gabby looked chastened and were whispering quietly to each other. Gabby spoke up. "I'm sorry. I didn't realize how much stress you were under, but of course that makes sense."

Elizabeth had a thoughtful expression. "Let's talk

through this. I mean really talk through it. That always helps my clients." Gabby and Jen groaned simultaneously, but Elizabeth carried on unperturbed. "Okay, let's talk about Giselle first. She was let go by the police. Why? She had motive and opportunity."

"They must know something we don't know," Jen said, throwing her hands up.

"Maybe," Elizabeth said. "Or maybe she gave them information that changed the game."

"What could she have said?" Gabby asked. They all thought for a moment but came up blank.

"Okay. Let's put a pin in that," Elizabeth said. "Jen, I know you don't think that Maya could have done this, but let's look at it rationally. The day after she returns from filming, her boyfriend's wife is killed with an overdose of the medication"—Elizabeth pointed at the *Women's Life*—"that she is now saying helped her lose all the weight. I'm sorry, but that's suspicious. What's that saying? The simplest answer is usually the right one."

"She hasn't been detained," Jen said, unsure of how to defend her friend.

"If we're talking about the simplest solution," Gabby said, "I don't know why the possibility that Bess took all those pills herself is totally unreasonable. I know what they said in the press release, that she knew about her medication and wouldn't mix, but couldn't she have wanted to off herself?"

"No way. Bess wasn't the suicidal type," Jen said. "But Maya isn't the murderous type either."

"What do we know that we *don't* know?" Elizabeth asked, pulling a notebook and pen from her purse. "Let's start with that."

"We don't know why Giselle wasn't arrested," Jen said.

"We don't know why Maya hasn't been arrested," Gabby said, shrugging to Jen.

"We don't know who put the XyloSlim in the tea."

"We don't know if the person who put the Xylo-Slim in the tea actually knew if Bess always took antianxiety medication before events or not."

Jen moaned. "We don't know *anything*. There are so many people that had access to the fridge in her dressing room. For God's sake, I had access to it. The VP of programming has cases of XyloSlim samples and leaves them all over the place, so anyone could have gotten those too—they're all over the office. I just know this is going to turn into one of those cold cases, and I'm going to be working with a bunch of crazy people for the rest of my life. I can't do it. I can't stand going back there."

"Maybe you shouldn't go back. Do you ever think it might be easier if you didn't work at the Yummy Channel?" Elizabeth asked. "It's one hundred percent completely about fattening food, and you are trying to change your life to be healthier. Maybe you'd be better off at a job where you weren't around food 24/7?"

"Elizabeth, I plan events for people. It's my job. Most of the time there's food involved. You see how that works?" She couldn't help bristling when Elizabeth put her life coach counselor hat on in their personal conversations.

"Calm down, I'm just saying I find it interesting that you took a job that deals with, in this case, food. It's interesting that you didn't find a job throwing a party for a bike shop's grand opening, or a marathon runner, or a charity walk-a-thon. The Olympics, the fashion industry, must I go on? Your job is to throw parties for the foodiest of foodies."

Jen blew out a gust of air, and a loose strand of her hair wisped up and away from her face. It fell back down across her forehead. "Maybe," Jen admitted.

Elizabeth reached over and patted Jen's hand. Jen looked at her for a long moment. "Now let's talk about people who are addicted to working out."

Elizabeth shook her head and protested, "I'm not addicted to working out, it just makes me feel good. It helps me deal with stress."

"Isn't that the definition of addiction?" Jen countered. "I used to feel the same exact way about cupcakes."

Later, after her friends left and Jen resigned herself to getting back to work, she found herself deep in thought about the diet industry and all the people who spend their workdays trying to get you to eat and/or not eat. So much money tied up in gyms and diet pills and food products, all so women can feel— what? What did she really want to feel above all else? Why, really, did she want to lose weight? There were many reasons, but the one that she kept coming back to was love. She wanted to feel lovable. She wanted to love herself, really and truly. She didn't want to chase fame and fortune and still end up miserable, like Bess Brantwood.

chapter thirteen

Jen carried the *Women's Life* under her arm on the way to the office on Wednesday morning and practiced what she'd say to Maya over and over in her head, getting the inflection just right. After her friends left yesterday, she'd gotten calls back from four chefs that confirmed their participation in Haley's Friday night event. A couple of other chefs called to pass, and grumble over the short notice. Two chefs had called back just to call her crazy for even asking. Everyone had expressed their condolences for Bess.

Early that morning, she'd checked her e-mail from home before leaving for the office. Tommy sent an e-mail forwarded from Bess's sister saying that the funeral would be held on Thursday afternoon at a Presbyterian church on the West Side. Jen would attend, in part because she could envision her mother's reaction if she decided to skip it. "Is that how I raised you?" Vera would ask. Her mom was right. She would go.

Jen rounded a corner onto crowded Sixth Avenue and gritted her teeth, mentally practicing her conversation with Maya. In the way up to the elevator, she prepared responses to any excuse Maya might offer for her rotten behavior. However, when Jen got to her office at five minutes after 9:00 a.m., she remembered Haley's revisions to the studio schedules. She checked the printout from the meeting, and sure enough, Maya was taping an in-studio special for her show *Khanfetti*. Rather than get into her workday and have her anger simmer down, Jen decided to go sit on one of the benches in the studio office and watch. Maybe she'd get some insight into the new, not-so-improved Maya by watching her at work.

The hallway leading to the studios was no longer blocked off with crime scene tape. She guessed the police department's investigators had done all they could do here, but with no one arrested, it was eerie to walk down the hallway. Jen avoided looking at Bess's studio, and the door was thankfully closed tight. In Maya's studio the audience lights were all the way down, with spotlights focused on Maya. Her set was decorated with pictures of cakes she'd decorated that looked more like art. There were rainbows of perfect sugar flowers atop a garden of frosting and cake, plaids of caramel and chocolate, or dainty little butterflies sitting atop cream cheese and gingerbread cakes.

Maya stood at the counter, really working the camera. She laughed out loud at herself, chatted naturally, and took her time with each piece of the decorating project she was undertaking. The undeniable charisma she'd always had was now accentuated by her sexy look. Jen noticed as she moved to get a new bag of frosting or one of the tools she used, she was stunning in an A-line dress and heels. She'd curled and sprayed her black hair so it fell in shiny, fat ringlets over her shoulders, and the cherry pattern on her apron matched her bright red lipstick. *XyloSlim,* Jen thought crossly, feeling frumpy in her jeans and blouse. She should feel great now that she'd lost five pounds, a huge step closer to her goal weight, but comparing herself to Maya she could tell she still had a long way to go. Jen sucked in her stomach and straightened her back as she watched Maya work.

Maya spoke to the camera, which was rolling with no one operating it. When Maya did these long shots that had to be edited together, sometimes the cameraman would take breaks. It looked like this was one of those breaks. "Listen, you can be as creative as you want. You can do as much or as little as you want. But the key is to trust your instinct and have fun with little experiments. You can always use a butter knife to scrape it off, and try something new."

Jen sighed and looked around the studio audience. This wasn't a show with a live studio audience, so only a few people sat along the benches. Jen recognized Maya's agent and the producer of *Khanfetti*. They were contractors with the Yummy Channel, and Jen hadn't seen them in a couple of months. There was no reason for them to come to the office while Maya was on the road. Jen noticed one other person, a woman who was hunched over. Jen didn't recognize her, but even in the dark, Jen could tell that her long blond hair was ratted and in severe need of a trim. Jen looked back to Maya, who was whisking white sugar with food coloring and powdered sugar to achieve a very shiny effect. Maya paused for a moment before continuing her monologue. Just then the producer's cell phone rang. Maya shot him a death stare, and he got up to leave the audience seating area. The agent followed closely behind, probably piggy-backing on the producer's interruption to make a call of his own.

A moment of silence passed as Maya fiddled with the mixture, getting it *just* right. The consistency had to be perfect, or it would look lumpy, she explained to fill the silence. Out of the corner of Jen's eyes, Jen saw the blond woman stand and start running down the benches toward Maya, hurling her petite frame forward with a surprising force. Jen stood nervously. Then the light from the set reflected off something shiny in the woman's hand. Jen squinted and saw that it was a long, serrated knife. Jen screamed, "Maya!"

Maya let out a shriek and dropped her bowl of sugar. It shattered into pieces all over the set's tile floor. Jen's anger at Maya melted away as she quickly decided what to do. The woman, who Jen could now see clearly in the light, screamed, "You bitch!" Her voice sounded strained. Her voice also sounded slightly familiar, and as Jen squinted at the woman's face, veiled beneath oversize sunglasses, she felt a flicker of recognition. Jen patted her pockets and cursed herself for leaving her cell phone on her desk in her office. She willed the producer or agent or cameraman to come back into the studio.

"Wha-what do you want? Who are you?" stammered Maya. Jen's eyes stayed glued to the knife, which had the same mahogany handles with the Yummy Channel logo as the set in this kitchen, in the *Deep Fried and Spicy* studio, and the *Bess's Bakery* studio. Jen knew who it was.

"Giselle!" The woman spun around so fast that the blond wig she wore slipped off, covering one eye. She clutched the handle of the knife and held it out from her body toward Jen.

"Giselle? Are you wearing a wig?" Maya covered her eyes and tried to see into the dark audience. "Jen? Is that your voice I hear up there? What are you two doing in here?"

"Shut up!" screamed Giselle. She reached up and yanked on the waxy blond wig and let it fall to the ground. Her dark hair was in a tight bun on top of her head and she looked even more skeletal. "Jen, get down here! God, why are you everywhere? What the hell?" She grunted a sound of guttural frustration. "Do you know they're going to arrest me? They let me go because my lawyer said he'd have the charges thrown out if they didn't find more evidence, but they will find more evidence. Because somebody is trying to frame me. Of course my fingerprints are on the bottle of tea! I packed the fucking bag for Bess. I did everything for Bess."

Maya stepped backward, but Giselle swung forward and in one swoop she brought the knife down hard into the cake Maya had been decorating. Frosting and the yellow guts of the cake flew everywhere. Maya screamed again. Giselle jammed the round end of the knife into a chunk of cake and brought it to her mouth like a demented cake pop. She took a huge bite, spewing crumbs as she spoke. "You ruined my life, Maya, and you're going to pay. Jen? Get down here." Jen eyed the door, wondering if she could get to it. There was no way. Giselle would beat her there, and even if Jen got out, Maya was still in danger. Jen needed to get close enough to Giselle to get the knife away.

"Giselle, did you kill Bess?" asked Maya in a hushed

voice. Jen cursed her. *Don't piss the crazy girl off,* she tried to mentally transmit to Maya.

"Shut up!" Giselle said again, and her voice seemed to shake less now. She took another bite of cake and answered matter-of-factly. "Yeah right. I know you did it. Sure, sometimes I wanted to take her out, but I didn't. I am, however, going to kill you because you ruined my life!"

Maya ducked down as Giselle waved the knife toward her, sending cake bits flying. "Why?" she called, moving her arms up to cover her face. Jen stared at the set and then she saw it. The huge studio camera, whose red light announced that it was still filming, was on wheels. If Jen could get down to it, she could shove it into Giselle before she even knew what hit her. Jen took a step forward.

Giselle shook. Her voice turned whiny. "You stole David away from me." She looked up to the audience, searching for Jen's face. "I should kill you too, Jen Stevens. Billy wouldn't be able to ignore me and go running to you every time he has a problem."

"What?" Maya stood straight up and crossed her arms over her chest. Her eyes flitted up to the studio audience. "What are you talking about?"

"Yeah, what are you talking about, Giselle? You sound crazy," said Jen, confused and thrown off-guard. She didn't even know that Giselle and Billy knew each other.

Giselle aimed her attention back at Maya. Her voice was a teakettle cutting through the room. "I am not crazy. You are crazy. Do you think no one knows you were seeing David Brantwood? *Everyone* knows. But it won't last. It won't. He loves me. He told me all the time, and it's just a matter of time before he comes back to me." Giselle moved forward and Maya stepped back again, her back against the set wall now. "Jen, you better get your fat butt down here now. I have no idea what Billy sees in you. When he showed me the diary, we were laughing our asses off at what Bess said about you."

"I'm coming. It's dark, and I'm trying not to fall," Jen said. Her cheeks burned. Could Giselle be telling the truth? She took another step closer to the camera and hoped that Maya wouldn't escalate the situation before she could launch it into Giselle.

No such luck. Maya howled, "Listen here, Skeletor. There is not a chance that David loves you. In fact, he's told me how gross he thinks you are. He likes a woman with curves."

"Oh yeah, is that why he only started screwing you after you lost thirty pounds? He never made *me* wait." Jen was now inches from the camera.

"You're lying." Maya's eyes were pure hate. "What we had was special, you bitch. We didn't consummate it until we were both sure we were in love."

"You didn't consummate it until you weren't so fat.

Isn't that right, Jen? Huh, Chubbster?" Giselle spoke evenly, without turning her head to look at Jen.

"Chubbster?" Jen choked, disbelieving. "Did you just call me Chubbster?" Infuriated, Jen pounced on the camera, jumping on the base around the bottom and sailing with the two-hundred-pound equipment into Giselle. Maya shrieked and cowered against the back wall, grabbing a rolling pin to protect her head.

The camera smacked into Giselle, pinning her against the wall. She screamed again. "My arm!" The knife clattered to the floor. Unfortunately, the impact sent Jen flying off the base and spinning around, completely off balance. She landed with a cool, wet thunk in Maya's destroyed cake. Of course. She looked up and grimaced. The camera was still rolling and pointing directly at her. *Why her? Why cake? Why again?*

Maya stood up and stepped toward Jen, but slipped on some icing, then righted herself. She kicked the knife away, far from Giselle's grasp. Giselle was still moaning in pain and trapped by the weight of the camera. Maya walked behind the camera and clicked on the brakes that held the wheels in place, trapping her further.

Maya opened the studio door and screamed, "Help! Somebody call 911!" She rushed back and helped Jen stand up. Maya looked to Jen. "You look like a kid after your second birthday party," Maya said, a loving tone radiating from her voice.

"Covered in cake again," Jen said. They laughed tentatively, their relief making them unnaturally giddy despite the fear pulsing through them.

Jen rubbed frosting off of her forehead and sniffed at it, considered licking the thick, fresh vanilla schmear from her fingers. She really wanted carbs and she was surrounded by them. She imagined the feeling she'd have by picking a big chunk off of her shirt and popping it in her mouth, and even though it was gross, her mouth ached and watered.

Next to her lay the *Women's Life* that she'd been carrying this whole time. It was crumpled in the chaos. Giselle began crying quietly behind them.

Maya looked at Jen. "Are you okay?" she asked, her voice tender.

"I'm fine." Jen sighed. "I can't believe she called me Chubbster." They looked at each other and both cracked a smile.

"Thank you for doing that. You probably saved my life," Maya said.

"Listen, we have to talk," Jen said, steeling herself for an uncomfortable confrontation. She glanced at Giselle, who was still crying. Jen opened the *Women's Life* to Maya's article.

Maya sighed and picked up a chunk of cake from the countertop, popping it in her mouth. After she chewed, she said, "I know it's cheesy, but it's extra money. And, I don't know, I'm proud of myself for losing all that weight."

"Did you really take XyloSlim? You don't even take asprin when you have a headache!"

"Well, not exactly," Maya admitted. "I just stopped eating carbs, mainly, and got a personal trainer. I took it once or twice, so the article's not a total lie."

Jen nodded. "This is so unfair to people who read it and waste their money on a stupid product. Who put you up to it?" Jen thought of all the diet commercials on the Yummy Channel. It was a multi-million-dollar industry that made its income on making women feel bad about themselves.

Maya was quiet for a moment. "Don't tell anyone," she said. "But Haley asked me to do it. She thought it would be good synergy for the companies to work together. She didn't want anyone to know, though. And she wouldn't take *no* for an answer." Jen's forehead creased. Before she could ask any other questions, Maya's agent walked back in. When he saw what was going on, he ran over to help. Within a few minutes, the room was filled with people. Tommy took Giselle out from under the camera and was holding her arm. She struggled for a moment but gave up, unable to escape the large man's powerful hold.

Jen's heart sank as she watched the scene. Her workplace would never be the same. She blamed pride and greed. She blamed hunger and the insatiable appetite of viewers. She blamed synergy and diet pills and carbs. She just had to get through this week, she told herself. If she could get through this week, she would update her résumé and put in her notice. The glamour of working at the Yummy Channel had dissolved with Bess's death. Her job had become more bitter than sweet.

chapter fourteen

Thursday, the day of Bess's funeral, was rainy. *Cliché*, Jen thought as she unfolded her purple umbrella and left her apartment to go to the office. She had plenty to do in the early morning hours of the day since the Yummy Channel would be mostly shut down for the funeral in the afternoon. Jen wore clunky rain boots and carried a pair of black heels in her bag to match her dress for the service. Instead of her usual tote bag, she carried a real leather purse. The purse was a mostly meaningless gesture of respect for Bess who'd let her views be known on Jen's "sloppy-looking bag lady" tote bag on more than one occasion.

Though it was already midmorning, it still looked dark as Jen stared out of the rain-spattered window of her office onto the street. She felt a pit in her stomach, and this time it wasn't just from her body adjusting to the low-carb diet. Billy's sister Robin had called her back, finally. Jen had been annoyed when she first answered the phone but was quickly quieted by the concern in Robin's voice. She asked if Jen had seen Billy, if she'd heard from him at all. Jen told her no, but she'd call her right away if she did.

When Jen hung up with Robin, she dialed Alex's cell phone number. He didn't answer so she left a voice mail asking if Billy's sister should report Billy as a missing person at this point? She suggested that maybe he or Detective Franklin could call Robin and talk to her about it, maybe put out an "APB." She read Robin's number into the recording. After she hung up, Jen wished she hadn't used the term she learned on *Law & Order: SVU*. Alex would probably think she was an idiot.

Jen was aching to know if they could shed any more light on Billy's relationship with Giselle. Last night, she'd tried calling both Gabby and Elizabeth to talk through the possibilities, but neither had answered. She called again now, but she guessed they weren't available to talk. She left voice mails. Loneliness and self-pity filled Jen, which then cycled around to full-on guilt for being so self-involved on the day of Bess's funeral. She tried to think good thoughts about the star.

After Giselle attacked her and Maya yesterday, Jen half-expected Haley and Tommy to cancel the event on Friday night, but Haley insisted that the show must go on. Luckily, the details of this event had been surprisingly easy to piece together, a blessing during this shockingly awful week. For once, all the vendors were easy to work with. Since they weren't renting a space but hosting the event themselves, and each chef was bringing his or her own food and supplies, Jen didn't have all that much problem-solving to do this time around.

The most laborious part had been the invitation list, but she'd e-mailed out the invitations yesterday. She'd already gotten nearly fifty responses. Apparently every blogger, reviewer, and chef in New York wanted to know what was going on in the Yummy Channel and were falling all over themselves to get an invitation, but Jen was determined to keep the numbers reasonable.

The prep kitchen in the Yummy Channel, where the event would be taking place, was a long, broad room containing nine miniature kitchens, each with a long marble counter, an oven, a deep sink, and a minifridge stocked with a few essentials. The room was used for getting food ready in various states for the shows as they were being filmed in the studio. The entrance to the prep kitchen was a wide six-foot doorway that opened on the opposite side of the hallway where the filming studios were situated. There were still a few remnants of the police investigation that had taken place here and in the adjacent dressing rooms. Jen stood in the prep kitchen and plucked a scrap of yellow crime scene tape that still clung limply against the wall. The door to Bess's dressing room was closed tightly. Will's was wide open, revealing his sprawling mess, complete with half-eaten sandwiches and stocked with cans of beer. There was a definite stink coming from his area, a mixture of stale food and cologne.

Jen planned to set up three round tables for the next day's event, each with ten chairs, along the wall opposite the prep stations. She knew there would be morbid curiosity about Bess's dressing room. She'd pulled white and gold linens and enough servingware for one hundred guests from their storage closet, though she had capped the event at a max of seventy people. Always better to have extras.

The air seemed desperate to shed its water weight when she left the office for the funeral. When Jen stepped off the elevator on the ground floor she felt the humidity hit her and realized her error. She'd forgotten her umbrella. She sighed and got back into the elevator to retrieve it from the workspace she'd set up in the prep kitchen that morning. The lights were off, but enough light streamed from the hallway so that Jen could see that the umbrella was just where she left it. The only other light was coming from Maya Khan's dressing room, which had been closed tightly a few moments before when Jen had left to go downstairs. *Strange,* Jen thought. She grabbed her umbrella and turned to go back downstairs. A thump from Maya's dressing room made Jen look over her shoulder. She listened for another noise and took a half step backward.

Maya's voice came from her dressing room. "Thanks for dropping this off—and waiting until the coast was clear."

"It's no problem," a female voice responded. Jen heard another thump.

"And David didn't find out?" Maya asked.

"No, it was easy," came the answer. Jen struggled to place the second voice. She didn't think she recognized it.

"How are you holding up?" Maya asked.

"I'm fine," the voice said. "Poor Charlie got reamed though. Apparently Bess wrote some stuff about him in a journal, that he was stalking her and he had to go defend himself for like three hours. He was mad."

"Oh," Maya said. "What about Billy Davidsen?"

A moment passed. "He's not violent or anything, but he's a little bit *off* sometimes."

"He just vanished, right?" Maya asked.

"I guess. Hey, I've got to go. Can we settle up here?"

The door to the dressing room widened and Jen hurried out. She didn't want them to know she'd been listening. When she got back from the funeral, Jen was determined to get in to Maya's dressing room and see what was in there.

It was already raining a few slow, fat drops when Jen got into a cab to go to the funeral and scooted across the leather seat. She longed for everything to go back to normal, though she wasn't 100 percent sure what normal even was anymore. It seemed clear that things would never go back to the way they were, at least not with Maya. Before she could slam the door of the taxi, a hand grabbed it and another person slid in next to her. "It's taken—" she started to say but then she fell silent.

Tommy Wegman slid into the cab next to her. "I'll catch a ride with you, if that's okay," the executive said. She hadn't spoken with him, or even seen him, since walking out of his office on Monday. Jen's breath caught in her throat and she started coughing and couldn't stop.

"Are you okay?" he asked, turning away to give directions to the cabdriver. He slammed the door, and the cab took off.

Jen finally nodded, tears filling her eyes. "I'm fine," she choked out. "Just swallowed the wrong way. Sorry," she apologized, cursing herself for adding to the awkwardness of the situation.

"I heard about yesterday's *situation* with Giselle," Tommy said. "You saved Maya?"

"It was nothing," Jen said. "I was in the right place at the right time." Jen sniffed the air. She smelled booze, she was sure of it. She looked at Tommy, wondering how many drinks he'd had. He was staring out the window now, watching the streets go down in numbers.

"Are *you* okay?" She directed the question at him now, not knowing exactly what to say to someone heading to their secret married lover's funeral.

A long moment of silence passed in the cab, the only noise the honks and whir of traffic. "I'm sorry I was rude to you on Monday. I'm not myself. I should have listened to you. Things are out of control at the network. Everyone's so goddamn selfish and greedy. Except you. I know you're a good person, I can tell. I feel like I can trust you, Jenny. It is fate that we're sharing this cab." Jen wasn't sure how to respond. She was flattered that he thought she was a good person, but wasn't sure she wanted to be in a position where he trusted her with personal matters. She felt like her head might burst from too much information—but too few real answers.

"That night," Tommy started, turning toward Jen. "The night of the party. I went there. I went to her dressing room. She told me to go away. She told me that she didn't have time for a fat, old loser. She wasn't acting like herself. I yelled at her, called her a whore. We argued. Then I took a walk, had a scotch, and went to the damn party." From Tommy's mouth came a strangled sound, a muffled sob. "I should have told her I loved her, Jen. It was the last time I saw her. I should have told her how lucky I was to have her in my life."

"I'm sure she knew," Jen said, her heart breaking a little bit.

"How do you know? She was in trouble and I wasn't there. That damn XyloSlim—I've always hated that product. Haley"—he cut off his sentence and gulped—"and that bastard husband of Bess's just wants all her money. Somebody ought to teach him a lesson. Whoever killed Bess should be six feet under." His voice grew steadily louder as he spoke, his words coming out in slurs.

"Tommy, do you want to stop and get a cup of coffee before we get to the church?" Jen asked.

"I'll be fine," Tommy said sharply. He took a deep breath. "Cabbie? Pull over here. I'll walk the rest of the way." He retrieved his wallet from his back pocket, then reached in and handed Jen a fifty-dollar bill. He was out of the cab before Jen could say a word, and the cab was off again. Jen took a couple of deep breaths, and thought about what Tommy said. She sympathized with his grief, and the ache rippled through her chest. She wished there was something she could do for him, like get him flowers or a card, but this was a wound only time would heal. *Time, and good scotch*, she thought. Nine blocks later, the taxi pulled up to the church. It was packed with people waiting to get in flowing down the stairs and out into the courtyard. Jen paid the driver and slipped on her heels before stepping out of the cab.

She filed into the church amongst chefs, restaurant owners, actors, producers, and agents, everyone dressed in their finest. The church echoed with their hushed voices while they waited for the funeral to start. Jen, for once just a guest rather than the master of ceremonies, just watched them interact, handing out business cards, schmoozing with one another. To Jen at that moment, they seemed like sharks in a tank, but she smiled and shook hands with everyone.

She sat next to strangers in a back pew and noticed David Brantwood walk in after her. Jen was relieved that Maya hadn't walked in with him. *What was Maya keeping secret from him in her dressing room?* David walked up and sat with the family, next to Bess's parents. Jen noticed them scoot over a few inches. Bess's father did not reach over to pat his back. Bess's mother did not look at him. The director of marketing and other employees from the Yummy Channel streamed in. Some of the employees from the bakery sat near her. Charlie Rosen was noticeably absent. So much remained unsaid between them as this group gathered together to mourn its fallen leader. Just as the music began, Tommy walked in and slid into the pew closest to the door.

The service started at noon. It was over in less than an hour and left nearly everyone in attendance in tears. No matter how cruel Bess had been at times, she'd touched all the people there deeply in some way, including Jen. The *truth* about how Bess treated people in real life seemed nearly irrelevant there. Bess Brantwood was bigger than her attitude, bigger than the flavor of her cupcakes. She had been an icon *and* she had been someone's daughter. The funeral made the loss palpable. Jen walked out of the church in a daze and down the stairs, letting the enormity of what happened to Bess settle around her. Unanswered questions churned in her head, a restless bout of mental heartburn.

Jen knew she'd have to go back to the office to get started on a long night of setting up the space in the test kitchen for the Comfort Food event. How Jen craved comfort. Bess's service and Billy's sister's call had left her feeling uneasy, like she had a hole that she needed to fill. With what, she wasn't sure. She began walking uptown, planning to catch a cab back to the office, but she passed block after block until she found herself in a part of the city she didn't know very well. A boom of thunder shook the city around her, and the first drops fell, landing on her hair and making big dark splotches on the pavement around her. It sprinkled for a moment before the sky opened up and poured rain down on her. She couldn't believe it. She'd left her umbrella at the church. She could picture it on the empty pew, the light from the stained glass falling on it.

Sopping and umbrella-less, Jen found a safe haven

in the closest shelter, a Wendy's restaurant, and when she swung open the door an immediate sense of familiarity surrounded her. Her mother had taken her to Wendy's on nights when they had wanted to avoid cooking. In high school, she'd worked at her local Wendy's—it was her very first job. She could still remember the feel of the visor on her forehead, and the greasy line of pimples it left. Jen hadn't been inside a Wendy's in a few years. She stood dripping in the doorway, soaked in nostalgia, sniffing the distinct aroma of fast food. The lunch crowd was still coming in strong at 1:30 p.m. Everyone was damp and shaking umbrellas and stomping their rain boots onto the slick brown tile floors.

People flowed around Jen as she stood in the center of the room, staring up at the menu. She was too tired to go anywhere else, too hungry to pick somewhere more healthy or trendy or posh. Wendy's was food for the anti-foodie; true comfort food. She knew what she was going to do as soon as she walked in the door. She looked around her, both ways, as if to make sure no one she knew was watching and then walked up to the counter and ordered a number four meal with large french fries and a large Frosty. All willpower vanished. It was more than that. She wanted to be so full that it hurt. She wanted to lose herself in a mass of salted french fries, eating them one at a time until all her cares went away and all that was left was the sweet and salty flavors on her tongue. She wanted to disappear into the flavors and just enjoy the experience of stuffing her face. She knew that she could stay on her diet, but chose not to. It would have been easy enough to order a Caesar salad instead of fries—fast food was pretty easy to tailor to a low-carb diet. But she didn't. She sat down, unwrapped her food, and took a deep, wide bite of the sandwich. She knew logically that food wasn't a reasonable way to rebel against the sadness she felt about work, her body, her friends, and life, but that's what it felt like as she dipped her fries in her Frosty and licked the grease off of her fingers.

The rain had slowed when she walked out of Wendy's and Jen quickly caught a taxi back to the office. She tried to wash the smell of fast food and total failure off her hands in the ladies' room and headed through the halls to the prep kitchen. She had to refocus on work: if she could get most of the event setup done tonight, tomorrow would be manageable. She was glad to throw herself into her work, glad for the complete distraction. And she had to see what was in Maya's office.

chapter fifteen

On Sunday afternoon, Billy had been on the first bus out of Port Authority after dropping the diary off to Jen. All he'd wanted was to get the hell out of dodge. He'd been running from the cops since he was a teenager, passing around pinner joints under the bleachers. He knew it was only a matter of time before they legalized it, but until then, he just needed to steer clear until the Bess stuff blew over and they caught who did it. He didn't know anything and he was too pretty to go to jail for accidentally concealing evidence. Giselle had wanted him to leave the diary with her, but he took it while she was sleeping on Sunday and—poof—disappeared.

The first bus out of Port Authority took Billy to Philly. He got there at midnight or something, because they had to stop in like every single town along the way. He went to his buddy Ted's house, a guy that he'd met when he'd visited an uncle in Arizona, who had relocated to Philly recently. They'd stayed in touch. It was pretty easy, you know, Facebook and everything. Ted was big on Facebook. Billy'd never met anyone who liked so many things. Ted let him sleep on the couch, though, and he relaxed into it. It smelled like beer, and Ted's rottweiler, a big thug of a dog named Bourbon, curled up on Billy's shins so he couldn't turn in his sleep.

Billy drank a six-pack that night, staring at reruns of *The Simpsons*. He mostly felt shitty about dropping such a big burden on his ex. He'd just been saying that he wanted to be cool with her. After he pulled that, he doubted that Jen would ever even talk to him again. Maybe they'd never even see each other again, because he sure as shit wasn't going back to work at Bess's Bakery. Those people were messed up. He never wanted Jen to find out that he was hooking up with Giselle. Giselle was good looking and everything, but not hot enough to be as crazy as she acted. Maybe he'd just stay in Philly. New York was for the birds. The only catch was that Bess's Bakery owed him one more paycheck. He'd have to talk to someone eventually if he wanted to get that money. He needed to think of a plan.

The next morning he walked from Ted's house to the Target to get a pack of boxers and left his cell phone on top of the sink in the bathroom, like an idiot. Of course it was gone when he went back to get it. He punched the wall without much commitment. He would have to figure out a way to call his sister. Ted had a laptop from the '90s that he only used to get on social media. Billy could probably use it to e-mail his sister if he could remember her e-mail address. Did they even make pay phones anymore? He'd figure it out tomorrow. On Monday he lay on the couch and finished his Stephen King novel. When Ted got home from work they watched the news. He and Ted passed a bong back and forth and watched *X-Men* on cable.

Tuesday was basically the same as Monday, except when he went to Target he saw a TV playing over the snack bar and Bess's face came up. He stared at it, remembering that face, slack and unresponsive, on Friday night. He bought Lucky Charms and fell asleep on the couch. He wondered if he could be suffering from post-traumatic stress disorder, or depression or something that he'd need professional help to shake.

Wednesday was Ted's day off and they packed up his dog Bourbon in the car, his stump of a tail wagging like mad, and drove to a hiking trail outside of the city. It felt good to get back to nature. Billy wondered if he could live out here. He figured he could manage for at least the summer. Something was nagging at him, though. Something he couldn't stop thinking about. He was trying to put it all together. It was like looking at one of those Magic Eye posters, and Billy couldn't do it for very long.

They were sitting on the couch early on Thursday morning and Ted was flipping through the television channels. He paused for a second and Will Riley's face filled the screen. *Deep Fried and Spicy.* Today he was showing viewers how to make a kick-ass fried sausage-stuffed calzone. Billy's mouth watered, watching it. "Gross," said Ted, who made a big deal about not eating red meat. Ted began flipping again.

Billy said, "Can you just turn on the news, man?" Ted flipped until he found a news program he liked. He started to change it, but Billy stopped him. "Can we just leave it here for a minute? I want to see if there's anything about—you know, the stuff back home."

Ted shrugged and Billy heard the sounds of cabinets opening and a bowl of Lucky Charms spilling into a bowl. Billy got through the local Philly news and when the national stuff came on, it was only a minute or two in before he heard the reporter start talking about Bess's Bakery, on the national news. Giselle had been arrested after attacking another Yummy Channel star and was also under investigation in the Bess Brantwood case. He tried to take a breath, but it felt raspy going in. He was a wanted man, and Giselle probably deserved to be locked up—in a loony bin, but not for murder. This isn't the way his life was supposed to go. He stared at the door and thought again about camping out in the woods indefinitely.

When the guy on the news, the anchorman, started talking about the way that Bess died, though, with mixed drugs, Billy felt a sick feeling creep over him. He thought she'd been, like, poisoned-poisoned. Not like medication poisoned. But if it was mixing up stuff in that tea—shit, he knew who mixed those pills into her tea. She stopped by the bakery all the time—*what was her name again?* She was from the Yummy Channel and acted like she owned the place, even though Bess didn't like her at all. She would just take those special teas from the bakery fridge and mix in the powder from the pills, then chug away.

Maybe he was wrong, though, but he stood up grudgingly. He had to go home. He didn't want to be with Giselle or anything, but he knew that she didn't do anything bad to Bess. He grabbed his backpack and headed for the door. "Headed back to New York, man," he called to Ted.

"'Kay, see ya," Ted's muffled voice came from the kitchen.

Bourbon ran up and licked Billy's hand. Billy patted him. "Good dog," he murmured. "Peace," Billy called out to Ted, letting the screen door slap shut behind him.

It was a mile walk to the bus station, and when he got there, the ticket booth lady told him the bus was boarding. He eyed the pay phone and thought about picking it up, but just hopped on the bus. There wasn't anything he could do from Philly anyway. The urge to nap dissolved and suddenly he knew what he had to do. He'd get back and go to the cops, like he should have in the first place. He checked the bus schedule and asked the lady sitting behind him what time it was. He'd go find Jen at work. If she didn't hate him for ditching out a few days ago, she'd probably help him. He could ask her, at least. He could use the moral support, and he wanted to find out what went down when she gave Bess's diary to the cops.

He fell asleep fifteen minutes into the ride. He woke up to a puddle of drool on his chin, docked at Port Authority. Billy jumped off the hunk of junk and started walking northeast toward Rockefeller Center, where the Yummy Channel offices were. He wasn't walking fast, wasn't walking slow, just steadily walking toward whatever fate was in store. The security guard at the front desk of the building was busy talking on the phone and Billy couldn't get his attention. He looked at the building directory while he waited, listening to the guard go on and on about a package being dropped off at the wrong building. *Cool it, man,* Billy thought. *Don't you know there are more important things in life?* The guard paid no attention and Billy ducked under the badge-access gate. He hit the elevator button and got off on the twelfth floor.

He'd never been up in the Yummy Channel offices.

It was crazy up here, totally different from the front-lines of the foodie world where he'd worked at the bakery. All these super close-up food pictures hung on the walls, and a couple of big, framed pictures of Bess, which was a little creepy. He wondered if he'd ever not feel slightly sick when he saw her face. The weird part about being in the Yummy Channel offices, though, was that it seemed dead silent. It was the middle of a workday and nobody was at work. Billy walked around, feeling like he was in one of those corn mazes you can get lost in. Then it hit him. Everyone must be at Bess's funeral. He'd heard on the news that morning that it was going to be held today. He turned a corner down a new hallway and started looking for Jen's name on all the door plaques. He was almost ready to give up and just wait at her apartment, when he saw *her*. The lady who mixed the pills in with her tea. He followed her down the empty hall. She had her hair up, but Billy was sure that it was her.

She took a right turn, then a left into a long corridor. The corridor opened into a room with a ton of counters and refrigerators, all much nicer than any he'd ever had in the apartments he'd lived in. *Who needed this many sinks?* he wondered. The woman opened a door and went into a dressing room. Billy cursed silently. He should have spoken up earlier. Now he would definitely scare her if he went up and knocked on the door. "Hello," he called out, hoping she'd turn and come back. She didn't. "Hello?" he called again, louder. He thought he heard low murmurs from inside the room. He tried to make out if the other voice he heard was male or female, but it was too quiet to tell.

He walked back toward the little room where she'd disappeared, making sure he stepped loudly, and knocked on the door. "Hey there—" He pushed the door open and took a step in. It was a little dressing room, with a table for ladies to put on their makeup.

Before he could take another step in, something hard smashed against his head. The sound was solid and metallic and echoed in the small room. Billy fell to his knees. He looked up and caught a glimpse of his assailant in the mirror. Disappointment flooded over him before his eyes flickered shut and he slumped to the floor. *Why, man? Why him?*

When he woke some time later, sore and sick feeling, he was in a dark room. The only light came from a small grate in the ceiling. He thought it was nighttime but wasn't sure. It felt like nighttime. His foot was tied to something. He tried to get the knot loose, but couldn't see well enough to unfasten it. His eyes adjusted to the light a little bit, pulling the room into focus. He inhaled deeply, then let his breath out in a steady stream. An eerie feeling raised the hair on his arms. He knew with a crushing weight just how screwed he was.

chapter sixteen

The Yummy Channel offices were technically closed that afternoon for Bess's funeral. Only a few people came back after the service ended. Jen was one of the few who came back. Will Riley was there as well, and doing everything in his power to make it difficult for Jen to work. Jen noted, as he walked back and forth to his dressing room, making a mess and distracting her from her setup, that he hadn't gone to the service. Maya definitely hadn't been there either. Jen didn't know if she should feel disgusted with Bess's costars for not attending, or relieved that they had not gone and made a scene.

Jen walked slowly, listening to her footsteps echo around the empty prep kitchen. When she was sure that not another soul was nearby, she tried the door-knob of Maya's dressing room. It was locked. She considered her options. She could call Officer Alex

D'Alby and Detective Franklin and tell them that something suspicious was afoot, but she wasn't sure exactly how suspicious it was. She could break down the door with her newly ripped muscles from self-defense class. Or she could just flirt with Phil, the studio manager and tech, and swipe his keys. She knew he'd be there, working hard as usual. Phil had not attended the funeral and Jen wasn't surprised in the least. Week after week, he bore the brunt of Bess's mood swings. Her lighting was always bad, or Phil had always attempted to trip her by taping down a wire incompletely. After waiting on Bess's whims for years, Phil was always happy to do a favor for someone who spoke to him with respect and kindness.

Jen found Phil today in the *Bess's Bakery* studio, changing some of the lighting and removing the set decoration. This filming studio would now be used for a reality-based program where six chefs competed each week to create dishes that would ultimately be used in a cookbook. After a few minutes of conversation, Phil high atop a ladder, he climbed down. He smiled a warm and genuine grin. He was wearing a backwards baseball cap and an old long-sleeved Rolling Stones T-shirt. Jen noticed the keychain on his belt loop and smiled even wider.

"Phil," she began, "it's been a really weird, sad week, right?"

"Sad in some ways," he said. "Definitely."

"Well, this morning, before I left for the funeral, I noticed something really weird. Maya got some sort of delivery to her office—I didn't see what it was. Did you notice anything like that?"

Phil was quiet for a moment, and brought his fist to his chin in concentration. "No, I actually went out for a long lunch with a couple of the other techs today, on account of it being so quiet." Jen raised her eyebrows, but Phil did not apologize for skipping the funeral. In fact, Jen could see a physical change now that he wasn't getting screamed at hourly for various infractions. He held his head higher, or at least Jen thought so.

"Well," Jen continued. She leaned in conspiratorially. "I'd really like to get in her dressing room and see what was dropped off. I think she's gone for the rest of the day, right? Almost everyone is gone."

Phil thought for a moment. He looked Jen in the eyes. She knew he could get in trouble for this if anyone found out. He took the baseball cap off his head and scratched his sandy brown hair. He replaced the cap. "Listen, I've got to take a walk through the prep kitchen and over by the dressing rooms. Why don't you head over in about five minutes and try the door again. Maybe Maya just forgot to lock it?" he suggested.

Jen was picking up what Phil was laying down. "Totally. I will. Thank you. Thank you!"

"Don't thank me. I'm not doing anything," Phil reminded her.

"Right. Got it." Phil gave her a wink and headed for the door, his keys jingling around his waist.

Jen sat down on the first row of audience seating in Bess's studio and gazed at the set. Even though Phil had removed some of the cute and kitschy decorations, the décor was still all Bess, with a real Americana charm. Jen could practically hear her Southern drawl here, instructing viewers to add a pinch of cinnamon or a tiny touch of lemon zest. "Plus butter 'n love," Bess had always said. It was late in the afternoon on the day of Bess's funeral and Jen wondered if she'd ever stop feeling Bess's ghost. How could she lay her conflicting, nagging feelings of responsibility to rest? She knew she wasn't responsible for Giselle, or Billy, or anyone else. Something protruding behind the fake kitchen window caught Jen's eye and she stood. As she rounded the wallpapered plywood that made up Bess's kitchen, the backstage area came into view and Jen shrieked out loud. She grasped the fake wall for support and blinked to try to understand what she was seeing.

Bess stared back at her, her blue eyes sparkling, a smile frozen on her face. It only took a split second for Jen to register. These were the life-size cutouts that Jen had carried over in Charlie's car less than a week ago to decorate the One Hundredth Episode celebration. Someone had moved them back from the bakery to Bess's studio. The four cardboard redheads stared at Jen, and she could feel their judgment. Jen had to help solve the mystery of Bess's death if she ever wanted to feel any peace here at the Yummy Channel. She knew where to start. Maya Khan's dressing room.

Exactly eight minutes later, Jen walked back down the hallway from the studios and through the prep kitchens. It was empty, with no sign of Phil or anyone else for that matter. She walked slowly toward Maya's door, pausing briefly to look around one last time to make sure no one was watching. It was unusual for this space to be so empty. She knew Will Riley could walk through the door again at any moment, so she moved fast, ducking into Maya's now unlocked dressing room—*thank you, Phil*—and closing the door behind her.

Maya's dressing room hadn't changed much since the last time Jen had sat in here a few months ago, before Maya went on the road to film *Khanfetti*. The pictures on the wall were the same and the bold blue curtains that framed the window hadn't changed. Small six-by-six-inch frames lined the room with beautiful, striking flowers of all the colors of the rainbow in full bloom. Where before Maya had only a few essential cosmetics on her vanity table, now it was crowded with tons of little glass vials and bottles. *All in the pursuit of perfection*, thought Jen. She looked to the door nervously, trying to determine if she'd heard a noise from outside and then dismissed it, chalking her jumpiness up to her nerves and an overactive imagination.

A few shopping bags from Bergdorf's were in the corner, their tissue paper still wrapping whatever newly purchased treasures they held. For a moment, Jen thought that the Bergdorf's bags could be the delivery that had arrived in secret earlier, but then a stack of five cardboard boxes caught her eye. Jen walked toward them and peered at them. The boxes were heavy duty and blank, with no logo or other detail. Jen furrowed her forehead and picked one of the boxes up. It was heavy.

Jen read the sticker on the top of the box. DE-LIVER TO MAYA KHAN. The Yummy Channel's address was scrawled across the bottom, but above it, in tiny letters was the East Village address of Bess's Bakery. Jen shifted its bulk in her hands, shaking it slightly, trying to guess what was inside. Whatever it was was stolen from Bess's Bakery. She thought of Billy and a rush of concern filled her chest. *Could Billy be a part of this?* Another emotion filled her chest as well. Anger. Anger at Maya, specifically. What was she doing? What good could come of stealing boxes from Bess's Bakery?

She put the box down and turned to leave but just as she took a step toward the door she heard the metallic scrape of a key entering the lock. Jen looked for somewhere to hide, but there was nowhere. In one swift motion, the door opened and Maya's sleek, trim silhouette filled the doorway. She saw Jen and put her hands on her hips.

"What are you doing in here? How did you get in here?" She sounded hurt, like Jen had betrayed her.

"It was unlocked," Jen said, telling the half-truth. "And what are *you* doing with these boxes from Bess's Bakery? How dare you?"

"It's none of your business," Maya said. "Get out of here."

"Maya, we used to be friends," Jen argued. "What is going on? Does this have something to do with Giselle? Or what? You need to tell me what's going on."

"I don't owe you anything, Jen. You just sit there and judge me for everything. Judge me for falling in love with David, judge me for saying that I used XyloSlim, judge me for every little thing that I do and say."

Jen realized that Maya spoke the truth. She had been judgmental, but everything had spun out of control so fast that Jen had barely gotten an opportunity to hear Maya's side of things. "Then explain to me," Jen begged. "Help me understand. What is this?" She pointed to the stack of boxes. "Why the secrecy?"

Maya crossed her arms over her chest. "It was supposed to be a surprise," she said finally, petulantly.

"What was supposed to be a surprise?" Jen prodded. "Please, explain."

"I just thought—" Maya broke off. "Oh god, it's so stupid." Tears began to leak out of her eyes. She dabbed at them with the back of her hand.

"Maya." Jen took a step toward her friend. "What?"

"It's the checkered plates from Bess's Bakery. The ones with the colorful rims, you know? I was going to give them to you for the Comfort Food event tomorrow night, but now I think it's too stupid. I just wanted to do something, anything, to honor Bess's success—especially after everything I've done to dishonor her over the years. I never even tried to be her friend, you know? I just always thought of her as this untouchable tyrant. Maybe she just needed a friend. I was the opposite of a friend to her."

Jen put her hand to her chest, touched at Maya's thought. She was relieved to see a trace of her old friend resurfacing. This was the Maya she loved.

"Maya. Bess wasn't the *friendly* type. You know that. You made some mistakes, yes, but Bess's social life was one of her own making. And your idea to use her plates is really sweet. Very, very kind."

"Daisy, the girl who works—worked?—I don't know, at the bakery, brought the boxes over."

Daisy's face clicked into place. Jen put her arms around Maya and hugged her tight. Maya pulled away and took out a plate. The familiar checkerboard pattern and bright green rim brought Jen right back to the Bess's Bakery dining room. "I'm going home," Maya said. "I'm going to call David and tell him too. I should have done that in the beginning. Use the plates or don't. I'm just so tired. I can't wait for this week to be over." Jen knew the feeling.

They talked for a few minutes and then Maya left, leaving Jen all alone in the prep kitchen. She sighed, feeling unsure of herself. On a whim, she tried the doorknob of Bess's dressing room and was slightly surprised to find it open. She walked in. Most of the remnants of the crime scene investigators' work in this space had been removed, but she picked up a stray piece of tape and crumpled it up in her hand. Bess's framed photos had been taken down and were stacked against the wall. The closet doors were open and the closet looked completely barren. Bess's wardrobe was gone. All the little jars and bottles on Bess's vanity were gone as well. Jen wondered where, and hoped that they hadn't reappeared in Maya's dressing room. She shook the thought out of her head, and tried to think only positive thoughts about Maya.

Another piece of junk on the floor caught Jen's eyes, and she stooped to pick it up. She barely glanced at it as she stuck it in her pocket, but retrieved it and turned it over in her hand. It was an Altoids box. She opened it and found a joint inside. She furrowed her brow. Why would this have been left behind when the rest of the room had been stripped? An intern, probably. She put it in her pocket, though she knew she should just throw it in the trash. She'd give it to Detective Franklin the next time she saw him. A refrigerator from the prep kitchen started whirring, but the sound made her jump. It was too quiet. She had to get out of here. She felt like a nerd for feeling like a criminal carrying a joint in her pocket as she pushed through the revolving doors into the evening.

It was after seven before Jen left the office, and nearly eight as she let herself into her apartment building wondering if she was still off the diet wagon, or back on the wagon. She stopped at her mailbox and unstuffed the usual credit card offers and department store coupons from her mailbox. As the dead bolt turned over, a scuffling sound inside her apartment caught her attention. She looked around, hoping to see one of her neighbors shuffling down the stairs, taking a dog for an evening stroll, but there were no other residents in sight. She heard another sound. A clunky-clanging, like dishes or baking pans, and voices whispering. Her heart started thumping. Could it be Billy again?

The noise stopped suddenly. Jen was frozen. She was petrified in place, dreading the sound that the key would make if she pulled it out of the lock, but also terrified to leave her keys in the lock. She heard another muffled sound, this time the distinct slamming of a cabinet door. Jen felt the blood drain from her face.

She reached for her purse but the strap slipped from her hands. She cringed at the noise she'd made and hoped whoever was inside didn't hear her. The police. Jen should dial 911, but her hands went on autopilot and dialed Alex instead. If she was going down, he was the person she wanted beside her. She squatted and felt around for the phone. In her tote bag it always fell to the same spot in the corner, but today she was carrying the unfamiliar leather purse. She kept one eye trained on the door as she tried to find Alex's number in her phone.

Before she could complete the call her heart took a nosedive. Her doorknob was turning—from the inside. She scrolled to Alex's number and hit "call" on her phone, ducking down and trying to remain as still as possible. At least if someone killed her, he'd be able to place the time of the call and know what happened.

"Surprise!" Two voices rang out into the hallway. Jen's head snapped up from her phone, and she saw Gabby and Elizabeth crowded into her doorway. Tears of relief filled her eyes. She quickly pushed "end" in rapid succession, hoping the call had not gone through.

"You guys almost made me call the police," Jen said, feeling a little bewildered.

Gabby and Elizabeth looked at each other and

laughed. "Are you okay, chica? We didn't mean to scare you!" Gabby asked, a concerned look spreading over her face. She knelt down to help Jen up.

Jen exhaled. "Yes, I'm good. I'm just a little jumpy. I just—I thought you guys were burglars or worse. Some awful thing that would be re-created using actors for a Lifetime movie. What are you doing here?" Jen asked. "I thought you guys would be busy tonight."

Gabby reached out and grabbed Jen's hand. "Never too busy for our friend." Gabby's sincerity touched Jen, then she sniffed the air. Her friends had been cooking.

"I agree," Elizabeth stated. "There is no such thing as too busy for Jen. Now get in here, we have a surprise for you." Jen gathered herself up and followed her friends into her apartment. "Actually, I have two surprises," Elizabeth said.

"Jenny Jen, it's your lucky day. Step in and see what we've got lined up here." Gabby slipped into a schticky used-car salesman voice, but broke out laughing. "It's *Fiesta time!* We have made a completely diet friendly fiesta for you," she exclaimed, gesturing to the living room like a game show model gesturing to a prize package. "You need a night to relax and not worry about work, or Bess, or carbs, or anything. Just relax. We're here!" Gabby hugged her tightly.

Jen's living room was small. *Homey* was the euphemism that leasing agents used, but Gabby and Elizabeth had used every square inch of available space to set the mood. Red, white, and green streamers were twisted over the bookcases, and sombreros hung on the wall in place of the framed photos. The coffee table was set with a platter of assorted veggies, meats, and cheeses, and three full-to-the-brim margarita glasses. "The lime is just for garnish—we didn't put any actual fruit in the drinks," Elizabeth said.

Gabby agreed, "Yeah, we knew fruit would mess up your diet. No fruit. Promise."

"No alcohol either." Elizabeth sighed. "Seeing as tequila has carbs too, sadly. It's actually just Mojito-flavored drink powder, but we added crushed ice and a Splenda rim to make it extra-fancy."

Jen laughed. "You guys are the best. I don't even know what to say!" She felt guilty and considered confessing her post-funeral trip to Wendy's. She didn't want to ruin the moment, though, so she bit her tongue.

"Say *cheese*! Because there's a lot of cheese on the menu tonight. Starting with . . . nachos." Gabby disappeared into the kitchen with a mischievous grin on her face.

Jen squealed, "You did *not* find a way to make carb-free nachos. Impossible."

"Bite your tongue. It's possible," Elizabeth said. "And while it's absolutely, completely unhealthy and disgusting—it's also kind of delicious."

Gabby emerged from the kitchen nook grasping a plate with one of Jen's worn pot holders. Steam rose up from the nachos. Jen squinted and leaned in to get a better look. The aroma nearly knocked her over. It smelled delicious. "What is that?" she asked, pointing at the base. It looked a lot like tortilla chips from across the room, and for a moment Jen feared that her friends were there trying to tempt her off the diet.

"Pork rinds!" Gabby and Elizabeth chimed together. They looked at each other and started laughing.

"We made spicy Salisbury steak with mashed cauliflower as well. We went all out! It's the least we could do to support you." She beamed at Jen. "You do look great, and I can tell the diet is really working for you. I'm here to support you, and so is Elizabeth."

"I love you guys," Jen cried. She felt giddy, and giddier still when Elizabeth unveiled the night's pièce de résistance. Dessert.

When Elizabeth walked in with parfait glasses filled to the brim with chocolate mousse, Jen couldn't find words. Elizabeth pulled the low-carb diet book off her shelf and flipped to the page where the recipe was printed, clear as day. "In case you don't believe me," Elizabeth preempted.

"You made me diet chocolate!" Jen thought she might actually cry. It felt so good to take a break from worrying and stressing about Bess and Billy, Maya and Will, and the Yummy Channel, and infinitely better to pig out on food that her friends had cooked with love.

"We made you diet chocolate," Elizabeth repeated, smiling. The ladies clinked parfait glasses, and even though Jen was stuffed from the other courses, she did not have any problems finishing off the entire chocolate mousse.

chapter seventeen

Friday morning dawned, and Jen woke up very worried that Thursday's Wendy's binge and fiesta feast would ruin her progress, but somehow, miraculously, the scale remained the same when she stood on it Friday morning. She couldn't believe it, but she'd take this unexpected mercy. She knew she'd be running around like a crazy person today, so she dressed in a comfortable sheath dress with a jacket and ballet flats. She tried to think of the scientific explanation for why she'd not lost weight, but not gained it back. Concepts like *metabolism* and *blood sugar* floated around her mind, as did more advanced weight-loss concepts like *Ketosis lypolisis*. Whatever was going on in there, it was working.

The phone rang, and she answered. Vera's voice on the other end of the line started in right away. "Good luck tonight, darling," she said. "I know you're nervous."

"I'm not that nervous, Mom. It's just strange. It *does* make me nervous that whoever killed Bess hasn't been caught yet. I don't understand why the channel's not totally closed down, totally mourning. It's all too fast for me."

"It's the New York City lifestyle," Vera suggested. "It's not a warm and fuzzy place you live and work, my dear. Listen, I read a lot of Agatha Christie," Vera offered. "I might be very useful in helping to solve this case if the police want to get in touch with me. Really, feel free to give them my number." Jen rolled her eyes. "I sent you a package," Vera said. "Did you get it?"

Jen realized that the night before her friends had caught her by surprise. She had never gone through her mail. She walked over to the table by her door and leafed through it. "Oh yeah, it's here. What is it?" She tore it open as she asked.

Vera answered Jen's questions at the same moment that Jen extracted a small metal tube from the padded manila envelope. "Pepper spray?"

"Just put it in your purse, be safe," Vera told her. "Look in the bottom."

Jen turned the envelope over and shook it. "Lipstick."

"It's called Warm Rose. It will look excellent with your hair color."

Jen rolled her eyes and thanked her mother for the call. "I've got to go now, Mom, thanks for thinking of me." She tossed both items in the bottom of her tote bag with a shrug. Neither could hurt. She remembered to remove the Altoids box she'd found in Bess's dressing room last night, putting it on her dresser for safekeeping until she spoke to Alex again.

That morning, Jen arrived at the office at 8:00 a.m. with a steaming cup of Dunkin' Donuts coffee in her hand. She knew she'd be running straight through on caffeine, protein, and adrenaline until the night's event was over.

The Comfort Food event was scheduled to begin at seven o'clock that night, and Jen had pulled off the unlikely feat of lining up nine of the best chefs in the city—with less than a week's notice—to prepare a small tasting portion of their favorite appetizer, main course, and dessert for seventy guests. The Yummy Channel brand had serious pull in the restaurant industry—being featured on the channel could really boost a restaurant's reputation. Thankfully, Gabby and Elizabeth both would be attending as well. Jen really needed the moral support today.

There were logistical problems Jen had to solve this morning, before the chefs began. She didn't bother stopping by her office before heading to the prep kitchen, where she planned to spend the entire day. She would work with the camera crews to make sure they had plenty of room to set up their equipment. The lighting team was supposed to be there in twenty minutes, at nine o'clock sharp, to hang a few extra mood lights in the area, and focus spotlights to shine on each chef. So much had changed since last week, that every detail of the event seemed to have a double meaning. They were a different company than they'd been a week ago. She was a different woman than she had been a week ago, she reflected, thinking again of her attraction to Officer Alex D'Alby and the five pounds she'd lost. She'd changed her outlook and her habits. She'd fallen off the wagon, and then climbed back on.

Jen set up her laptop, making a temporary work-space on one of the prep kitchen counters. She concentrated on printing out labels for each chef, and postcard-size menus with the names of the dishes they'd e-mailed in to her. After an hour of printer errors and toner replacements, she finally got everything in order. Now she could eat, and she had a left-over Spicy Salisbury Steak in an insulated lunch box in her office with her name on it. "Hey," she heard a voice yell. "You Jen Stevens?" She nodded and walked over to the delivery driver who was dropping off a load of food for one of the chefs that night. She checked her watch. They were early. She showed the driver where to unload and set up. Another driver showed up, and Jen helped him too. Soon the pantries in the prep kitchen were overflowing, and a nonstop parade of traffic was coming in and out of the room.

So much food. Fresh fruits and vegetables, fragrant

cheeses soft and firm, homemade bread, butter, purees, and soups. Bottles of red, white, and bubbly were un-crated and placed on each chef's counter. All off-limits to Jen. Then there were the desserts. Restaurant staff carried in chunks of chocolates bigger than Jen's head, toffee, peanut brittle, creamy artisan ice cream. Jen felt overwhelmed by the cornucopia. She felt like an orphan in a Dickens novel, holding her tin cup out, begging, "Please, sir, just a taste. Please, may I have some more?"

Jen felt shaky with hunger at three o'clock in the afternoon when things calmed down for a moment miraculously. She didn't think she could make it back to her office without fainting from hunger, though. Well, she probably could, but just in case she would stop at the vending machine on the way to get a beef jerky. The lights were shining down, and Jen stepped forward into the puddle of a spotlight. She blinked, and when she looked up, a figure stood in front of her blocking her path. She blinked again and held a hand up to shield her eyes from the light. David Brantwood stood in front of her.

"Jen?" he asked. He adjusted the load he was car-rying, boxes stacked and held in front of him.

"David," she said. "What are you doing here?"

He flinched. Jen thought he might turn around and walk away, but he cleared his throat, held his ground, and continued.

"I, um—" He paused and took a deep breath. Jen

had never seen him so vulnerable, so speechless. "I made cupcakes. Well, Maya and I baked them. Last night we went to the bakery and stayed up all night making them, using Bess's recipes. It's a strange way to honor her, I guess, but it's our way." He sounded apologetic and tired. "They're for the event tonight. Maya told me you were working hard to make sure that the network honored Bess. I just wanted to say thank you. I—" He stopped again and sniffed, pressing his lips tightly together. "I did love her once, you know. We had problems, of course, but I did love Bess. There was something special about her. And when I was there last night, I swear I could feel her with me. I could just feel that I wasn't alone. These little noises, little groans. It was like she was trying to communicate with me."

Jen put her arm out to touch David's wrist. He pulled back slightly, and the boxes stacked on his arms teetered. "Take these," he said. She did, and before she could thank him, he'd turned and walked back down the hall.

She carefully placed the boxes on an empty square of counter. Her stomach growled more insistently, and stacked right next to her was her favorite food in the world. Cupcakes made by Maya Khan from Bess Brantwood's special recipe. Possibly the best cupcake recipe in the world, as far as Jen was concerned, brought to life by one of the best artisan bakers Jen had ever met. She opened the top box and saw the familiar swirls and decorations of cupcakes. The apple pie cupcake with its perfect crumb topping, and the s'mores cupcake with the little triangle of graham cracker sticking out like a flag.

She and Maya, in the old days—pre-diet, pre-affair, pre-XyloSlim days—used to have long conversations about the exact balance of the perfect cupcake. Maya insisted that the ideal consistency was spongy, less sweet, and she preferred leaving the cake unfilled, intact, finished with a light frosting, decorated to perfection. "The eyes have more taste buds than the tongue," Maya pointed out. For Jen, there was no rival to Bess's butter-rich, impossibly sweet and moist cake, flavored with chunky pieces of fruit, swirls of chocolate, thick rivers of caramel.

She looked around for someone to save her from her lascivious memories and pressing hunger. Why was her willpower wavering so much? One minute she was confident and strong, the next she was quivering before a cupcake. She wanted to tell someone that she was on a diet. She wanted to tell someone that she'd just lost five pounds, like that, and snap her fingers. There was no one to confide in, though, except herself.

You don't need it. But I want it.

You've been so good. So I deserve it.

You are stronger than this. I am more than the sum of my carb intake.

Her mind still churning, weak with hunger, buzzing with emotion, she carried the box into Bess's studio and closed the door. She sat down, letting her body block anyone from walking through the door, and bit into a cupcake. *This was happening. Oh yes.* A rush of excitement muddled with recklessness spurred her forward in her sin. It was chocolate heaven, with a center of chopped caramel corn in an ecstasy of cream. Light cream cheese frosting drizzled with a hardened chocolate sauce and tiny flakes of caramel corn sat atop, and a rush of excitement shot through Jen's mouth and her jaw trembled slightly as she chewed and swallowed. Her fantasy come true. Her dreams made reality. Her worries momentarily escaped.

She licked her fingers, the cupcake's rich flavor still haunting her mouth. *One cupcake isn't that big of a deal,* she tried to tell herself. Jen knew, however, it wasn't going to be just one. Like a bear after a picnic raid, she'd developed a taste for people food again, with its sugar, its flour, its incredible rich deliciousness. She had to see this through, simply had to take another break from the monotony of string cheese and Caesar salad.

Jen looked around as she bit into her next cupcake, a ginger cream sparkling with brown sugar and red hot sprinkles. She wondered what Bess would say, watching her rip into her cupcakes from above, but Bess wasn't there. Jen tossed back the second half of her ginger cupcake and stuck her finger in the frosting of a banana cream pie cupcake topped with graham cracker crumbles and savored the fruity flavor.

"Jen?" The heavy tread of footsteps interrupted her sinful moment. Officer Alex D'Alby stood in front of her. She wiped frosting from her mouth. She couldn't decide if she was more annoyed that she'd been *caught* pigging out by a handsome man whom she'd started to miss, or that he'd *interrupted* her binge.

"Alex, hi," she said, and tried to subtly close the top to the box. He put his hand on top to look inside.

"What's that?" he asked, peeking into the box. "Cupcakes. They look good. Well, actually, I don't really like sweets. I never have."

She glared at him. Of course he didn't like sweets. He was naturally healthy. She looked at him. He looked so handsome in his uniform, with his hazel eyes sparkling, that her irritation floated away. "What do you like?" she murmured.

"Oh, mostly veggies," he said. Then he broke into a smile. "Just kidding. I'm a meat eater. I never met a cow or pig I didn't like. I'm a big barbecue fan."

Jen smiled. There might be a future for them yet. Jen looked down and wiped crumbs off her shirt. "I swear, I am not always covered in food," Jen lied. "I've just been working to set up this event and didn't get a chance to have lunch."

Alex shrugged. There was no judgment in his eyes. "I wanted to let you know that Detective Franklin got in touch with Billy Davidsen's sister yesterday after your call. He's been officially reported as a missing person. Thank you, again, for getting in touch."

Jen reached up and touched her cheek, and all the energy drained from her. She sat down on a stool. "Oh no. You came here just to tell me that?"

"Not only that. I came to provide a police presence at the Comfort Food event tonight. Tommy Wegman put in a request for extra security tonight, and they asked that I come since I've been helping Detective Franklin with the case."

"Tommy didn't mention that to me. Well, welcome," Jen said. "Thanks. Do you want me to show you the setup for tonight?" She looked at the big wall clock and wondered where the afternoon had gone. "The chefs should be arriving any minute."

They walked together around the prep kitchen, and stopped at each counter. "There's where the bar is going to be." Jen pointed over to a folding table covered with a linen cloth. They paused at each counter in the large room, and Jen explained each restaurant's reputation and the chef's unique style to Alex. He listened as she talked, nodding occasionally and asking questions. Alex put her at ease and seemed at ease around her.

Chef Peter Jaworski, who ran the kitchen at a popular Williamsburg restaurant, cleared his throat in the doorway. "Sorry to interrupt," he said.

"Hello, Peter," Jen welcomed him and stuck her

hand out to shake. "This is Officer Alex D'Alby." Peter nodded his head solemnly.

"It's a pleasure to meet you." The two men shook hands. Jen led Peter to his counter in the prep kitchen. On his menu for the evening were pierogies filled with cheese, local potatoes, and squash from the Brooklyn farmers' market, and homemade sausages stuffed with poultry and pork from a coop farm just twenty miles out of the city.

As Peter described the menu items, Alex looked at Jen, eyes wide. "If there are extras, I hope the peace-keeper can have a sample."

"Undoubtedly," Jen agreed.

"You're the first one here, Peter, and the other chefs will be arriving soon," Jen explained. "The camera crew will start filming in about an hour, and the guests will be here at seven o'clock. Thank you so much for coming, we feel so lucky to have you here with us. Let us know if you need anything at all." Peter beamed at Jen and thanked her. Alex had found a place to stand out of the way, along the back wall, and Jen could feel him watching her. She was proud to have him here, watching her do what she did best.

Next, chef Wen Fu and his partner walked into the kitchen. They each carried an orange plastic bag with even more fresh ingredients from Chinatown. A table never stayed empty long at Fu's Asian Fusion Kitchen in Tribeca. Their menu had creative interpretations of

Chinese-American classics: crisp wontons folded over savory greens, egg rolls encasing finely chopped vegetables and seafood, and noodle dishes showcasing Chef Fu's roasted meats.

Jen welcomed Wen and two other chefs who streamed in afterward. Smells began simmering and emanating from the different stations, and before Jen knew it the production assistants began buzzing around the space, setting up shots, talking to the chefs to prep them for their interviews. Soon the prep kitchen became a sea of savory and spicy aromas. The smells tantalized her, and she had to muster all her willpower to behave professionally and not become the office's new Food Freak, now that Giselle was behind bars for attacking Maya. Then she made a decision. Tonight, she'd enjoy this rare feast of New York's finest chefs. Tomorrow, she'd try again.

The plate of pasta that she collected from Cogli l'attimo, the Italian restaurant, was completely antithetical to the low-carb diet, and Jen felt rebellious as she ate. As she dug in, each bite of the delicious, starchy, cheesy dish stretched from the fork to her lips and gave her taste buds a kick of sweet tomato, spicy Italian sausage, smooth, buttery cheese. Their turkey meatballs actually were low-carb, and Jen asked for the recipe.

The gourmet pizza topped with Gorgonzola and caramelized onions and pears blended savory and aromatic. Then there was the Sesame Lo Mein, and the

Cuban Empanadas. She didn't refuse herself a single taste.

None of the guests did either. They began flowing in as scheduled at seven, and the sounds of laughter and lively chatter filled the room, along with the occasional clinks and clanks of kitchen equipment as the chefs and their staff worked their magic in front of the crowd. At least sixty people now crowded the space, and wherever Jen turned she saw smiles, the pink tips of tongues running over lips to capture every bit of flavor, or eyes half-closed in an ecstasy of flavor. The crowd seemed to be relaxed, happy, and unstressed. Jen had watched for Haley to make sure she didn't set out the requisite samples of XyloSlim, but hadn't seen her yet that night.

Jen bit into a soft brown bun with warm barbecue at the center and looked over at Alex. Alex was biting into an eggroll, though she could tell his eyes were scanning the crowd. Gabby and Elizabeth pushed their way through the crowded room just as Jen bit into a long churro, letting powdered sugar sprinkle down her shirt like snow. Both her best friends had the glow of a free cocktail or two on their faces as they walked up.

"Jen, there you are. Off the wagon?" Elizabeth asked in a singsong voice, snatching the churro and taking a bite. Elizabeth wore a pair of slim-fit slacks with heels and a fitted blouse. Her hair was up in a ponytail, and she looked casual but lovely.

"That's mine," Jen exclaimed, snatching it back. "Yes, I suck. I have no willpower, no self-control, and I'm totally off the wagon. Go ahead, make fun of me."

Instead, Gabby wrapped her friend up in a hug, slyly snagging the last bit of churro. "You don't suck. You'd have to be certifiably insane if you could be in this room without tasting everything," Gabby assured her, biting down and closing her eyes in ecstasy for a moment. When she snapped back to the conversation, she continued. "You're just human!"

"You're Catholic, right?" Jen asked Gabby.

"I'm Catholic-ish." Gabby laughed.

"Do you know if communion wafers have carbs? Because I think I'm in desperate need of some divine intervention."

Gabby choked on the last of the churro. She sputtered, half laughing, "Hold on. Need water," and walked toward the bar.

When Gabby came back with three glasses of champagne, Jen and Elizabeth were discussing the effect of transubstantiation on carb count. Gabby looked horrified.

"Sorry." Jen looked embarrassed. "Bad joke. I'm just kind of drowning here. My motivation just seems to waver so much, and with everything going on in the world, I'm thinking it's just the wrong time for me to try to lose weight."

They moved toward the closest counter to get out

of the way of Chef Fu, who was walking in for a one-on-one on-camera session. The closest counter was a local chef who had made her name by using fresh, leafy herbs in surprising ways. A green-tinted fresh basil and peppermint shortbread cookie was on her menu, which Jen couldn't wait to try. The chef, an extremely tall, pretty woman with glowing pink cheeks, used a spatula to put a new batch of cookies on a platter for serving.

Gabby was thoughtful. "I know we were sort of talking about this before, and I don't mean to be a broken record or anything, but I just recently read this article in *Vogue* about the top five reasons why diets fail, and one of the biggies is thinking of the diet as a temporary situation instead of a lifelong eating shift. Like, your natural state should be eating healthful foods, and when you don't, that's the aberration."

"Look, tomorrow's another day," Elizabeth said, smiling at Jen. "Your diet is not supposed to ruin your life, it's supposed to make your life better. You've been under a lot of stress and shouldn't beat yourself up. You can stop anytime and still enjoy the rest of your evening. Moderation is key," she finished in an upbeat tone.

"Elizabeth, I just don't think I'm wired that way," Jen protested. "I know that works for lots of people, but for me it just seems to be all or nothing. And I'm scared to go back to nothing. I don't want to gain back this weight. I still have so much more I want to lose."

"How much more?" Gabby asked. "You look great right where you are."

Jen smiled back, sincerity and gratitude rushing through her. "Thanks guys. I'm so glad you're here." They clinked glasses. "It's a nice event, right? It turned out well despite being borne of tragedy, having no time for real planning, having guests that are mourning, and needing police presence."

"Speaking of police presence, he can't take his eyes off you," Elizabeth said. "I have to be honest; I think he's a little turned on by your vigor for food." Jen looked over at Alex, and they met eyes for a minute. He nodded at her and smiled.

"Guys like a woman who can eat!" Gabby exclaimed, gesturing with the notebook she was using to make notes about the event for her blog.

"Clearly." Elizabeth laughed, reaching over to wipe powdered sugar off of Jen's shirt. "And this woman can eat!" She bumped her hip into Jen. Jen, noticing that the new platter of basil-peppermint shortbread that she'd been craving earlier was almost gone, snatched one off the plate. She broke off pieces for Gabby and Elizabeth, and kept the biggest piece for herself. They bit in, and Jen's taste buds popped with delight. It was so herby, so minty. The combination was familiar, and suddenly, aided by the aromas, pieces of something came together in Jen's mind. The Altoids box she'd found. It belonged to Billy. She recognized the smell of herby pot and breath mints. It was his smell. Billy had been here, in Bess's dressing room. It didn't make sense, but it had to be true.

She mentally scrambled over the events of the last couple of days, trying to piece together what had happened. She'd found the box on Thursday night, after the funeral, and she'd been in the prep kitchen all evening. Billy must have come before that, but the only time she was gone that day was when she—and everyone else—had been at Bess's funeral. Only Will Riley had been walking through after that. Jen looked around the party to spot Will. She saw his spiky blond hair disappear into his dressing room, a cute brunette following behind him.

"I have to talk to Alex," she said to her friends, and pushed her way through the crowd.

Alex listened to Jen's description. She felt panicked and her voice was quavering. She spoke too fast and was stumbling over her words. "Billy—he smokes pot. It's the reason he didn't want to come to you in the first place, but—"

Alex raised his eyebrows and began to respond, but Jen cut him off.

"Please, just listen. He has an Altoids box. I think it's his, but I didn't know it was his. It's at my house, but I found it yesterday, here, after the funeral. I know it's his. It all just came together for me. I know he was here, or at least someone who saw him and could have gotten the Altoids box was here."

"Show me where you found it," Alex said. Gabby and Elizabeth had followed Jen over and walked arm in arm behind Jen and Alex toward Bess's dressing room. Jen opened the door and turned on the light and pointed to the place where she'd recovered the small box.

"Was anyone else back here yesterday?"

"It was really empty, because of Bess's funeral. Maya was here. I was here. Will Riley was here."

"Is Will here now?" Alex asked. As a group, they moved toward Will's dressing room. Jen looked around for Maya as she was stepping toward Will's dressing room. She'd said she'd be there. Alex knocked on the door. "Will? Open up," he yelled. "This is Officer D'Alby. I need to speak with you." His commanding voice boomed through the prep kitchen and a handful of guests formed a semicircle around them.

A young woman opened the door. Jen recognized her as the intern from the marketing department. She was flushed and visibly upset. Will lay flat on the couch in his dressing room. His face was pale white and beads of sweat gathered around his forehead. The mousy-haired intern was gripping her shirt to her chest, tears leaving trails down her cheeks. "I think . . . he's dead," she said.

chapter eighteen

Alex amazed Jen with his lightning-fast response. He was beside Will in less than a heartbeat, expertly feeling for a pulse, listening for breathing. After a second, Alex stood up. "He's alive," he assured the girl, and then repeated it to the small crowd who was now watching. "He's breathing. We'll get the paramedics up here." To Jen, Alex said quietly, "I'm pretty sure he's just really inebriated."

The paramedics arrived a few minutes later. Will Riley was conscious again, but barely, and was batting away a team of professionals who were prodding him with various devices and speaking to one another in acronyms and codes. "I'm fine," he slurred. "I'm fine."

"Can I talk to him?" Alex asked. Alex called Detective Franklin, but he had been called out on another case. The paramedics moved back to let the officer crouch down next to Will.

"Will," he said. "Look at me."

Will looked up and tried to focus on Alex's face, but his eyes rolled around his head. "What did you drink?" Alex asked.

"I already told them—those guys," he said, pointing to the paramedics. "I just had a few shots of whiskey."

"Yeah, if a few equals twenty," Elizabeth quipped quietly to Jen. Gabby and Elizabeth stood against the wall, trying ineffectually to comfort the girl in Will's dressing room. Jen checked in with them every few minutes but was doing her best to manage the crowd. She'd made an announcement to the guests, thanking them for coming, and suggesting that those who wanted to leave should take a cupcake to go. Two-thirds of the crowd had taken her up on it, but the other third, including the chefs and several big bloggers in the foodie world, stayed. Jen knew that the Yummy Channel's reputation was seriously tarnished if even their tribute to Bess ended in disaster.

"Will, listen—Jen said she found some pot in an Altoids box in Bess's dressing room yesterday. We know you were back here. Tell us where it came from?"

"I didn't do nothing," Will said. "I'm just a cook. I didn't invite that kid in here. I just like to fry things. I'm a fryer, not a fighter," he slurred.

"Did you fight someone?"

"Nahhhh," he said. "I put him in the basement for

her, that's all, just down the stairs. I'm just a fryer. She's the one. She's the fighter. She hits hard for a gir—" He closed his eyes again, his head nodding to one side.

"Who?" Alex asked. "Who's the fighter? Will? Who's the fighter?" But Will was out again, and the paramedics moved back around him.

"We're going to take him in to monitor him," one of them said to Alex. "For a man this size, his blood-alcohol level is pretty high." They put Will on a stretcher and pulled him toward the elevator.

"Sounds like drinking on a guilty conscience to me," Gabby said. "Do you think he really put someone in a basement? What does that mean? Was he even talking about Billy?"

"I don't know," Jen said quietly. Her full belly slowed her down and zapped the energy from her. She looked around at the people. "These people should just go home. This is no time for a party."

Alex, who had been talking on the phone to Detective Franklin, walked over. "I can fix that." He walked to the center of the room and pointed at the door. "Folks, we have a medical situation here, and we're going to have to ask you all to please get your things and head for the doors in an orderly fashion."

Jen grimaced at Alex's stern tone and quickly ran from counter to counter. Her career was falling apart in front of her eyes. She tried her best to thank the chefs for attending, and help them gather their things, but her thoughts were on Billy. Where could he be? She was in a daze and wanted to go door to door, searching every basement in town until she found the one that Will Riley was talking about. But his drunken ramblings were so vague; Jen didn't even know for sure that he was talking about Billy. Unfortunately, when Alex gave his command, even the employees from the staffing company they'd hired to bartend and clean up left. Gabby and Elizabeth helped Jen throw away the extra food and deal with anything that would start to smell if left overnight.

Detective Franklin had gone to the hospital to wait for Will Riley to answer more questions. Officer D'Alby said he needed to speak to Giselle Martin again, and drove back to the holding cell where she'd been since her arrest on Wednesday afternoon. Before he left, he made Elizabeth and Gabby promise to get Jen home safely, and told Jen he'd call her in the morning.

"I'm trying to figure out what pot has to do with XyloSlim," Gabby said, after a few minutes of working in silence. "And I just can't think of any connections."

"Pot makes you want to eat, and XyloSlim makes you not want to eat," Elizabeth offered.

"One's illegal and one's over the counter," Jen said.

"One makes you jittery and one calms you down," Gabby added. "Really, I don't think they have anything to do with each other."

"The question I have," Jen said, "is why did Billy come here to these offices? Why didn't he call? And what happened to him afterward?" Her eyes filled with tears, not for the first time that night. "What an idiot. Why didn't he call?" she said again. She tried to identify why she was so upset about a guy she barely knew anymore. Their shared history was imperfect, but her time with him had made her who she was today. She felt a unique responsibility for him, and she knew that would never change. "I have to find him," she said to her friends.

"Who is the *she* that Will was talking about?" Elizabeth asked. "I think it's Maya."

"It's not Maya," Jen said, but her voice was weak. She wasn't convincing herself, let alone her friends.

"Then who?" Gabby asked. "You said yourself that Maya was acting strange lately. Wait, was she at the funeral yesterday?"

Jen thought about it. "I don't—I don't think so." Jen tried to remember the last time she saw Maya. She didn't show up at tonight's event, even though she'd promised to. Would Maya and Will ever really collaborate on anything, though? They were such rivals that it seemed incredibly unlikely. A sinking feeling came over Jen. She could no longer ignore the possibility. She ran her hand through her curls, now frizzy and poufy.

She sat down on the counter closest to the wide,

open doorway and put her head in her hands again, wanting to just sink into bed and never get up. When she looked up, she saw the cupcakes that David had dropped off, arranged neatly on a platter over near the bar. She stuck her finger in one and licked it. No one's frosting recipe was better than Bess Brantwood's.

She looked up and scrambled to her feet. "Oh my god. I know where Billy is!" she shouted.

chapter nineteen

The temperature had dropped a few degrees during the afternoon, and now a cool breeze reminded them that it wasn't quite summer yet. Jen, Gabby, and Elizabeth slid out of the cab on a corner in the East Village, trying to muffle the smooching sound of the leather seats on their thighs and the clack of their shoes on the pavement. It was nine-thirty on Friday evening, and a few bars on the block were picking up steam. Jen sent Alex a text explaining where they were headed—and why.

Jen explained to her friends how Maya had gotten the decorations from Bess's Bakery, and then David had dropped off cupcakes for Bess's tribute. He had mentioned that he didn't feel alone in Bess's Bakery. David had attributed the muffled noises he heard to Bess's spirit. At first Jen thought he was dealing with his feelings of sorrow and guilt since Bess's murder, but now Jen thought differently. What if Billy was in the basement the whole time, trying to signal David? Anyone who worked at the Yummy Channel, including Will Riley and Maya Khan, would know that Bess's Bakery would be totally empty this week.

As they walked stealthily toward the darkened Bess's Bakery, Gabby whispered, "So what's the plan?"

"I don't know!" Jen whispered.

"This gives me the creeps," Gabby said, clutching her purse close to her chest, her eyes glued to the dark sky. "Maybe we should wait until tomorrow morning and come back."

"You're probably right," Elizabeth said. "Let's at least go check it out?" She took a few steps, heading toward Bess's Bakery. Her heels clicked noisily on the pavement. "So loud," she whispered over her shoulder to her friends. "Sorry." She pushed up on her toes and tiptoed a few more steps.

Jen heaved a sigh. "No, Gabby's right. Nobody's here. This is dumb. Why would they put Billy here?"

"Everyone in the neighborhood knows it's closed," said Gabby, offering a good reason. "They probably didn't expect that David would come here to make cupcakes in his grief."

Jen considered it. "The cops are looking for Billy. What if Will and the 'she' he's working with are trying to frame Billy for Bess's death? Is my imagination running away with me?" she wondered aloud. "Do things like this really happen?"

"Shhh," Elizabeth said.

"Oh, I'll be okay," Jen assured her.

Elizabeth stuck a bony elbow in Jen's side. "No, shhh!" Elizabeth pointed at the upper level of Bess's Bakery. "Look!"

A light in the top window flickered on, and from the street Elizabeth, Gabby, and Jen could see shadows skittering across the wall.

"Someone's in there for sure," gasped Jen. They were huddled close to the curb, about six feet away from the front door, and their view was mostly obstructed by window displays and brown paper they hung up to prevent passersby from lingering. There were only a few inches on the bottom left uncovered. Outside the front door, people had created a makeshift vigil, leaving flowers, notes, stuffed animals, and other gifts to honor the deceased celebrity.

"I'm going to get a closer look," Elizabeth hissed. She stooped down and tottered in her heels toward the blush of the window, pushing aside some of the flowers. She peeped in the window.

Gabby and Jen stood back, watching motionless, too nervous to breathe. Suddenly Elizabeth spun around and clapped her hand over her mouth. Gabby let loose the beginning of a little shriek, and Jen reached up to quiet her. Elizabeth motioned to Jen and Gabby to come look.

They both shook their heads fervently, scared to get any closer. Jen's fingernails dug into Gabby's arm until Gabby wrenched loose.

"Sorry," Jen said.

"I thought you were the one comforting *me*," Gabby said, rubbing her arm.

Elizabeth pointed at them and motioned again, nodding her head up and down, her eyes wide and emphatic. The message was clear. Jen crouched and crab-walked over by the window to squat next to Elizabeth. Gabby followed. They all peeked inside, making sure to stay down out of view of whoever was inside.

Inside they saw a large, messy pile of papers and boxes gathered together in the center of the room. It looked chaotic, as though someone had ransacked the dining room. One of the display cases for the cupcakes was shattered.

"Guys, I'm calling Alex." She dialed and pressed her phone to her ear.

He answered after one ring. "Jen. I just got your text. Where are you?"

She whispered her answer. "I'm at Bess's Bakery. Someone's in there. And someone trashed the place. You should get here quick. But be careful, we think Billy might be in there. It could be stupid but—"

"It's not stupid. Detective Franklin just called from the hospital. Will Riley's awake and told us—"

A sound inside the bakery made them all jump. "Hold on, Alex," Jen whispered as she looked carefully. A movement behind the counter caught their attention and they stared, trying to make out what was happening. A loud crash made them jump again, as they saw that chairs were being dropped from the upper level. A long shadow began making its way down the staircase, growing more distorted with each step. Like a specter floating in from above, Jen felt her stomach drop as the shadow grew ominously bigger and stretched nearly the whole length of the shop.

"This is crazy," Gabby whined. "I might just head home."

"You're not going anywhere, toots," Elizabeth said. They all held their breath as a messy blond bun emerged first from the shadows followed closely by bright red lipstick and a pair of stiletto heels. It was Haley Parnell.

Jen whispered into the phone. "Are you still there?"

"Yes, and I'm on foot, almost to your location."

"It's Haley Parnell," Jen said. "Haley Parnell is at Bess's Bakery."

"That's what I was going to tell you," Alex said. "Will Riley regained consciousness and confessed. According to him, she's the one who *intentionally* slipped Bess Brantwood the overdose of XyloSlim. I'll be there in less than five minutes. Do not go in there without me." Jen hung up the phone, in shock.

Elizabeth and Gabby looked at each other and crouched lower. Inside, Haley had disappeared again. When she appeared next, Billy was staggering in front of her. He tried to run for the door, but Haley tackled him and took him to the ground with a single move.

"She is a fighter," Gabby said. "Poor Billy."

"I can't believe how strong she is," Elizabeth said in awe. "She's so tiny."

Haley clacked around the shop, moving faster now. Her white teeth practically glowed behind her blood-red lipstick as she smiled at Billy.

"I can't hear anything," Jen said, so worried about Billy that she thought her heart would burst from her chest. "I need to hear what she's saying to him." She looked back at the street impatiently, looking for Alex. Scanning the storefront, Jen saw a box air conditioner above the door, and Jen thought she could hear through the vents.

"I need to get up there." Jen pointed. "There's a gap—"

Gabby looked dubiously at the small hole. "How are you going to get up there?" she asked.

Jen looked around and thought for a moment. "Elizabeth, you used to be a cheerleader, right?"

"Yes, varsity in high school. Why?" Elizabeth looked over to Jen.

"Did you do those pyramids?" Jen asked.

"Yes, Jen, we did the pyramids. Why?"

Jen smiled at Elizabeth.

A second later Elizabeth spun her head toward Jen. "Wait a minute, *noooo*, you want me to lift you up there?"

Jen nodded. "I'll sit on your shoulders!"

"No way." Elizabeth shook her head.

"It's time to put those muscles to good use. Oh, but if you don't think you're strong enough . . ."

Elizabeth groaned. "Fine. Okay, let's do it."

"I adore you," Jen gushed.

"I'm just glad you went on that diet so it's a little less to lift," Elizabeth joked as she slipped off her heels and scooted over past the window under the vent. Jen hiked her skirt up, and using the wall to stabilize herself, she threw one leg over Elizabeth's shoulder. Elizabeth grabbed it, and braced herself. Jen put her other leg up and used the wall to take some of her weight off of Elizabeth. Elizabeth grunted.

"Are you okay?" Jen whispered.

Another grunt.

"A little to the left," Jen said as she leaned over and put her head against the vent.

"Can you hear them?" asked Gabby, who had moved over in front of the neighboring storefront to spot the precarious human ladder her friends had built.

"I think so." She pressed her ear against the splintered wood and willed the sound waves to come to her ears.

For a moment she heard only silence coming from the inside of Bess's Bakery, but then Haley's voice cut through the night. "Why did you come back?"

Billy muttered something. Haley asked, "What was that?"

"I said *I don't know*." He shuffled his feet. "Do you really have to do this?"

"Well," Haley said, shrugging her shoulders. "You could go to prison willingly instead, say that you made her drink the stuff. But I'm guessing you think you're too pretty for prison."

Billy let out a strangled laugh. Jen could hear rustling and footsteps and peeked inside the gap. She saw Haley sifting through the papers in the file. She walked around behind Billy.

"I won't tell anybody," Billy said. "The cops don't know anything."

"That might have been true if you hadn't come back," Haley said. She looked at him coldly, then delivered a sharp kick to his ribs. He groaned. "Do you have any idea what this will do to Yummy Channel ratings? Never mind, why am I even talking to you? You're a moron."

"I just don't get why you'd burn it up."

"I am not burning it up, sweet Billy," Haley said. "You are."

"No. No." Billy shook his head. Haley kicked him again.

"The thing is," Haley said, "there are a lot of people who want to work together with me. I am very good at creating synergy. Maya Khan, for example. Maya was happy to work with me to promote XyloSlim. I don't have any patience for people who don't want to work with me."

"Like Bess?" Billy asked. "You did it on purpose."

"I didn't give it to her at all," Haley said. "All I did was accidentally put my bottle of tea with an extra dose of XyloSlim into her minifridge. That inadequate girlfriend of yours did the rest." She paused. Jen craned her neck atop Elizabeth's shoulders to see what was happening. "You think I didn't know that you and Giselle were dating?"

Jen gasped and teetered on top of Elizabeth's shoulders. "What?" Gabby pleaded. "What is she saying?"

"Shhh, I'll tell you everything in a second," Jen whispered, her ear glued to the vent, desperately trying to make out what Billy was saying now. Elizabeth grunted again and put another hand on the wall to brace herself.

"Jen," Gabby said again. "You have to come down!"

"Gabby, hold on," Jen whispered.

"No, it's Alex—"

Jen felt a tap on her back and spun around. Her

motion caused Elizabeth's grip on the brick wall to slip, and Elizabeth took a couple of staggering steps, trying to regain control. Jen waved her arms wildly on Elizabeth's shoulder, trying to right the situation. "Oh god!" exclaimed Elizabeth as her knees gave out slightly. At the jolt, Jen's grip loosened and she felt herself falling fast toward the pavement.

chapter twenty

"Umph," Jen said as she hit. Her eyes were squeezed tight. It took her a moment to realize her fall had been broken by something other than Elizabeth's bony body or the cement of the sidewalk. She opened her eyes a tiny slit and saw Alex. He was looking down at her, a look of concern across his face.

Jen was so relieved to be not lying broken on the pavement that she couldn't stop a bubble of laughter from escaping. "Thank you for coming," she said. He smiled at her, and she could see relief on his face as well.

"A little help here?" Elizabeth interjected. She'd fallen down on her knees. Alex helped Jen down to her feet and then offered his hand to Elizabeth. She had only a skinned knee. Not too terrible an injury considering their perilous endeavor.

"Give me your hand," Alex said, helping her up.

Gabby spoke up, "Haley Parnell and Billy," she told Alex.

"You have to get in there. Haley's going to burn the place down! Haley killed Bess too. She set Giselle up. Now she's setting Billy up. She keeps kicking him. I can't believe it."

Alex crouched down and put his hand on his gun holster. "You can explain more later. I'm going in. You guys get back to the other side of the street. Backup is on the way."

"Alex?" Elizabeth said. "She heard us. She's looking right at us."

Sure enough, Haley had peeled back the brown paper covering the window and was peering out at them. She disappeared, and they heard a clatter from inside.

Alex took his gun out of its holster and ran toward the front door, shouting, "Freeze. Police." Alex slammed his shoulder into the front door. He brought the butt of his gun down onto the windowpane, and put his hand inside to turn the dead bolt. He pushed the door open and stepped in just as Jen saw smoke start curling out of the window. She pointed.

"Oh my god," yelped Elizabeth, who stood huddled together with Gabby and Jen.

Jen couldn't catch her breath. "I have to go in there," she panted. "I have to see what's going on and try to help them." Before her friends could stop her, she ran up to the front door.

As she ran up, Jen saw Haley pull aside the NO ADMITTANCE sign and scamper down the basement stairs. Alex was standing over the flames. He looked around for something to douse them but finding nothing nearby he started unbuttoning his shirt. Jen was transfixed as he peeled off his shirt and fanned down the flames, smothering them out. With only an undershirt and bulletproof vest, he reached for Billy. A cracking sound came from above them, and Jen saw a thick golden liquid ooze down over the edge of the balcony. "Watch out," she said, but it was too late. A river of melting butter poured onto Alex and Billy. Haley must have put it on the balcony so that the place would go up in flames faster. Jen's mouth fell open as she saw Alex fall, and slip, unable to get up. Billy rolled over, but couldn't stand. The butter quenched the rest of the flames, but neither man could move, and they dripped with the gooey liquid.

"Haley Parnell," Alex's voice boomed through the room, and he tried to move toward the kitchen door. He took a step toward the basement stairs and slid. Jen stepped in, moving around the butter, trying to help them.

"Jen!" Alex yelled. He took another step and his feet slid out from under him. Jen screamed as she saw him slide to the basement stairs, where he tumbled downward, crashing and thumping on each step.

"I've got to go down there," Jen said. "We have to

help him." She edged around the gooey mess to the top of the stairs. Haley Parnell was down there alone with Alex, and Jen had to help him. She started down the steep stairs, clutching the banister so that she didn't slip on the buttery mess.

"Be careful," Gabby shouted after her. A flash of love charged through her. Her friends were already inside Bess's Bakery, trying to find something to mop up the gallons of butter, helping Billy up and out. They were the most loyal friends on the planet.

"Haley?" Jen called. "Hey, we know you're down there." Silence met her and she took two more steps down. She blinked, trying to get her eyes to adjust to the dark.

Alex lay at the base of the stairs. He was conscious, but just barely. His eyes flickered shut. Jen felt panic spread through her. Her heart raced. In the murky dark of the basement, Jen saw a spark. A moment later a waft of sulfur touched her nose. Jen bit her lip. She knew exactly what Haley must be planning.

"Don't play with matches, Haley. Please, you'll kill us all." Jen cleared her throat and lied: "I have a gun. And I know how to use it." A bang of metal against metal made Jen jump nearly out of her skin. *Bang.* Haley was trying to unlatch the basement doors that let out onto the sidewalk.

"Haley?" Jen tried again, "Let's just talk." *Just stall her.* She couldn't let Haley burn the bakery down and escape. Jen moved back toward the stairs and tried to pull Alex up. She hooked under his armpits and tugged. He didn't budge. He was solid muscle.

Clank. Bang. And then another spark. Jen could make out shelves lining the walls now, loaded with jars and cans. Big barrels of oil were stacked next to them—Jen shuddered when she thought of those catching fire. A pallet loaded with giant bags of flour jutted out into the middle of the space. Jen moved around the stacks, squinting, trying to see where Haley was standing.

Something whizzed through the air at her, landing and exploding at her feet with a loud crack. Jen leapt back and fluid splattered all over her shoes. Jen laughed. "Eggs? You're throwing eggs at me?" But when three more came flying out of the darkness, Jen ducked. *At least they're low-carb,* Jen thought as she stepped down the last two steps into the basement, clutching her pan by the handle.

Jen could see the thin beam of light coming from the street exit. Haley had forced the metal up a couple of inches, which given her small stature was almost enough for her to slither through. A shadow moved and Jen ducked as another couple of eggs hit the wall and burst above her. Jen thought about what to say to her to calm her down, and most important, to get her to stop throwing the salmonella grenades.

"This would make for a good show on Yummy

Channel, huh?" Jen said, trying to start a conversation—trying anything to distract Haley. "Think of it: the drama, the suspense, the, um, yolk. It would get great ratings."

Silence.

"Haley, just tell me why," Jen reasoned. "If you just tell me why, I'll come over there and help you open the door. I have nothing to lose by helping you get away. Think about it." She was terrified that Haley would find out that she was holding a cast-iron pan instead of a gun, but she'd keep the illusion up as long as she could.

Jen took another step into the darkness. She found cover behind some jars of canned peaches and pineapples. "You're so pretty and skinny," Jen said, trying to appeal to Haley's vanity. "I can't believe you were smart enough to mastermind this whole thing."

"Well, when you're pretty and skinny, not a lot of people think you're smart," Haley answered from the darkness. "You get away with a lot more." A flash of blond hair stepped out from behind a vat of oil.

Jen cleared her throat and started to speak, but Haley continued, talking over her.

"But I didn't do anything, Jen. I've got nothing to be ashamed of," Haley said. "As the VP of programming I noticed that our main demographic was overweight. So then I started thinking about what types of advertisers would want to reach those viewers most."

"Diet pills?" Jen guessed.

"Exactly. First I looked for advertisers to sell our ad time to. When I met the people at XyloSlim they cut me a deal. I sell them ad space at a discounted rate and then make a percentage on the pills. Synergy. Simple business plan."

"Clearly," Jen said, blown away by Haley's blasé attitude. "So what happened?"

Haley snorted. "It's complicated. Turns out Xylo-Slim isn't the *safest* diet pill. Bess was going to tell and take the whole business down. Do you know how much money is in diet pills? But Bess wanted more and more money, a bigger and bigger share, to keep her mouth shut. She had it all anyway, the greedy bitch." Haley's voice quivered, and this scared Jen more than anything else. Haley had never been out of control, not in the entire time Jen had worked for her.

"So you killed her?"

"She was pathetic," Haley said. "She would have ruined everything. She was so high and mighty. Miss Perfect Bess Brantwood. Her poor anxiety. When I found out she took those pills and that's why she'd never try XyloSlim . . . I knew her weak spot."

Jen shook her head. "You have to be so in control that you've lost control of everything."

Jen looked back, hoping to see Alex moving but he lay still. *Please don't let him be dead.* While Jen was distracted, Haley lunged, knocking the pan out of Jen's hand. Jen fell to her knees, then tackled Haley by the calves. They both tumbled down together. Jen tried desperately to remember her self-defense moves as she and Haley fought bitterly for control of the pan. Haley managed to drive her stiletto into Jen's hand. Jen yanked her hand back, and Haley rolled over on top of her, her knee in Jen's chest. Haley picked up the heavy pan and held it above Jen's head.

Haley laughed. "Nice gun." Jen shielded her face with her hands. She could make out Haley's narrowed eyes. Haley spat, "These chefs? They're a dime a dozen. Any of those idiots you got to show up at the Comfort Food event would kill for a shot to be on the Yummy Channel. And now they'll get a chance."

Jen doubted it. "But how could you just kill her?"

"Technically, I didn't kill her," Haley said lightly. Jen could see the gleam of hard metal in her hand and a glint in her eye. "I put a few XyloSlim pills in a tea that I was intending to drink, and accidentally left it in Bess's dressing room at roughly the same time she popped her prespeech antianxiety pill. Ooopsie."

"You're so sick," Jen said.

Haley was silent a moment. "I need things to be in control. I was just trying to get everything in order."

"By killing people?"

"By *solving problems*," Haley said fiercely. She took

a step toward Jen. "And I'm about to solve another one right now." Finally, Jen heard footsteps thumping above them. The backup had arrived, thankfully. Jen groped around behind her, feeling for something she could use to protect herself. While Haley was turned away, Jen grabbed the object nearest to her and swung it at Haley.

The bag of flour hit Haley in the stomach and doubled her over. Jen scrambled backward against the shelves as Haley righted herself and raised the pan. Jen ducked, and the crash of the pan smashing a crate near her head thundered in her ears. Haley had missed by an inch or so, and the force of the smash had torn open a bag of sugar on the shelf above Jen. A fine waterfall of sugar was pouring down on Jen's face, coating her hair and eyelashes. Jen stuck out her tongue and licked her lips. Nothing had ever tasted better, which was good, because it might be the last thing she ever tasted.

Haley pulled herself upright one more time. Her red lipstick had smeared on her face, and her hair had fallen out of the bun. She limped on her single high heel. Jen felt strangely calm. She'd fought as hard as she could. If she had to go, she was glad to go with a sweet taste in her mouth.

"Jen?" Alex called. He was alive.

"Don't come any closer," Haley called out. "I'll smash her face in." The thumps on the stairs made

Haley cagey. She swung the pan toward Jen again. Jen ducked to miss the full impact but the pan hit the side of her head and made her ears ring.

Officer Joe Romano, Alex's partner, paused only a second before launching himself onto Haley, pulling her down into a stack of Crisco cans. They clambered down and he wrenched the pan from her hands. He tugged Haley to her feet and held her wrists behind her back. "Are you okay?" he asked Jen.

"I'm okay," she answered. "Haley, on the other hand, is a cold-blooded killer. She's the one who killed Bess. She admitted she put the XyloSlim in her tea." Officer Romano tightened his grip on Haley's arms. She struggled against him.

"You people just don't get it!" Haley gave a high-pitched shriek. "You don't understand how this industry works."

"Well," Alex said, sitting up against the wall and pulling himself up, "that may be true. One thing I do understand, though, is murder. And you are under arrest for the murder of Bess Brantwood."

Officer Romano read her Miranda rights and led her up the stairs slick with eggs and through the butter-splattered dining room.

Jen walked up behind them and into the arms of her friends. The paramedics helped Alex onto a stretcher and hoisted him out. Gabby and Elizabeth folded in around her, and hugged her tightly. They stood behind the counter of Bess's Bakery, taking in the damage that Haley had caused.

Out in the street, Billy was already on a stretcher. Jen walked over to him and opened her arms. He lifted his arms up to hug her too, and groaned in pain. Jen took his hands and said, "You are an idiot, but I love you. Completely platonically, but I love you. Don't ever scare me like that again."

"Thanks for rescuing me. That lady's scary," Billy said.

"Oh yeah," Jen agreed. "That was my boss."

"You're a tough gal, Jen Stevens."

"Thanks, Billy." She looked over and saw Alex on a stretcher. "Hey—I'm—"

"Go," Billy said. "Go talk to the cop. He has the hots for you."

Jen made a face at Billy and walked over to Alex. He was laid out on the stretcher, the paramedics working on his leg. She stood next to him and he turned his head to look at her.

"You are sweet," Alex said, staring into Jen's eyes, brushing her hair out of her eyes. "But what were you thinking when you went into that basement?" He wiped grains of sugar from her hair off his hands, laughing quietly. He winced as the medic eased his leg up on the stretcher.

"There was no way I was going to let her hurt you more," Jen said. "And you're sweet too." The lights from the police cars parked everywhere outside, at odd angles, halfway up onto the sidewalk, filled the room with alternating red and blue. Policemen moved all around them collecting the grease-soaked paperwork. Haley was barricaded in the back of a police car. To gawkers on the sidewalk it looked like total chaos, but Jen felt calm and relaxed for the first time in a week, knowing that Bess's killer was really behind bars.

"Look, I've been thinking," Alex said. He paused, and Jen's stomach flipped in anticipation. "Anyone who's as sweet and crazy as you, well, I want them on my side." He looked from his hands into Jen's eyes. "Do you want to be on my side?" he asked.

"Do you usually call people crazy when you're asking them out?" Jen smirked at Alex.

Alex laughed, his eyes sparkling. "Okay, you're not just crazy and sweet. You're smart, brave, and beautiful. I've thought so since the first time I saw you." His voice was muffled as a paramedic put a face mask pumping oxygen up to his nose and mouth.

Jen smiled. "That's more like it." She reached over and took his hand. "So what is required of someone who is on your side? Is it a full-time job? Because I'm looking for one. There's no way I'm going back to work at the Yummy Channel."

Alex thought about it. He raised his eyebrows at Jen. "The job description is way too complicated to explain here, but maybe I can fill in the blanks over drinks and dinner?"

"Absolutely," Jen agreed. "When?"

Alex scratched his head, wincing when he touched the bump. "How about every night this week? How about that?" He reached up and gently eased his face mask down, holding eye contact with her the whole time. He pulled her face down toward his. He kissed her lips lightly, and then kissed them again more firmly.

Jen nodded, her lips hovering centimeters from his. "Every night this week sounds good to me."

epilogue

The first few days she was unemployed Jen did very little. She slept late and went for walks with Alex during the day when he was off duty. She went back on the diet, with more vigor. Eventually, she updated her résumé but didn't send it out yet. She knew she could last only so long without an income, though.

It had been about two weeks since the Comfort Food event. Jen was eight more pounds down—thirteen in all—and out to dinner with Alex. She allowed herself to have a glass of wine, and over candlelight, they talked about her options. "I just got so caught up in the Yummy Channel fame game," she said. "There's something amazing about working with celebrities. Maybe I could work for ESPN or Lifetime Channel or something?"

Alex thought a minute. "Yeah, you could, but why don't you work for yourself?"

"Oh, I don't know, I think I need the support of a company." But as she thought about it, she realized that maybe she didn't.

"You should talk to your friends," Alex said. "Between a food blogger and a life coach, you could probably get some pretty exciting gigs."

Jen thought about it. She was slimmer and feeling more confident about her body, but since leaving the Yummy Channel she'd been feeling more like herself than ever before. She remembered all the things she liked doing besides eating, and to her that felt healthy.

"You know, Alex, I think you're right," she said. She looked up at him. "Cheers. To Jen Stevens Event Planning."

Alex clinked glasses with her. "You should make it Jen Stevens Event Planning/Private Investigator Business."

Jen let out a big laugh. "Better not," she said. "I hope I never have to solve another mystery."

"Hmm." Alex wrinkled his face. "That's not really going to work for me. You see, I just got a promotion to full-time detective with the New York City Police Department."

"Oh my goodness!" Jen said. "Congratulations." She beamed at Alex.

"Thank you, thank you. But just a reminder—you promised to be on my team, remember? And that means solving the occasional mystery, skinny girl."

Jen shrugged, tickled that he'd called her skinny. He noticed her weight loss! "Fine," she said. She reached over the table and squeezed his hand, then picked up her fork and took a bite of her grilled salmon. "You know what I was thinking?" she asked. He shook his head. "Let's order dessert. Let's ask if they have cake." Alex raised his eyebrows. Jen raised hers back. The night was just getting started.

Jen shrugged and noted that light called her skinny.

He reached her waist-level. "Fine," she said. She reached over the mike and squeezed his hand, then picked up her fork and took a bite of her grilled salmon. "You know what I was thinking?" she asked.

He shook his head. "Let's order dessert. Let's ask if they have cake." He arched his eyebrows. Jen raised him back. The night was just getting started.

skinny mystery recipes:
a diet to die for

Caesar Salad with Grilled New York Strip Steak

1 lb sirloin steak

Salad
    6 cups romaine lettuce
    2 tbsp shaved Parmesan
Marinade
    balsamic vinegar
    1 tsp salt
    1 tsp pepper
    1 tbsp olive oil
Dressing
    ¼ cup mayonnaise
    1 tbsp pasteurized egg substitute
    1 tbsp Parmesan cheese
    ¼ cup water
    1 tsp olive oil
    1 tsp lemon juice

1 tsp anchovy paste
1 clove garlic
dash pepper
dash salt
dash dried parsley

Mix balsamic vinegar, salt, pepper, and olive oil. Cover steak with marinade and refrigerate for 3 to 6 hours.

Use a blender to mix all the dressing ingredients for one minute and refrigerate dressing.

Use a knife to cut the romaine lettuce into 1-inch pieces. Put the lettuce into a large bowl. Cover with the Parmesan shavings. Toss the salad with the dressing and divide into three servings.

Grill the steak for 4 to 6 minutes per side over medium heat and let rest for at least 10 minutes. Slice the meat at an angle into 12 pieces. Arrange 4 pieces on top of plated salad.

Servings: 3
Total carbs per serving: 8.4 grams

Fiesta Friday Pork Rind Nachos

  1 lb lean ground beef
  1 packet of taco seasoning
  3 4-oz bags of pork rinds
  2 cups shredded cheddar cheese
  1 quart (32 oz) pico de gallo
  3 tbsp pickled jalapeños
  ½ cup sour cream

Brown ground beef. Drain off grease and add in taco seasoning.

Preheat the oven to its highest heat, or a broil setting.

Spread pork rinds onto a cookie sheet, cover with taco meat and cheddar cheese. Put in oven and cook until cheese is melted.

Place pork rinds on a plate and top with pico de gallo, jalapeños, and sour cream.

  Servings: 4
  Total carbs per serving: 10.2 grams

Spicy Salisbury Steak

½ cup beef stock
1½ lbs ground beef
¼ cup grated Parmesan cheese
1 egg
¼ tsp salt
1½ tbsp prepared horseradish
⅛ tsp red pepper flakes
3 cloves garlic, minced
1 tbsp Worcestershire sauce

In a large bowl, mix together all the ingredients. Shape into 6 oval patties.

In a large skillet, over medium-high heat, brown the patties on both sides. Pour off the excess fat.

Servings: 6
Total carbs per serving: 2.8 grams

Low-carb Chocolate Mousse

2 tbsp cold water
1 envelope unflavored gelatin
4 tbsp boiling water
1 cup granulated zero-calorie sugar substitute—try
    Truvia
½ cup unsweetened powdered cocoa
⅛ tsp salt
1 cup heavy whipping cream
½ tsp almond extract
1 tsp vanilla extract
1 tsp whipped cream

Put a large mixing bowl into the refrigerator a half hour
before beginning your recipe.

Place cold water in a medium bowl. Sprinkle in the
envelope of gelatin. Add the boiling water and stir until
all the gelatin is dissolved.

Take the bowl that's been chilled out of the refrigerator.
Combine sugar substitute, cocoa powder, salt, cream,
and the almond and vanilla extracts. Use a mixer on
medium speed to beat the mixture until stiff peaks form.
Beat in the gelatin mixture.

Serve in parfait glasses with a dollop of whipped cream
and a dusting of cocoa powder.

Servings: 4
Total carbs per serving: 7.3 grams

Chicken Breasts Stuffed with Pesto and Cheese

    4 boneless skinless chicken breasts
    2 cups packed fresh basil leaves
    2 cloves garlic
    ¼ cup pine nuts
    ½ cup extra-virgin olive oil
    ½ cup Parmesan cheese
    ½ lb fresh mozzarella cheese
    toothpicks

Preheat the oven to 350°F.

Pound the chicken breasts flat using a rolling pin or kitchen mallet.

Make pesto by blending together basil, garlic, pine nuts, olive oil, and Parmesan cheese.

Spread pesto over uncooked chicken breasts.

Cut mozzarella into ⅛-to-¼-inch slices and lay over the pesto on the flattened chicken breasts.

Taking one end of each chicken breast, roll the pesto and cheese up inside. Lay on a baking sheet and use a toothpick to secure the chicken.

Bake for 40 minutes, remove from oven, and let set for 10 minutes before serving.

    Servings: 4
    Total carbs per serving: 4.6 grams

Mushroom and Green Onion Omelet

   3 oz cremini mushrooms, or your favorite type of
      mushrooms
   2 tbsp chopped green onions
   3 large eggs
   ½ tbsp water
   Salt and pepper to taste
   1 tbsp butter
   ¼ cup of grated cheddar cheese

Finely chop mushrooms and green onions. Whisk eggs
together with water, salt, and pepper. Warm a nonstick
pan over medium-high heat, and melt half of the butter
in the pan. Add mushrooms and most of the green
onions. Sauté 3 minutes, stirring the contents of the pan
from time to time. Add the rest of the butter and allow
it to melt. Then pour egg mixture over the sautéed
vegetables and cook until omelet is set. Lift up the
edges with a spatula to let uncooked egg flow underneath, and cook for about 2 minutes. When the omelet
is mostly cooked, add the grated cheddar cheese. When
cheese begins to melt, fold both sides of omelet.
Transfer to a plate and sprinkle omelet with a few
remaining onions.

   Servings: 1
   Total carbs: 7 grams

Chunky Chicken Salad

    2 boneless skinless chicken breasts
    2 tbsp mayonnaise
    3 tbsp water
    salt and pepper to taste
    2 stalks of celery

Place the chicken breasts in a pot and cover them with water. Bring to a boil and cook for thirty minutes, until the chicken registers a temperature of 160 degrees or higher with a meat thermometer.

Lay the chicken out on a cutting board and cool until comfortable to touch.

In a large bowl, whisk together mayonnaise and water. Add salt and pepper.

Chop the celery and the chicken breasts. Add to the water-mayo mixture and toss to coat.

    Servings: 4
    Total carbs per serving: 4 grams

acknowledgments

Thank you so much to my mother and my husband for their unwavering support.

Thank you to all the amazing people at Gallery Books and Simon & Schuster who work so hard to publish great books.

Thank you to all my amazing girlfriends for the countless conversations we've had about dieting, and thank you to my writing group for all the feedback.

Finally, a special thank-you to chocolate for always being there when I needed you most. Without you, none of this would be possible.